CASSY OAK

Their Fire Queen

Copyright © 2024 by Cassy Oak

All rights reserved. No part of this publication may be reproduced, stored or transmitted in any form or by any means, electronic, mechanical, photocopying, recording, scanning, or otherwise without written permission from the publisher. It is illegal to copy this book, post it to a website, or distribute it by any other means without permission.

This novel is entirely a work of fiction. The names, characters and incidents portrayed in it are the work of the author's imagination. Any resemblance to actual persons, living or dead, events or localities is entirely coincidental.

First edition

Cover art by Canva

This book was professionally typeset on Reedsy. Find out more at reedsy.com

For all the girlies who want to set people on fire while being worshiped by three smoking hot men.

Contents

Triggers   iv
1   Chapter One: EMBER   1
2   Chapter Two: ACE   12
3   Chapter Three: EMBER   18
4   Chapter Four: RYKER   24
5   Chapter Five: EMBER   28
6   Chapter Six: EMBER   33
7   Chapter Seven: EMBER   39
8   Chapter Eight: CAYDEN   46
9   Chapter Nine: EMBER   50
10   Chapter Ten: ACE   56
11   Chapter Eleven: EMBER   60
12   Chapter Twelve: CAYDEN   67
13   Chapter Thirteen: EMBER   71
14   Chapter Fourteen: EMBER   80
15   Chapter Fifteen: EMBER   89
16   Chapter Sixteen: CAYDEN   97
17   Chapter Seventeen: EMBER   99
18   Chapter Eighteen: EMBER   106
19   Chapter Nineteen: RYKER   113
20   Chapter Twenty: EMBER   118
21   Chapter Twenty-One: EMBER   123
22   Chapter Twenty-Two: ACE   129
23   Chapter Twenty-Three: EMBER   135

24	Chapter Twenty-Four: EMBER	140
25	Chapter Twenty-Five: ACE	145
26	Chapter Twenty-Six: EMBER	150
27	Chapter Twenty-Seven: EMBER	155
28	Chapter Twenty-Eight: EMBER	160
29	Chapter Twenty-Nine: CAYDEN	165
30	Chapter Thirty: EMBER	169
31	Chapter Thirty-One: RYKER	178
32	Chapter Thirty-Two: EMBER	181
33	Chapter Thirty-Three: ACE	191
34	Chapter Thirty-Four: EMBER	197
35	Chapter Thirty-Five: EMBER	202
36	Chapter Thirty-Six: Cayden	208
37	Chapter Thirty-Seven: EMBER	212
38	Chapter Thirty-Eight: EMBER	217
39	Chapter Thirty-Nine: EMBER	225
40	Chapter Forty: Ryker	229
41	Chapter Forty-One: EMBER	231
42	Chapter Forty-Two: EMBER	239
43	Chapter Forty-Three: ACE	247
44	Chapter Forty-Four: EMBER	253
45	Chapter Forty-Five: CAYDEN	261
46	Chapter Forty-Six: EMBER	268
47	Chapter Forty-Seven: RYKER	271
48	Chapter Forty-Eight: EMBER	275
49	Chapter Forty-Nine: ACE	281
50	Chapter Fifty: EMBER	283
51	Chapter Fifty-One: CAYDEN	288
52	Chapter Fifty-Two: EMBER	292
53	Chapter Fifty-Three: RYKER	297
54	Chapter Fifty-Four: EMBER	301

55 Epilogue: EMBER	307
Acknowledgements	310
About the Author	311

Triggers

Triggers Warning:

This book contains:

- Abuse
- Child Abandonment
- Mentions of Suicide
- Homophobia
- Cannibalism
- D/s dynamics
- Spanking
- Bondage
- Daddy Kink
- Exhibitionism
- Kidnapping
- Needles
- Drugging
- MM
- MMMF
- Stalking
- PTSD
- Panic attacks

- Anxiety
- Eating disorder
- Slut Shaming
- Cutting by Another Person
- Stockholm Syndrome
- Violence
- Gore
- Torture
- Mutilation
- Murder
- Burning People Alive
- Fatphobia
- Attempted Sexual Assault
- Sexual Assault
- Death
- Explicit Sexual Content
- Human trafficking
- Mention of Sex Slaves

These are not necessarily in order. Please take care yourself and your mental health, Ace, Ryker, Cayden, and Ember would want you to. You are loved.

1

Chapter One: EMBER

Well fuck me...

The roar of the crowd was deafening, their energy was electric. A light sheet of sweat coated my forehead as I stood in the center. All focus was on me and the four men I shared the ring with. A large hand on my shoulder brought me out of my head and into the moment.

I looked at the three men that surrounded me. Each twice my size, towering over my 5'6 frame. I attempted to shrug the hand from its tight grip on my shoulder. The hand only tightened, and I looked up at my captor. Ace. His piercing dark, almost black eyes, bored into my blue wide ones. His lips pulled into a sadistic smirk which made me shiver. He nodded his head towards the center of the ring.

It was event night. Rival Hitting Wrestling or RHW's weekly show. My twin brother Lucas and I were the babyfaces or good guys. He was being attacked by the Bloody Wolves who were the heels or bad guys. Although I didn't wrestle, I joined my brother by the ring as his manager. Despite knowing the three men in the Bloody Wolves for years, I was still hesitant around them. They were dangerous and hated Lucas both inside and outside of the ring.

Cayden and Ryker, Ace's teammates, were beating the shit out of Lucas, my twin brother. Ace's tattooed hand kept me in place no matter how much I fought him. Tears welled up at his punishing grip. I could do nothing but watch with the crowd at what came next. Blond hair, identical to mine, was driven into the ground. The golden color was now turning to a red similar to my own. The only difference, mine was from a box, his was from blood. I tried to cry out, but no sound escaped. A wordless scream and a few tears later, I was being forced closer to my bleeding brother. I didn't mean to cry, I was just overwhelmed, this was my first major storyline in RHW.

"Hit him!" Ace growled in my ear. His voice was one that romance readers would kill for. It was deep and dripping sin, one that would make the girls and the gays fall to their knees.

I was helpless to do anything other than shake my head. He shoved me forward to where Cayden and Ryker held up Lucas's beaten body. They all laughed and tried to urge me to punch Lucas. The crowd was getting louder, their boos filling my ears. The peer pressure from both sides was getting too much. The fans were screaming, "No! No! No!" over and over. I agreed with them, I was not going to hurt Lucas.

Lucas's eyes met mine. A silent plea for his sister, his twin to punch him. He wanted to end my torment, my suffering even if it meant more pain for him. I shook my head, and my brother was shoved to the side. I would never hurt my brother. He protected me, no matter how bad of a sister I was. Now was the time to make up for all my previous sins. I was safe with everybody in the ring, I reminded myself.

CHAPTER ONE: EMBER

"You do what we say!" Ryker demanded as I was shoved to the ground. Shaking, I curled into a ball as more verbal abuse was screamed at me. I covered my head and let out a whimper as a foot tapped me. Despite it being more of a nudge, I pulled my limbs closer to my body. My eyes squeezed shut and I silently pleaded for the torment to stop.

Loud music blasted through the speakers and answered my pleads. Three men from the roster came running out to save Lucas and myself. My three tormentors ran away and Ramero, my best friend, placed a hand on my back. I was still shaking as he and his friends helped Lucas and I up. I kept my head down as I was helped away from the crowd.

As we stepped out of the lights, Kai and Grant, Ramero's friends, helped Lucas to the trainer. Somebody called Ramero away and I was left alone in front of a large individual. His dark eyes shined with amusement and curiosity.

"Didn't scare you too badly, did we baby girl?" Ace asked, with his signature cocky grin.

I shook my head, "You ain't that scary!" His grin seemed to grow, causing me to desperately fight squeezing my thighs together. Why was he so sexy?

"We aren't?"

I jumped with a yelp. "Ryker! You shouldn't sneak up on people like that!"

"Like this!" Cayden whispered in my ear. I jumped again with a curse. "What a naughty mouth you have, princess." I blushed as Cayden smirked.

"You were crying out there. Did we make you cry?" Ace questioned. I struggled to determine if he was concerned or being an ass. There was a genuine note to his voice that wasn't there during the earlier teasing.

Ramero joined us, "Leave the poor girl alone. Bad enough you tortured her out there, don't continue it back here! Come on." Ramero led me away from the men and outside the building. "So, you like 'em?"

I blushed again and shook my head, "Like them? Hell no!"

Ramero's six-foot-five frame towered over me. A smile spread across his face, "Body language conveys somethin' different. You can lie to yourself, but you can't lie to me." Nothing could ever get past him; he knows me too well for that.

"Shut up," I mumbled, rolling my eyes. I noticed Lucas talking to a petite brunette dressed very provocatively. He glanced in my direction and walked over. Ramero mumbled something, gave me a quick hug before walking away.

Lucas put an arm around my shoulder, "You did good tonight. You were crying out there. You good?" My body tensed slightly; touch wasn't my favorite thing.

I nodded, "I thought it was my job to play the damsel in distress? What about you? They really hurt you!"

"I'm fine Ber. You cool if someone else brings you to the motel? Someone kinda asked me out for drinks." He looked at the brunette who was staring dagger at me. If she wants to be his focus, so be it. I love my brother, but a break might be nice.

I bit my lip, "Yeah, I'll figure it out. It's about time you went on a date! Make sure you tell your date that you have a psychotic twin who will fuck them up."

He playfully rolled his eyes, "I'll make sure to tell her. Now, go find a ride!"

I went back into the building, searching for Ramero. Instead of him, I stumbled across Cayden. He gave a lazy smile, "Hey,

CHAPTER ONE: EMBER

pretty girl. Where are you off to in such a hurry?" I really hope he can't see how the blush that I feel rising.

I huffed, "One, don't call me that. Two, have you seen Ramero?" It took all of my self-control not to slap him as he cocked his head.

Cayden shook his head as Ryker and Ace joined him. "You guys seen Ramero? Our sweet firestorm is asking." I blushed at the nickname and sighed as they shook their heads. I get that my hair is red, but I am not their anything.

"Don't call me that, I'm not yours or anybody's. Thanks anyway. I should be going." I muttered and turned to leave.

A heavy hand landed on my shoulder, and I was pulled back into a solid chest. I squirmed, trying to get away from my captor. It's almost as if he enjoys feeling me struggle. "Hold up baby blaze. That brother of yours left, how are you getting to the motel?" Ace questioned, tilting my head so our eyes would connect. Why was that innocent move so hot? What was with the nicknames, they have never been this forward.

He held me still and looked down expectantly. My tongue darted out to wet my lips, "T-that's why I needed to find Ramero. Now, let me go numbnut!" I wiggled and he let me go.

Ryker smiled, "Let us drive ya back!" His genuine offer took me off guard. Ryker was never sarcastic; it was almost like he was a robot. I looked at the other two who agreed.

"I would rather walk, thank you though." I winked and gave an innocent smile before turning on my heel.

"Brat!" Ryker called down the hall after me. I laughed and flipped him off.

* * *

Maybe a break was a bad idea. I was sitting in the motel room that I was supposed to be sharing with Lucas. Alone, yet again in a dirty motel room. Don't get me wrong, I'm happy for Lucas. He deserves all the happiness in the world, but I wish he was here. The walk back was cold, dark, and scary. Every noise made me jump and as my luck would have it, it started raining.

I took a quick shower in the disgusting bathroom, running out when I saw a roach. It was times like this that I wished Lucas would let me work more hours. He rarely let me pick up shifts at the local grocery store. I pulled the blankets up close, shivering from my wet hair and cold night. A loud crash of thunder made me jump and I pulled the sheets over my head. I shouldn't be cowering from something so childish. A flash of light filled the room, and I yelped as thunder shook the motel. I closed my eyes, tears leaking out and started counting. I longed for my headphones and lighter that were sitting in the backseat of Lucas's car. The lighter helped me feel better about the dark. Lucas burned me with it a few times when I almost set the motel on fire. It hurt, but they were punishments that I deserved.

There were three loud rasps at the door. I shook my head, of all times to forget his key. The carpet felt filthy under my bare feet. Normally I would be disgusted by walking on it, but right now, I didn't care. I was shaking and really wanted Lucas to hold me. Craving to be protected, I rushed to the door. My trembling hand made it a challenge to unlock the door.

I wiped my eyes, no doubt that they were red and puffy, before opening the door. "Luc, this is the-"

"Are you okay, princess?" Cayden pushed open the door,

CHAPTER ONE: EMBER

concern lining his face. I looked behind him to see Ace and Ryker mirroring his expression.

I nodded and squealed, betrayed by a monstrous crack of thunder. Shaking, I tried to stop the tears that leaked from my eyes and the tightening in my chest. "P-p-please, l-leave," I whimpered, feeling like a child. I tried to close the door, push them out into the storm. I was used to feeling scared and helpless, but I didn't want to feel that way around them.

They never made me feel like I was in danger, nothing could hurt me when they were around. Ace, Cayden, and Ryker were almost like silent protector, always watching out for me. Several time over the past few years, they saved me from Lucas when he got worked up. My brother could be explosive and mean at times, but I was never hospitalized because of it.

Cayden shoved his way in and grabbed my arm. Ace and Ryker followed suit, closing the door. I was pressed into Cayden; his wet shirt sent a shiver down my spine. Being so close, I could feel his abs and the tight muscles that made up his chest. I felt heat rise when I realized his dick was hard and pushing against my back. He led me further into the room. I heard the door close, and the lock snap shut. The three men curled their lips in disgust at the room. It clearly was below them.

"Please Cayden," I started.

"Shh," he murmured into my ear, the sound was almost comforting. He pushed me onto the bed, and I was quickly surrounded by the three men. "Why didn't you look before you opened the door?" My eyes bounced between the three of them.

I thought back, two years prior. *Cayden, Ace, and Ryker surrounded me after beating up Lucas. We were in a dimly lit parking lot; I was screaming for my brother. Cayden laughed and kicked Lucas hard in the ribs. Ace grabbed me and forced me to watch the assault that followed. Blood dripped from my brother's mouth and nose as he begged for the men to spare me. Even with Lucas's blood covering them, I found them attractive. The blood may have even heightened the appeal. What is wrong with me?*

As I kneeled in front of Lucas's broken body, he told me not to piss off the wrong people. I later found out he took five dollars from them for our rent. I cried over him at the hospital, then cursed him for being so foolish. He knew I could have picked up an extra shift.

As these men surrounded me, I knew that something bad was about to happen. They just stood there. Watching me from the edge of the bed. Ace had a stupid look on his face, Cayden and Ryker grinned. I turned and launched myself off the bed. I didn't make it very far and was caught before my feet even left the bed. Ryker held me in his arms for a second before throwing me back on the bed. A loud crash of thunder forced a scream from me.

I placed my hands over my ears and squeezed my eyes shut. I did the only thing I could think of at the moment, I begged. "Please! I-I-I, please!" I didn't know if I was begging to be left alone or to be held. Did I want to be comforted or alone in a dark, dirty motel room? The answer had to be comforted, but not be these men. Right?

"Please what, baby blaze?" Ace taunted. He took a step forward and placed a thumb under my chin. I felt like a deer being stalked by a hunter. "What are you begging for?" I struggled against his iron grip and lost. My watery eyes met his commanding ones. His thumb wiped a tear that escaped as he hummed, clearly waiting for my answer. An answer that I wasn't ready to admit.

CHAPTER ONE: EMBER

I tried to shake my head, but Ace's hand did not let me. "Cat got your tongue?" Cayden teased; a smirk spread across his face. Ryker just stared, showing an unknown emotion. Out of all the men, he had the shortest temper and was most of the time unreadable.

"Now, this is how tonight is gonna go," Ace started without letting go of me, "you are gonna come with us." I started to squirm and fight his grip. I was not going with them. What would Lucas think? Why did they want me with them? I shook my head, ready to voice my disagreement.

"Stop it, little flame. Listen to Ace." Ryker said firmly. I fought the shiver that rose from the nickname. He took a step closer and crossed his arms. When I nodded, he said, "Verbal answer."

"O-okay." I need to get my shit together, be strong and stop stuttering. Is that even possible with the three men surrounding me?

Ace smiled and used his other hand to pat my head. "Good girl. As I was saying, you will come with us. Lucas made a mistake; he must pay for it. You will pay for it." I shook my head and Ace lost his beautiful smile. "You can come willingly or by force, you have five seconds to choose."

What the fuck did Lucas do? Why was I just hearing about it? When did he do anything? "Five." Cayden said. Shit! I need to make a decision. I can't go with them. Would I be safer with them? It hurt to want to be protected from my twin. They protected me before, are they protecting me now?

"Four," Ryker counted. If I go with them, maybe they won't hurt me. Did Lucas steal from them again? We had enough money for tonight. I knew that I couldn't go with them. Lucas would kill me if I went with them. A crash of thunder made me jump and whimper.

Ace pulled out a syringe, "Three." I pressed myself into the headboard. Did he steal money to go on his date? What could he have done in the short time we were apart?

My eyes were wide as tears leaked from them. "P-please. What are you-"

"Two," Cayden licked his lips after cutting me off. He dragged a hand through his unkempt blonde hair. If this was any other person, I would dare think he was hot. His body seemed to be sculpted, the memory of his dick against my back still very present. I pulled my knees closer to hide the need to squeeze my legs shut. Why was I aroused by this? Lucas would be furious to know this. Thinking of Lucas and the fear he struck into me killed the aroused feeling.

"One," Ryker finished the count. His lips twitched, like he was trying to hide a smile. He wanted to kidnap me; he wanted me to choose the hard way.

Tears were free flowing as Ace pulled me towards him. "Please! Let me go!" I begged, "Don't do this!" I fought with everything in me. I slammed my fist into his chest, causing him to chuckle. He tilted his head and lifted me to my feet. His hands moved to circle my wrists, capturing them in one hand. I flailed my legs, trying to kick him where I could. Without an effort, he turned us so I was held captive on his lap. His long legs draped over mine and his hand still held my wrists as the other held the needle. "I can't," I whimper, "I can't go with you."

"That's a shame, princess." Cayden shook his head. "I really wish you chose the easy way." His face was inches from mine. My breath caught when his tongue darted out and licked the salty tears that leaked from my eyes. He pulled back and gave

CHAPTER ONE: EMBER

me an inhuman grin. "Such as shame, my sweet firestorm, such a shame."

Ryker and Cayden switched with their friend. The pair held me down as I screamed for help. Ryker moved from holding just my arms to put a hand over my mouth. His large hand covered my nose as well, making each breath a struggle. My face was growing redder as my lungs screamed for air. Ace tilted my head to the side giving him full access to my neck. I was sobbing as he kissed my collarbone. He moved up my neck and nipped at my ear. Whispering sweet nothings in my ear, a sharp object poked my neck. This ripped a shriek from deep in my lungs. Lucas is going to kill me because of them.

"Good girl," someone said as my world faded to black.

2

Chapter Two: ACE

She smells as good as she looks. For such a tiny thing she can sure put up a fight. I rubbed my chest where her puny fists bounced off of. I looked at the two men that make up my family. Between their grins and the way they look at Ember, it was obvious we made the right choice.

Cayden twirled a strand of our girl's blonde and red hair, "Did you see the way her thighs squeezed shut? Do you smell her?" His face dipped down towards her sweet pussy.

Ryker's eyes darkened but decided to put a stop to Cayden's antics. "Cayd, we do not touch or smell her," he pulled the other man away, "while she is sleeping. Soon we will get to smell, taste, drown in her pussy, but not while she is unconscious."

I laughed as Cayden flipped off the dark-haired male that challenged him. A cockroach scrambled out of the bathroom towards us. Cayden stomped on it in disgust. "Roaches. This fucking place is not safe for our girl."

Shaking my head, I hoisted the girl onto my shoulder and gestured for one of the men to get the door. We weren't

CHAPTER TWO: ACE

worried about getting caught, our incredible team got the cameras covered. In this neighborhood, nobody would bat an eye to us, which is why she should not be here. This is not a safe place for a precious flame like her.

Watching her from afar for just over two years has proven to be a challenge. The number of times we almost intervened when her asshole brother decided to hit her... again. A few times we distracted him, but it was never enough to truly save her. The final straw was the fear we saw out in the ring tonight. The fear wasn't from us, no matter what she has convinced herself to believe. She looked at Lucas with true fear despite us kicking his ass.

Cayden threw his jacket over her, shielding her body from the majority of the rain. We sat her in the backseat of my dark blue pickup truck. Ryker buckled her in and sat with her head on his shoulder. Despite what she might be thinking, we don't want to hurt her. She will understand that someday soon.

I jumped into the driver's seat with Cayden next to me and threw the car into drive. The rain was coming down hard, lightning flashed every few minutes. Maybe it was a good thing Ember fought, the poor girl was terrified of thunderstorms. Lucas would comfort her during the storms. It seemed the only time he was a good brother was when she was scared of something other than him. It was like she could only be scared of him.

I glanced up every so often to peer back at her. Ryker was playing absentmindedly with her hair. I fought the pang of jealousy, but I knew that I would get my time with her.

We pulled into the driveway of the home we shared. It wasn't a mansion, even though we could afford several. This house was perfect for us, we weren't home much anyway. The rain had slightly let up, which allowed us to quickly get her into the house without getting her too wet. We should be the only ones that get her wet. I need to calm down before I get overly jealous by the rain.

Ryker carried her downstairs into a bedroom that we created just for her. Cayden grabbed a towel and dried her off before getting a blow dryer for her hair. We exchanged looks when we noticed how old and dirty her pajamas actually were. They had holes in them and were covered in a thin layer of dirt. They didn't smell horrible, our girl could never smell terrible, but they had an unclean smell to them. Our beautiful girl should only have the best of everything. With us, she will never have to sleep in pajamas or any piece of clothing again.

I longed to change her into something nicer, maybe one of my t-shirts. However, we didn't want her to wake up scared and in new clothes. Her brother hammered into her head that she wasn't pretty. She could never wear anything that didn't fully cover her shape without him hitting her. We saw this through the cameras that we put in her hotel.

Ryker finished with her hair; he was good at that stuff. You wouldn't guess it, but that's what made me love him even more. I loved all the people in this room with an unexplainable passion. I carefully lifted her to a sitting position and placed her body on a chair.

Glancing around the room, I smiled at our work. The pink comforter, blue sheets, and purple blanket gave the room a homier feel. We don't want her to feel like she is in a prison; we want this to be her bedroom until she is ready to sleep with us. Cayden even picked out a stuffed bear that we hoped would provide a sense of safety.

Both of my men frowned as I produced four zip ties from

CHAPTER TWO: ACE

my pocket. I sighed, breaking the silence that formed when we first brought her to the truck. Unfortunately, we needed to make sure she doesn't run and get a video taunting Lucas. Lucas needs to see that he can't hurt the woman we love and get away with it. He also needs to see that he did this to himself by aligning himself with Trevor Ashben.

Trevor has been a pain in the ass since he was born. He also killed our ally, his own father, George Ashben. Cayden, Ryker and I are on a hunt for him, however we needed to get Ember out of the way. Lucas would do anything to protect himself, that includes throwing his own twin into the skin trade.

I let out a heavy sigh, "I don't want to either, but we have to. We have to get that video and hope that she doesn't hate us too much." I handed one to each man who tied her wrists to the chair. I put one on each ankle and connected them to the chair as well. The only reason we are using zip ties is to make her seem like a more believable hostage. From now on, she will only be tied up with bondage ropes that are safe for her skin. Ember will also be a willing, awake participant in the future. I just hope she doesn't struggle and hurt herself now.

Ryker cleared his throat. "Do you think she will forgive us? We are imprisoning her! Are we any better than her fucking brother?"

For the first time in years, I saw Cayden flinch, "We are definitely better than her brother! We aren't gonna fucking hurt her or beat her! Never compare me or any of us to him again! Am I understood?" The fire in his voice would make anyone shrink back in fear. Ryker was no acceptation.

Ryker was always the most submissive out of the three of us. We found that out when I first yelled at him for doing something stupid in high school. Ryker nodded, bowing his head slightly. We are no strangers to having kinky fun with each other, maybe the two of them need a release.

"Ryk, Cayd, I think you guys should go into the dungeon. I'll stay with her; she shouldn't wake up for another hour or two." Despite framing it as a thought, it was a command. Both men submitted to me during scenes. We were equal partners during work, but not during play.

Ryker looked hesitant, glancing between me and Ember before nodding. Cayden seemed like he was going to argue, but one raise of my eyebrow got him leaving. "Leave the door open!" I yell after them.

We also learned in high school that both Cayden and Ryker are switches. As much as they enjoy being Doms, they both have explosive tempers and need someone to even them out. The dungeon is soundproof, we play rough, and we don't want our neighbors calling the police. With the door open, I can still hear and jump in if I feel the need to do so.

I watch Ember's unconscious form, listening to Cayden direct Ryker into the position he wanted. I heard a slight whimper from Ryker and my cock started to harden. I unbuckled my belt and pulled out my throbbing dick. Less than a minute later the hard smack of a paddle meeting flesh echoed down the hall. I wrapped my hand around my cock and pumped to the rhythm of Cayden's paddle.

Ryker yelped and I knew Cayden moved to the back of his thighs. I groaned, picturing the dark red Ryker's ass must be. Ryker let out several loud moans, meaning Cayden must be fucking his ass. My breath now came out in short pants before I exploded to the sight of Ember and the sound of Ryker and Cayden's howls.

I sighed, tucked my dick back into my jeans. I looked at the

CHAPTER TWO: ACE

blanket on the bed that was now covered in my come. Within the hour, the blanket was in the laundry and the three of us were sitting on the bed. On the side table was a glass of water with a straw for when our girl wakes up. Ryker leaned his head on my shoulder, and we sat in silence, our eye glued to the beauty in front of us.

3

Chapter Three: EMBER

My mouth was dry, my throat was on fire, my neck throbbed. Every bone in my body hurt like I had just been hit by a truck. I tried to shift, but something was keeping me in place. I slowly peeled my eyes open but closed them again as a bright light burned. The pain coursing through my brain threatened to spilt my head in two. I dug my fingernails into something hard, wood I think. I was sitting up so this must be a chair.

I jumped, forcing my eyes open when a gentle hand was placed on my thigh. "Looky here! Princess is awake," a rough voice laughed. Cayden's blurry figure was looking up at me. He was kneeling on the floor, his blue eyes stared through me. "Drink," he ordered as Ace held a straw to my lips. I shook my head, instantly regretting it. "Drink, *now!*" Cayden's command had me shaking. His grip tightened on my leg, and I bowed my head slightly before taking the straw to my mouth. His grip wasn't tight enough to hurt me but kept me aware of his ability to crush my leg.

I took a small sip; the water was cold and eased my sore throat. I let the straw fall from my mouth. Ace shook his

CHAPTER THREE: EMBER

head and put it to my lips once again. "More." Ace said as his partner lifted his brow. At Cayden's look, I drank more water. As much as I wanted to fight them, I felt better as the water slipped down my throat. They didn't have to give me anything, so I decided to take advantage of it while they were being kind.

"Good girl," Ace murmured in my ear and took the cup away. My body turned to mush at his words. Like most women, I wasn't immune to being called a good girl. His voice however, intensified the wonderful words.

Cayden had his signature smirk. It was strange to see him on his knees before me. His eyes spoke more than his smirk. They held something that appeared to be caring and kindness. Somehow, I recognized the sincerity in them, saw them as more than just pity. I was their captive, why were they being nice to me? They could just as easily torture me to get back at Lucas.

"You are going to send a nice message to your brother. You will tell him that you are unharmed and safe as long as he pays what he owes us. Understand?" Ace held up his phone, ready to film. Lucas was going to kill me no matter what, a shock of fear went through me. Lucas wouldn't want to save me, I was stuck here until they kill me.

My tongue darted across my lips. Cayden's eyes followed the action, his smirk faltering for a moment. "B-but that's not true. W-we don't have money to pay y-you!" I couldn't keep the fear out of my voice or hide the trembles that racked through my body. I wish I was stronger. After everything Lucas did to me, I should be.

Cayden let out a sharp laugh, "You're so naive! Now pout those pretty lips and say what we told you to." What was I missing?

Ace nodded, confirming that he was filming. I exhaled, "Lucas, I am safe as long as you pay them. Please, help me!" I fought the tears that threatened to spill. I don't want to cry in front of them... again. Lucas hated when I cried, he would probably think I was too pathetic to save.

"Very good, that should be convincing enough," Ace muttered before walking away. I took this moment to look around the room. It was also when I realized that Ryker was nowhere to be found. Where could he be?

The walls and floor were cement. There were no windows and two doors. I was tied to a chair across from a bed and table. There was also a wardrobe near the closest door. The room wasn't small, but it was small enough for me to feel claustrophobic.

Nothing personal was on the table, the only thing that showed any color was the baby blue bed sheets and pink comforter. It was another odd sight. I imagined my captors trying to wrestle the light blue bed sheets on the bed. I wondered if they ordered the comforter or had to go to a store and buy it. I fought a giggle at the idea of them buying a bright pink comforter and carrying it through the mall.

"What's so funny, sweet firestorm?" Cayden sneered and I shook my head. My eyes drifted above his head and then darted around the room. I looked around and noticed a camera in each of the ceiling's corners. "Those are for us," Cayden told me, following my eyes. I nodded slowly; my head still throbbing. Cayden got up and walked towards the door closest to the wardrobe. "This is your bathroom."

"What?" I asked. I have a bathroom, does that mean they plan on keeping me? For how long? Thousands of questions

CHAPTER THREE: EMBER

fly into my head making the pain worse. "Let me go!" I said suddenly.

"No." He flatly said. I opened and shut my mouth at his bluntness. It was no use arguing with him. "Alright Ember, I'm gonna untie you and you are gonna behave. Understand?"

I dumbly nodded. Cayden walked over to me and untied my right wrist. He rubbed it gently before doing the same to my left. Frozen in place, I watched him stand up and walk to the door. "One of us will be down with food later, I suggest getting some rest. You can shower if you want, there are clothes in the wardrobe and towels in the bathroom. Put something clean on. Unless you fuck up, there are no cameras in the bathroom."

As the door slammed shut, I peeled myself off the chair. What has Lucas done this time, I wondered.

The clothes in the wardrobe consisted of lingerie that left nothing to the imagination and men's shirts. The only pants there were shorts that would cover nothing. How did they get my size? I nervously looked at the camera above the bed. Were they watching me?

Shaking my head, I grabbed a shirt, the shorts and a matching baby blue lace bra and panties. Despite being alone, my face burned red, and I fought the urge to scream. My pajamas that I was currently wearing were old and had many holes in them. I got them a thrift store a few years back. The pajamas were a few sizes too small now, but they did their job. They were also dirty, as I was unable to wash them for over a week. Cayden's words echoed in my head, was it obvious that my clothes were dirty? Did they smell that bad? I blushed at the thought of smelling bad around my three captors.

I scanned the bathroom for cameras. The walls were white,

with gray tile on the floor and light blue tile in the shower. The shower was a combination shower and bath with a blue shower curtain that matched the tile. As I undressed and stepped under the warm water I sighed. My thoughts drifted to my twin.

At nine years old, we were thrown out into the world. He became protective instantly. He found us food, shelter and even bargained for clothing. I helped him with his schoolwork, and he helped me survive. Although his anger sometimes got the best of him.

At thirteen I wanted to go out with some friends from school. Lucas told me no and I began to argue.

"It's not fair, Lucas!" I had exclaimed. "We are just going to the mall and then I'll come straight back here! I promise!"

"I said no, now stop it!" I knew I should have stopped, but I didn't want to miss all the fun.

"Luc-"

"Ember Breelyn, I said no!" Lucas never used my middle name, he said he hated it. It was my maternal grandmother's name; she hated boys and hated him. I huffed and he grabbed my shoulder harshly, "Do not give me attitude, I'm the only reason you are alive!"

As his grip tightened, I muttered a quiet apology. His eyes stared daggers into mine and he gave my shoulder a final punishing squeeze. He shoved me towards a desk telling me to do my homework and his. I bowed my head, fighting the urge to rub my bruised shoulder and started on our algebra.

How I wish I was back doing algebra. Lucas kept me safe; he would save me now. At least I hoped he would Somehow, that thought didn't comfort me.

I quickly rinsed the conditioner from my hair and used the coconut body wash and a washcloth to clean my skin. My

CHAPTER THREE: EMBER

eyes slid shut as I imagined my three captors watching me bath. I could almost picture Ace's eyes flaring, Cayden's smirk, and Ryker's intense gaze upon me as I washed every inch of my body. Before I knew it, my fingers were circling my clit to the image of being watched. Tearing my hand away from my pussy, I washed the remaining soap off and jumped out of the shower.

Wrapping a towel around my body, my eyes flashed to the mirror. Ugly, they would never think my fat body littered in scars was theirs to worship.

4

Chapter Four: RYKER

I want to worship her. Watching Ember is quickly becoming my new favorite hobby. Watching her in the motel was fun, but knowing she is so close makes watching her so much sweeter. She was so cute, especially when she tried to hide herself from the cameras. My little flame also angered me when she tried to hide herself. My mouth watered at the thought of licking and kissing all of her beautiful curves.

It pained me to think that she believed that she was anything but beautiful. It also made me want to kill her piece of shit brother. He always put her down, making her feel like she wasn't a goddess. The number of times I watched her sneak onto the scale in the locker room when she thought nobody was looking is disheartening.

I glanced at the cameras in her brother's motel room. Originally these were just to watch Ember; but after we first saw him hit her, we knew we had to get her out. Lucas was currently tearing the room apart and punching holes in the wall. Cayden and Ace sat next on either side of me as we watched the cameras.

CHAPTER FOUR: RYKER

Ace had sent a video of Ember begging for help to Lucas. This video was meant to mock him, our girl will never be in any danger around us. She is our world; she has been for months now. Lucas didn't want to save; he was just mad that we had her. He planned on selling her anyway.

Ace's phone rang, the caller ID showing Ember's best friend and our right hand Ramero Gutiérrez. He had been working with us since he was eighteen as our lead trade and hit man. Despite being only 22, his skill rivaled Cayden's in murder.

Ace, Cayden, and I started and currently run ACR Empires. The rumors of us being mafia men or working within the skin trade are not true, but nobody needs to know that. In reality we are far worse than mafia men and we would never force women to do anything, let alone sell them. We aren't good men, but women and children are off limits.

Ace answered the call and Ramero's panicked voice came from the phone, " Ace! Ember is missing! I just got a call from Lucas. You kidnapped her!"

Ace let out a laugh that lack humor, "Ramero, watch your tone. We both know that I do not owe you any explanation. Now, we understand you are her friend and that you care about her; therefore, I will tell you she is safe."

The call was silent for a moment, "Can I talk to her?"

"No." Cayden said bluntly.

Ramero let out a rush of breath, "Are you going to hurt her?"

"No!" All three of us barked at the same time.

I could almost picture the relief on his face. "Gentlemen, I trust you guys and I know you don't owe me an explanation, but can you give me something? A reason why? She is my best friend and I have done a lot of good work for you recently."

I glanced at Ace who thought for a moment before nodding.

Ace always tried to be fair, and I knew that he liked Ramero. "You know her brother is an asshole; she needs to be protected from him." That was it, that was all he was going to give.

"He is an asshole. Just know, she has PTSD from Lucas and is going to need a lot of love and patience. If at any point you need me to, I can hide her. Be patient with Ember. If you need anything let me know. I am going to check out the Ashben warehouse, Austin will be in my ear. I'll let you know if anything happens."

He hung up the phone and I knew he was frustrated. Cayden cleared his throat, "That went well. Hopefully the Ashben situation will be handled, and we can reward Ramero by allowing him to see Ember." We all nodded our agreement. With Austin, our tech wizard in his ear he should be fine.

Ember turned over, letting out a groan. Ace got up and disappeared into the kitchen. Cayden and I watched Ember sprint into the bathroom. The blanket around her shoulders was like a cape, our little superhero.

Ace returned a few minutes later with a plate of food. I stood up quickly and reached to take it. Cayden placed a hard smack on my sore ass. After our impromptu session, I was feeling tender. As much as I loved topping Cayden, it was just as important to submit to his delicious torture.

Only hours before I was tied to the spanking bench in our playroom. Cayden standing behind me with his favorite paddle spanking my ass. I was getting hard just thinking about the way he fucked me and put a large glass plug in my ass. It was still there, shifting every time I moved, reminding me of who I belong to.

I looked between Cayden and Ace before asking, "Can I please take the food downstairs? You wouldn't let me see her when she first woke up."

Ace nodded and handed me the plate. "Ryk, you weren't in a good headspace to see her. You know we would never keep you away from her unless it was necessary."

I tipped my head before another stinging slap got me saying "yes, sir."

With the approval of my two boyfriends, I headed towards the basement stairs. Taking one last lingering look at the cameras, my feet carried me down the stairs.

At the bottom was four rooms, Ember's room was the second door from the staircase. Not wanting to seem too hasty, I slowed my steps and took a second to calm my breathing. I couldn't show my nervousness or seem like I was anything but in charge.

Just as I reached her down, a loud scream echoed in my ears. I gave one harsh knock before unlocking the door and rushing in.

5

Chapter Five: EMBER

I felt much better after my shower. A good cry was necessary for me to feel even remotely better. I had brushed my teeth with the toothbrush and toothpaste that were sitting on the sink. Nerves hit me as I grew the courage to open the door. The t-shirt covered me enough, but I still felt fat. I weighed more than most women and didn't have a flat stomach. I glanced in the mirror; the shirt was a little short because of my belly. I sighed and hoped my thighs didn't jiggle too much when I rush to the bed. The door slightly creaked as it opened, and I was exposed to two of the four cameras.

 I stepped out and ran over to the bed. I quickly covered myself with a purple blanket. It wasn't there earlier, so I assume that one of my kidnappers put it there. The material was soft against my bare legs which gave me a small sense of comfort. It was warm, like it was fresh out of the dryer. Under the blanket was also a small stuffed bear that seemed to ask for cuddles. I snuggled into the blanket, shivering slightly from my wet hair. I was going to regret not brushing it, but I didn't have the energy. Pulling the bear close, I closed my

CHAPTER FIVE: EMBER

eyes. For what seemed like hours I begged sleep to come, but it never did.

I laid staring up at the ceiling, replaying the events of the previous night over and over in my head. My stomach gurgled, reminding me that I had to eat at some point. I sat up with a sigh and stood. I wrapped the blanket around me like a cape and held it tight. This would at least cover me, I thought. I put the bear on the pillow and grabbed the wooden hairbrush that was on the side table.

I wandered towards the only unlocked door in the room. Closing the bathroom door, I dropped the blanket and attempted to brush my hair. For the millionth time I thought about shaving my head. The tangles were frustrating, especially without detangler. My hair was thick and often unruly. Unless I have some sort of product, it would hurt like a bitch to get the tangles out. I let out a frustrated scream as a large knot prevented the brush from passing through.

A loud knock on the door caused me to yelp. It swung open to reveal Ryker. He stared at me with a concerned look on his face, "Are you okay, little flame?"

I rushed to grab the blanket as I felt his eyes slide over my body. I nodded with a deep blush. He didn't look convinced, "Come here," he demanded, adding "now!" when I made no attempt to move. His tone had me scurrying out of the bathroom. I prayed he didn't see too much. I was shaking really badly and flinched when a large hand was on my back guiding me to the bed. I was waiting for him to command me to drop the blanket or do some other degrading act.

"Why were you yelling?" Ryker asked calmly when I was sitting on the bed. The chair I was tied to earlier was dragged over. He sat, placing a plate of food on his lap. I was so distracted by him, I failed to acknowledge the food that was on the side table. A turkey sandwich was on a white paper plate. There were also apple slices and a handful of barbecue potato chips. My mouth watered at the sight. I couldn't remember the last time I ate, let alone that much. Lucas never let me eat.

He looked at me expectantly, my eyes darted from the food and him. Why did he care? He kidnapped me, he is supposed to hate me! "I don't hate you, little flame. Never think or say that. Do you always think out loud?" I hide my face under the blanket. Even the promise of food couldn't save me from the embarrassment.

He chuckled, "Don't hide from any of us either. Now, that is two questions that you ignored, a third and you get punished. Understand?" Punished? What did that mean? Ryker removed the blanket from my head, allowing me to keep it covering my body. I nodded, remembering that that would be the third question. He grabbed my chin, "I want to hear that pretty little voice of yours. Verbal answers only."

"Yes," I squeaked, my eyes wide.

He smiled gently, "We will talk about this more later, but you have no reason to fear us. We won't hurt you." His grip never changed, it didn't hurt, but I wanted to look away. I struggled in his grasp, "Before I let you go, answer my first question. Why did you scream?"

I swallowed, "I couldn't get a knot out of my hair. I'm sorry."

He nodded and let go of me. "No need to scream or be sorry. Just ask for help next time, okay?" His voice held such a gentleness that made me wonder if it was forced or not.

"Okay," I whispered. Ryker picked up half of a turkey sandwich and held it out to me. "I'm not hun-" I started when my stomach let out a large rumble. He laughed and held out

CHAPTER FIVE: EMBER

the sandwich again. "Is it poisoned?" I asked cautiously.

"Why would it be?" When I still made no move to take it, he sighed. He took a bite and chewed. "Okay? Now, you are going to eat everything I give you. Don't make me force feed you." His tone made me realize that he would force feed me.

I gulped and took the sandwich. He shifted, almost uncomfortably in the chair. I was almost like it hurt him to sit. The next ten minutes consisted of me chewing and him watching. Ryker's intense stare made me shiver. Why was he watching me? What did he mean earlier? It was awkward and embarring to be watched while I ate. He didn't seem to notice or care. Questions flew through my head, and I looked away from him. My gaze fell upon the wooden wardrobe.

"Why are there no clothes in the wardrobe?" I asked, curiosity finally getting the better of me.

Ryker followed my eyes. "There is," he answered plainly. He smiled, "If you have a problem with those clothes, you don't have to wear them."

"Then what would I wear?" I asked. His grin grew and I blushed again looking away. Gross.

He stood up and put the now empty plate on the table. I had eaten more than I had in a year and felt uncomfortably full. I watched as he rose and grabbed the hairbrush from the bathroom. I bit my lip nervously. Ryker came back and told me to sit in the chair. I shook my head. "Ember, the chair, or my lap. Choose!" I leapt into the chair, was he serious? I did not want to find out that answer. "Thank you," he growled in my ear.

I jumped when his hand touched my hair. "What are you doing?" I tried to sound demanding.

"Brushing your hair."

I sat silently, groaning when he started detangling a knot. Ryker was surprisingly gentle and took his time making my hair soft. He hummed softly, a song that I couldn't quite name. "Ryker?" He paused and I took that as a sign to continue. "Why are you doing this?"

"Doing what?"

"I don't know. Brushing my hair? Caring if I ate? Keeping me here?"

Ryker did not respond, instead he finished brushing my hair and pulled it into a ponytail. Where did he get the hair tie? I was broken out of my thoughts when he put the brush on the table. He grabbed the discarded plate and left.

I sighed; guess I wasn't getting an answer today. Who I wouldn't kill for a lighter right now. I love fire, the dancing flames always calm me when I am upset. Throwing myself onto the bed, I pulled the warm blanket over me and allowed myself to fall into a fitful sleep.

6

Chapter Six: EMBER

Silence. I woke up to silence. I kept my eyes shut wondering where Lucas was. Why wasn't he snoring next to me? I rolled over and opened my eyes. Where am I? The room looked different from the dirty motel that I had grown used to. This room was clean and didn't smell like BO and weed.

The fear paralyzed me for less than a minute before everything flooded back causing my head to pound. Panic took over as pieces of the night prior came back. The ring segment, the storm, the kidnapping, the moment with Ryker.

I scrambled out of the bed and ran to the door. I didn't know what time it was; I didn't care. I shook the knob, locked. I started screaming, banging on the door. "Help!" I yelled, "Help!"

The door was suddenly thrown open and I screamed. Three worried faces stared at me as I stumbled back. "What's wrong, baby girl?" Ace asked, stepping forward. As the others entered the room, they cleared the doorway. I bolted out the door. Heavy footsteps followed me as I ran. I glanced behind me, Cayden was close. I picked up my pace.

I didn't register anything but get to safety. Just keep running until safety. They will beat me if I get caught. They will kill me if I get caught. I took the stairs by two, doing my best not to fall. I made it into a living room and kept going.

Then the ground was coming towards me fast and someone or something had wrapped their arms around my waist. I landed hard on the mystery person's chest before being flipped to be pinned to the floor. I squeezed my eyes shut, trying to will the person away.

"Open your eyes, Ember." A harsh voice said. I shook my head while someone pulled me to my feet. "Ember, I will not ask again. You are already in trouble."

I hesitated. Wrong move, a heavy hand landed on my ass. I squealed and tried to move away. Another smack and my eyes flew open. "I'm sorry!"

Ace's hand rested on my ass as Cayden held me in place. Ryker was staring at me, an unreadable expression on his face. I blushed and looked away from their hard stares. "Ember, you understand what you did was wrong, correct?" Ace asked. I nodded and he continued, "I expect verbal answers from now on. You need to be punished for this stunt."

I tensed, eyes tightly shut, preparing for a slap, or beating from the larger men. I fought the images of the bloody mess I would be when they are finished. These men are huge, they could easily hurt and kill me. "Princess, relax. Look at me, Ember," Cayden said softly. His fingers tipped my chin up and I forced my eyes open. His dark blue ones bore into mine. "What do you think is about to happen?"

I bit my lip, "I-I don't know?"

He tsked, "Ember, I don't like liars. This is your only pass. Answer my question."

CHAPTER SIX: EMBER

His grip tightened and Ace's hand squeezed my ass. Although I couldn't see Ryker, I knew he was listening closely. "A-Are you g-gonna b-b-beat me?" I stutter out.

"Beat you?" Ryker demanded, pushing Cayden out of the way. "Is that how your piece of shit brother treated you? Like a fucking dog?"

I flinched and tried to back away. I didn't get very far; Ace was standing too close to me. Ace turned me around and wrapped his arms around me gently. I was pulled into his chest as Ryker cursed. Burying my head into him I fought the urge to cry.

I breathed in his scent for a long while. Something about his larger frame and strong muscles was comforting, not terrifying. He was warm and smelled of sandalwood and leather. Lucas was smaller built and was never good at comforting. His hugs were always stiff, where Ace is someone I can melt into.

Cayden was saying something to Ryker, but it was too quiet for me to hear. I instead focused on Ace's breathing and slowing my own. "I'm sorry," I mutter to no one in particular. Ace rubbed my back slowly, soothingly. My body craved the comfort that he provided.

"I want you to breathe. Once you are relaxed, we'll talk." Ace whispered to me. He held me for a few minutes longer before I was deemed calm enough. He sat me in front of him on a couch. The three men surrounded me, blocking my view of the room.

"Ember, we are not going to beat you. We will come back to that later though." He was speaking slowly, but firmly, "Now we want to get this over with, okay?"

I lowered my eyes and nodded. The butterflies in my

stomach turned to wasps as my nerves worsened. Clearly, they were going to do something, but what was my punishment? Cayden looked at me, "My sweet firestorm, as soon as this is done, we will forgive you. We are going to correct your behavior; I promise that we are not going to leave marks or cause long-term harm. Ace is the most clear-headed, go over his knee."

"What?" I asked, shocked. Was he about to-

"Ember, I will not ask again." Cayden growled. I jumped up, shaking and walked over to a second couch where Ace sat. Ace's face was calm, he wasn't angry or at least didn't appear to be. Despite knowing what was coming, I was surprisingly less nervous.

Ace pulled me over his knee gently. "Relax," he rubbed circles on my back. I blushed when he pulled my pants and panties off. Before I could protest, I felt a hard smack on my ass. The sudden pain caused me to gasp and struggle against Ace's grip. "Stop Ember. If you take your punishment like a good girl, we can put this in the past." He held me tighter and I placed my hands on the ground to balance myself.

I closed my eyes and rested my head on his leg. I bit my lip as tears fell. Two hard spanks landed on my left cheek, two on my right. He spanked me harder over and over. He spanked me until his handprints were engraved on my ass. Tears fell, I kicked despite my mind telling me to stop. His leg trapped my two and I was stuck. My face was red, but my ass was probably more so.

"Please," I choked out. "I'm sorry!" I whimpered, wanting the pain to stop. I wasn't scared of him or the spanking, I was just tired and in pain. This was a different pain than I was used to, more caring. He didn't say anything, didn't stop,

CHAPTER SIX: EMBER

just kept going. Soon, all I could focus on was the pain and tiredness I felt.

"Five more," Ace said gently, "these are going to be the hardest." And he was right. On the fifth one, I screamed before collapsing and sobbing. He was rubbing my back once again, letting me cry. I never registered being moved to sit carefully on Ryker's lap.

Ryker's strong arms wrapped around me as he rocked us slowly. He whispered sweet nothings in my ear and told me that it was over. I did nothing, said nothing, just let him hold me. Was this what love feels like? I've never felt so safe and content. Soon my cries turned to sniffles and Ace and Cayden knelt in front of me.

"Do you understand why we had to spank you?" Ace asked, looking up at me. When I nodded, he said, "Verbal, babygirl. Speak."

"Yes, sir."

"Why?" Cayden tilted my chin slightly.

I felt my face heat up again, I didn't want to say anything. However, Cayden's impatient look told me to speak. "I tried to run away."

"Good girl. That was very dangerous, princess. You could have gotten hurt or ran into very bad people. From now on, you will stay where we put you. Our goal is to keep you safe; we will talk more about this later. You can trust us. Now, I can see that you are tired. We will have that conversation, but tonight we'll just relax. What movie do ya wanna watch?" Cayden asked.

Why would they want to keep me safe? I was their captive. "Um, I don't know. Maybe a comedy? The one with the old English guys who are trying to find Jesus or God or something."

The three men chuckled. I blushed and hid my face. Ryker moved my chin to look at him and I tried to get up. "Ember, where are you trying to go?" I bit my lip, Ryker's tone startling me. I froze and he continued, "Unless you want to sit on your sore ass, you will stay on my lap."

I nodded and muttered an apology. Cayden sat down next to Ryker and rubbed my leg soothingly. Ace got a bottle of water and set up the TV. "Here, drink." I looked up cautiously. "Ember, you are dehydrated and need the water. Drink!"

I flinched and took the bottle. We locked eyes as the bottle was placed at my lips. He watched as I took a long sip. "Keep going, I want that water gone by the time I get back." Ace then walked away, leaving me with the others and the water.

"Drink the water, little flame. Ace ain't afraid to put you over his knee again." Ryker urged. With wide eyes, I finished the water and handed Cayden the bottle. Ryker smiled, "Thank you little flame."

Ace came back with some blankets and hot chocolate. He smiled when he saw Cayden with the empty water bottle. "Good girl! Now, let's watch the movie!"

7

Chapter Seven: EMBER

After the movie, I was left with Ryker. Cayden had to go to the store, they asked what I liked to eat so he went to get me my favorites. Ace left to start dinner. We spent the time in comfortable silence watching cartoons. Finally, I started to squirm.

"Stop it," he growled, grabbing my hips.

"I have to go to the bathroom," I whimpered, between the water and the hot chocolate I was ready to burst.

He was reluctant to let me use the bathroom, "If I let you up, are you gonna run?" He had turned me to face him. If I didn't have to pee so bad, I would be embarrassed to straddle him.

I shook my head, "Please Ryker! I'll be good! Please, please, please!" I really had to pee. I felt like I was going to explode if he didn't let me up.

He smirked and placed a palm on my face, "So pretty when you beg. You have to pee really really badly, don't you, little flame?" I nodded and pouted my lips. Ryker picked me up and carried me over to the bathroom. He placed me in front of the toilet and walked to the door. He leaned against the wooden door frame and watched me.

I blushed, "W-what are you doing?"

"You said you have to pee. So, the bathroom is yours to use." Ryker said, making no attempt to move or leave.

"Can I have privacy?" I asked, already knowing the answer.

I bowed my head as he responded, "You lost that when you ran. You have one minute, use it wisely."

I gave him a final, embarrassed look before accepting my fate. My ass hurt, I was tired and scared. I pulled down my pants being sure to cover myself and sat carefully on the toilet. I winced and looked at the tile on the wall.

It was green, almost seafoam. It covered the entire bathroom and combined with the decor, gave the room a very beachy feel. There were starfish and seashells on a shelf in the corner. It also held extra toilet paper, books, and magazines. The books were all war and military books, with the exception of a memoir of some old wrestler. The magazines were much the same, with guns and 'manly' things on the covers. The magazines were the only sign that men use it.

Looking anywhere but at Ryker seemed to do the trick and I was finally able to pee. I sighed with relief as my bladder was finally empty. I grabbed some toilet paper and Ryker watched me closely. I quickly finished my business and pulled up my pants, making sure that all my intimate areas were fully covered. I flushed the toilet and washed my hands, silently.

He gave me a wicked grin, "Pull down your pants and put your hands on the sink."

I shook my head, "P-Please, I'm already sore! I-I-"

"Relax!" Ryker commanded, "I'm not gonna spank you. I need to check your ass for bruising. If you do as you're told I'll even put arnica cream on you."

CHAPTER SEVEN: EMBER

I gulped, "Promise you won't spank me?" Lucas would say he wouldn't hurt me and then would, why would Ryker be any different?

"I promise little flame. Nothing but look and lotion." He gave me a gentle smile and leaned me over the sink. "I'm gonna pull these down now." I tensed as he pulled down my pants and panties. "Ace spanked you good, he always did know how to make a sore ass. Just be careful, you don't want to meet Cayden's paddle, that shit hurts."

"H-How do you know?" I dared ask. Hindsight told me that was stupid and that I shouldn't have said anything while I was so vulnerable.

Ryker reached for a bottle on the shelf behind me, "Do you know what a switch is?"

"Someone who is both a top and a bottom?"

"Exactly. Hold still, I'm about to put the cream on." I took a breath as jumped slightly as his hand touched my hurting ass.

"I'm sorry! I didn't mean to move!"

"Deep breath, love. I'm not mad, I know it hurts." I nodded at his comment. "Anyway, I'm a switch and they spank me sometimes when we play. I actually felt the paddle yesterday, it was both pleasant and painful."

Spankings can be pleasant? They hurt so much and they're embarrassing! I was aroused because of Ace's body, not his hand spanking me. Right?

"Alright little flame, come on. Dinner should be ready any minute and you have to set the table." Ryker said cleaning his hand and righting my clothes. He reached out his hand. I thought about ignoring it but thought better of it. My ass hurts now, imagine another spanking?

"Thank you, sir." I murmured.

"You're welcome little flame." His voice was kind.

Taking his hand, he led me to the kitchen. Ace was stirring something in a pot and smiled when he saw us. "Hey, Ember!" I looked at the ground. I hated being the center of attention and that was all I seemed to be here. Lucas never gave me any good attention like this. "Aww," he cooed, "is baby girl being shy?" My cheeks reddened.

"She just had to piss; I think she is." Ryker huffed. My face felt like it was on fire. I felt like shrinking into a ball and throwing myself into a ditch never to be seen again. "Here," Ryker handed me four plates, a stack of napkins and four forks. He then gestured for me to place them on the table. I did and he came behind me and placed down knives at three of the four placemats. The table was a rectangular table with six chairs, three of the dirty placemats told me where they normally sat. The only odd thing was one of the dirty placemats sat further from the head of the table. A clean one next to it.

I was then asked to get drinks for everybody, dragging me out of my thoughts. Beer for Cayden and Ace and water for Ryker and myself. I was surprised when Ryker told me that he didn't drink. He seemed like a whisky kind of guy, but I guess I just stereotyped him.

Cayden walked into the kitchen wearing flannel pajama pants, which was a change from his usual attire. Ace was putting spaghetti on the table which looked so good. Cayden gave me a kiss on my forehead and sat down on the left side of the table. I noticed that he sat next to the clean placemat. I hurriedly gave him his drink before debating on where the other three go.

"Ace sits at the head of the table and Ryker is sitting on the other side. You, princess, are next to me." He smiled and I

CHAPTER SEVEN: EMBER

mumbled a quiet thanks before setting the drinks down.

Ace and Ryker came to the table, and I moved around to my chair. Pulling it out and I noticed a pillow had been placed there. I let out a breath of relief at the fact of not sitting on a wood chair. I sat cautiously and bowed my head. Cayden served everyone, including me, a large helping of pasta and tomato sauce. Ryker also placed two pieces of warm bread that dripped with butter on my plate. My mouth watered at the sight. The men all started to eat and engage in simple conversation, I kept my head bowed.

"Aren't ya gonna eat, Ember?" Cayden asked.

I looked at him, knowing better than to get hopeful. "Am I allowed to eat, sir?" I asked, worried about getting in trouble for even entertaining the thought.

"What do you mean? Why the fuck couldn't you?" Ryker exclaimed.

Ace put a hand on his arm to calm him down. "Ember, you can eat. You never have to ask to eat. Although we will make sure you get two to three meals a day, if you are ever hungry, tell us. Understand?"

I nodded, "Yes, sir." He held eye contact with me, for a second then told me to eat. I did as I was told happily. Ace was an amazing cook and I made sure to compliment him on it. He shrugged it off, but deep down I knew he was happy with my comments.

We ate in a comfortable silence. At the end of the meal, I helped with dishes. I wasn't allowed near the knives however, but I helped with everything else. After cleaning up, I was brought back downstairs to my prison.

"So, baby girl, we need to talk." Ace started, "Do you know why we took you from the motel the other day?"

"Lucas owes you money," I whisper, pushing myself into the corner of the bed. My attempts to hide failed as Ace pulled gently towards the center of the bed.

"No," Ryker said harshly, "he is a no-good son of a bitch. You are ours. We protect what is ours. Especially from punk ass, dumbass, bitchass, asshats like him!"

I flinched at his words. Sure, Lucas had his moments, but we all do. He was my brother; he would never hurt me. I was a bad girl, a bad sister, he was just disciplining me. I deserved it. "That's not true! My brother is a good man, and nobody owns me!"

Ace lifted his eyebrow, "Has Lucas ever hit you? Not spank you. Hit you? Slap you across the face?"

My mind went back to a week ago. *After a show we were in the car. I was hungry and asked if we could get food. Lucas yelled and told me I had already eaten, and he didn't want a fat sister. I tried to explain that I needed more than an apple, but he told me that I was already fat enough and needed to lose weight. We stopped and he got food for himself before going to the motel. He ate in front of me, made me watch. Lucas told me when I am one hundred pounds, I could eat with him. I talked back. He smacked me across the face and punched me in the stomach three times. On the third time he told me "Maybe these punches would flatten your stomach," before going back to his meal.*

"I-I deserved it. I misbehaved." I said, weakly.

"No-"

"Yes," I stated, "I talked back. I should just lose the weight and be a good sister. A sister he is proud of."

"Ember you should not please that dirtbag and what the fuck do you mean lose weight? You are perfect!" Cayden argued.

CHAPTER SEVEN: EMBER

I shook my head, "I currently weigh 215 pounds, that is too much. Lucas says when I weigh a hundred pounds, I can eat with him again! So, I need to lose it." I put a hand on my stomach, regretting eating dinner.

Ryker stormed over to the bed from where he leaned on the door frame. A shriek left my mouth as he grabbed me. I tried to kick and pull myself from his grasp. I received two warning spanks before finally settling down. "Little flame, I don't care what your piece of shit brother says. You are beautiful. Now, do I have to strip you naked and worship every inch of your body or will you believe me?"

I was shocked at his forwardness before shaking my head dumbly, "I'm sorry for upsetting you sir."

He exhaled sharply, "Understand that your brother is abusive. Little girl, we noticed you have been weird the past few events and we saw Lucas punch you."

I tried to get out of his grip, and he let me. The three of them surrounded me, throwing facts about my brother's quick temper and its effects. They told me about what they witnessed, why they beat up my brother outside of the storyline at the last event. It all became too much. Their much larger bodies around me, the horrible memories they brought up, the stress of the past couple of months.

"BLACK!" I screamed, before the waves of dread came over me and the room was no longer clear.

8

Chapter Eight: CAYDEN

Black? What the fuck did that mean? I looked up with wide eyes at Ace and Ryker. I caught Ember as she fainted, the unexpectedness had me falling to my knees. I cradled her head in my arms, trying to figure out what was going on.

Ace was the first to react. He lifted our girl off of me and carried her over to the bed. Ryker helped tuck her in and we all stood in a stunned silence. Ramero said that she had PTSD, but we never thought she would have a panic attack around us. We are supposed to keep her safe, not be the cause of her fear.

"I'm gonna go get her some water." I got up and walked out the door. Needing a minute, I grabbed a bottle of water from the fridge and a straw. I looked out the window above the sink for a minute before hearing footsteps behind me.

"You okay, baby boy?" Ace asked, rubbing my back gently.

I shoved him away, "Don't touch me! We caused her to pass out. She was so scared that she fainted because of us!" My voice rose, causing Ace's eyebrow to raise.

"Cayden, I understand you're upset, but do not raise your

CHAPTER EIGHT: CAYDEN

voice." His demand sent a shiver down my spine.

"Or what?" I challenged, needing the release that that threat promised.

He let out a slow breath, took the bottle and straw from my hand. "Bend over the sink. Put your hands on the window."

His calm demeaner only made him scarier. I slowly turned and placed my hands against the window. I tensed when Ace pulled down my flannel pants.

"You have a nice ass. I like that you went commando, makes my task easier." He whispered in my ear, rubbing my ass in slow circles. "Keep your hands there and stay as silent as possible."

Nodding, I murmured, "Yes, sir."

A loud slap echoed through the kitchen before being followed by several others. I stayed still, leaning into the pain. Small groans escaped my mouth without control. The sting of Ace's palm felt like heaven and hell all wrapped up together. Ace paused for a spilt second before the sharp smack of the spatula filled the air.

Ace always knew what I needed. Without stopping his rhythm, he reached his hand around to play with my balls. Tugging on them and lightly squeezing them caused me to let out a whimper. He was teasing me, tugging them in time to the spatula bouncing off my ass.

I almost took my hands off the window when his hand left my balls. Ace clicked his tongue, "You take your hands off the window this will turn into a punishment with ginger involved."

I pushed my weight onto my hands at his threat. I needed a release, not to have ginger shoved up my ass. The spanks came to a stop and Ace's hand began rubbing my stinging cheeks.

"I am going to let you come and then we are going to go downstairs and take care of our girl." His fingers slowly moved up and down my dick. Using my precum as lube, his movements got faster. "Keep your hands where they are. If they come off the window or you do anything stupid in the basement, I will take you into the dungeon and you will wear a chastity belt for the next month."

Whimpering at his words, I nodded. "Yes, sir! Please let me come! I'll do anything!" It felt so good, the rush of blood to my dick didn't allow me to think of anything but my own pleasure.

Ace didn't make me wait long, "Come for me baby boy."

I shouted my release as his hands worked my cock until it was limp, and I was satisfied. Ace turned my panting form around and pulled me into him. As much as I would never admit it, hugs were one of my favorite things.

His warmth radiated into me and the way he rubbed my back made me feel loved. The whole stereotype that men have to be strong and not show emotion is bullshit. My parents refused to let me even acknowledge my emotions, Ace always dragged them out of me. Ever since we were kids, the three of us shared a bond and my love for them will never make me weak. We make each other stronger. Even as I try to keep from bawling my eyes out in Ace's arm, I am not weak. If we didn't have our sweet firestorm waiting on us, I would be sobbing.

After a final pat on the back, Ace opened the bottle that I got for Ember and had me drink some. He then got another bottle, and we walked downstairs to see if she woke up.

Disappointment in myself threatened to surface when I saw

CHAPTER EIGHT: CAYDEN

she was still out. Ryker was leaning by the bathroom when we entered.

"She woke up for a brief moment, before falling asleep again." Ryker told us, moving to lean on the door frame.

Ace set the bottle on the side table and stood over by the bathroom door. I decided to lean against the wardrobe watching the sleeping girl on the bed.

"Are we good? We need to be united without scaring her again. Ryker do you need a guilt spanking or are you okay?" Ace asked, causing Ryker to blush a bright red.

"I needed one, nothing to be embarrassed about." I say, trying to eliminate the embarrassment that he was feeling. Ryker always overthinks and feels embarrassed for admitting his needs. He felt bad, that was obvious, but he didn't seem to be beating himself up as badly as me.

He shook his head, "I think I'm okay. My ass still hurts from that cursed paddle. I don't think I'll sit for a year if Ace spanks me on top of this." I laughed and shook my head, I guess I wield a wicked paddle.

A low groan followed by a loud whimper caused my head to turn. My sweet firestorm is awakening.

9

Chapter Nine: EMBER

I don't remember how I got onto the bed or under the warm comforting sheets. I briefly remember waking up, but the warmth and stress of the past couple of days lured me back to sleep. My head hurt, causing a groan to come from me. I whimpered with confusion as I sat up looking quickly around the room. Ace stood at the bathroom door, Ryker by the other door and Cayden leaned on the wardrobe. They were as far from me as they could without being out of the room.

"Ember?" Cayden asked gently. They were all staring at me. I looked down at my hands. Watched them as they fidget and my thumbs twiddle. I took interest in my half-chewed nails and how ugly they were. Another thing that made me unwanted. Unlovable. Ugly, as Lucas used to tell me.

"Baby girl?" Ace kept his voice low and even. He slowly took a few steps forward, like he was trying not to spook an animal. He kept his hands in front of him, showing that they were empty. "It's okay. You are safe." He repeated these words until he reached the bed. My eyes shot between him and the other two. I jerked back when Ace went to touch me. "I'm

CHAPTER NINE: EMBER

sorry!" He rushed out as he pulled his hand away. Despite my fear, it hurt to see him upset because of me.

"What does black mean?" Ryker asked gruffly.

I shrugged and tried to crawl deeper into the corner of the bed. Ace sat perched on the edge of the bed. His concerned eyes told me everything that I needed to know. Cayden and Ryker had the same look, pure concern and fear. They cared. They wanted to help me. They held a look Lucas never gave: love.

Was I stupid for thinking it as love? They kidnapped me, are holding me hostage, but they love me? "Panic attack." I mutter, embarrassed at my own mental health. These men clearly had no fear of anything, no mental health problems.

Despite not looking up, I felt Cayden and Ryker move closer. Their presence is always overwhelming, even more so now. Footsteps echoed in the now silent room. "Black means you are going to have a panic attack?" Cayden asked, cocking his head to the side.

I shook my head quickly, "Having a panic attack."

"Oh," Ace gave me a soft smile, he placed a hand on my foot. The action was slow, a move meant to not startle me. A thing a person would do to gain the trust of an animal or a small child. "Do you have a color system?" I nodded. "Can we know it? We want to make sure that you are okay at all times." Another hesitant nod of approval. "Are you scared to tell us?" I gave a third nod, slightly embarrassed.

"What are you afraid of?" Ryker asked. His bluntness contradicted what his two friends were trying to do. They wanted to make sure I was okay, Ryker wanted to know facts.

I bit my lip, "I don't want it used against me." Something about them compelled me to spill everything. It seemed the only right thing to do was be honest. They were probably going to kill me anyway, so it couldn't possibly matter that I was scared.

Cayden gently grasped my chin, "Stop biting those beautiful lips, princess. We would never hurt you, just like you shouldn't hurt yourself. Listen, we will never, and I mean NEVER use anything you tell us against ya."

"Promise?" I half whispered half whimpered. Whether I want to admit it or not, I need them.

I need them.

Cayden released his grip and held out his hand. I looked at it for a moment before taking it, sealing my fate. I trust these men.

I trust them.

Tears threaten to spill again at that realization, at the kindness that they are showing. At these men for being themselves. Cayden pulled me easily out of the corner and off the bed. I hated when people touched me after a panic attack. It was just a reminder of my fears and how I've been hurt. However, when he pulled me into his chest in a bear hug, I melted. He whispered in my ear, "we promise, princess, we promise."

He pulled away before picking me up and placing me in Ryker's lap. Cayden took the chair that I had first woken up in the other day and moved it in front of the bed. Ace moved closer to Ryker, and I was surrounded by them. We sat in silence for a moment or two. I used this time to herd my racing thoughts into comprehensible sentences. The patience shown was something to be admired. Even Ryker waited for me to speak first, instead of his normal harsh questions. His hand trailed down my spine in slow movements.

CHAPTER NINE: EMBER

Finally, my voice filled the room, "I adopted a color system with Ramero and a few of the others to rate my anxiety and if I need to be removed from a situation." They stayed silent, waiting for me to continue. Almost fearing I would stop. "I'm gonna go over the colors." My voice felt heavy as I explained, "Pink is no anxiety, which I never feel. Green means I'm on edge, but not to worry. Green is my baseline color. I feel that color when I'm with Ramero. Yellow is that I'm anxious, but okay. That's what I normally feel during events or when I'm out in the ring with Lucas." I paused and gave them a chance to think. Glancing around I realized I had their full attention. "Blue means I'm starting to have an anxiety attack because of a trigger. Gray means everything is too much and the trigger or I needs to be removed. Finally black means there's no stopping a panic attack. According to Kai, I may have something called vasovagal syncope. I lose consciousness when emotionally triggered." Kai is studying psychology in college.

When I finished Cayden smiled, "What color are you now?"

Ace and Ryker watch my answer carefully. I thought about it for a moment, contemplating what color I truly was. "Yellow." I responded honestly.

The men nod in unison. Ryker asked roughly, "Lucas wasn't included in the people who knew about the color system, why?"

Ace elbowed him and Cayden shot him a look. I shifted uncomfortably, but Ryker pressed, "Was he what you meant? Would he use this against you?"

I looked at the ground and gave the smallest nod possible. He's my brother, my twin. I should not fear him or fear giving him personal information. Ryker let out a curse and tightened his arms around my waist. I fought against them, and he let me go immediately. I jumped off of his lap and back to the corner of the bed. It gave me a sense of comfort that he let go so quickly.

"I'm sorry! I didn't mean to make you angry!" I insisted.

Ryker cursed again and gave me an apologetic look. "Little flame, *you* did not make me angry. Your brother did. I promise I'm not mad. Come here, beautiful."

I looked at Cayden and Ace, they both smiled and nodded encouragement. I slowly moved back towards him. He patted his lap gently and I gave him a small smile before settling down on his lap. His face lit up in a goofy grin and he wrapped his arms around me. Ace's hand gently grasped my chin, "Thank you for sharing, baby blaze. We won't take your trust for granted." He leaned down and kissed my forehead.

After the rough few hours, I relaxed and held an easy conversation. We started to talk about wrestling. They asked me about joining them in the ring and if I would like to start wrestling.

"I've never been asked that," I admitted. I did want to be a wrestler, but years of being called weak have deterred me. According to Lucas, women like me should not wrestle. I had no idea what that meant, but he would laugh every time I asked to train with him. "I want to wrestle." I stated.

Instead of laughing or mocking me, to my shock, they offered to train me. To teach me what I thought was once impossible. I'm going to be a professional wrestler, I thought excitedly.

"Time for bed, little flame." Ryker announced. My first thought was to argue, but a yawn stopped me.

I got off Ryker's lap and waited for Ace and him to get off the covers. As they did, Cayden got up too. "Are you going

CHAPTER NINE: EMBER

to be okay for the night?" He moved the chair away from the bed and joined the other two men.

I nodded, but quickly remembered the one main rule, "Yes, sir."

I made my way under the covers. When I was comfortable, each man kissed my forehead.

"Good night, baby blaze!"

"G'night, sweet firestorm!"

"Sleep good, little flame!"

Before the three of them filed out of the room, turning off the light in the process. I heard the lock click, which reminded me that I am a prisoner here. But in a sick, fucked up way, I'm okay with that.

10

Chapter Ten: ACE

Leaving Ember was difficult. I wanted to watch her sleep, make sure she felt safe. Unfortunately, business had to be taken care of. Cayden and Ryker sat down on the couch staring at me as I paced.

"Ace, sit down. Let me tell you about the Ashben place and get that over with." Cayden said with a sigh.

I gave him a sharp nod before sitting down on the reclining chair. Ryker handed me a glass of whiskey before taking his seat next to the blond-haired man. I gave him a confused look, wondering when he left. Instead of asking, I took a sip of the drink to calm myself.

"Ramero and I took a group of men to raid the Ashben warehouse earlier this evening. We found three women tied up that appeared to have been beaten and raped several times." Cayden took a long drink from the beer in front of him. "The women are being treated by our doctors at headquarters. None of them speak English, we are working on finding a translator for Berber."

"What is Berber?" I demand, feeling slightly guilty for my

CHAPTER TEN: ACE

tone.

Ryker cleared his throat. "Berber peoples are a group of people from North Africa. They are also called Amazighs and often speak several languages including Arabic and French. These women however were kidnapped and sold only knowing Berber and the few English words they picked up from the monsters who held them captive. We determined they are from Egypt by giving them a map." Ryker always knew odd facts, which often came in handy at times like this.

"We are working on getting them home. I know we don't deal with the skin trade often, but Trevor Ashben is our target and helping a few women never hurts. Plus, we can hand over any information we find to Presley and Jeremy." Cayden added.

I nodded thoughtfully. Presley Archer and Jeremy Hawke lead for a small organization that works to take down local slave rings. That's how she met Harper Sinclair, Presley's girlfriend. We worked with them on many occasions.

"Fill them in and see if they know a translator or can find a way to communicate. This isn't our specialty, but those women deserve better." I said before knocking back the rest of my drink.

"I'll tell Ramero to get on that. We also have two of Ashben's men in the headquarters' basement. We killed eight out of the ten, most were just lackeys doing their assigned task. The two we have are a little higher up. Austin is working on getting the information as we speak." Cayden leaned back into the couch. "You think Ember realized I wasn't at the store?"

Ryker shook his head, "You had showered before she saw you. We had an interesting moment in the bathroom, so she couldn't have been sure when you got home."

Cayden smirked, "Did ya now? What happened?"

"Cayden," I warned. He liked tormenting the poor guy.

"What? I'm just wondering." He tried to sound innocent as he batted his eyelashes at me.

Rolling my eyes, I stood and wrapped a hand around his neck, "You and I are going to talk on the way to headquarters. We will get what we need and then come back before Ember knows we were ever gone." I lift him by the neck and give Cayden a gentle shove towards the door. "Ryker, you keep an eye on her. Protect her with your life."

* * *

Wiping the blood on a towel, I turned away from the man tied to a chair. He was missing six fingers, his right eye and part of his left ear. The prick gave us the information for his boss, Topher Randell. Randell was the lead guy when it came to Ashben selling humans. He corrupted the former Ashben family and convinced Trevor that the money was more important than his morals. He didn't know much else and passed out from blood loss after his ear got sliced off.

Cayden slit the guy's throat, "Nothing. He gave us absolutely fucking nothing."

I threw him a clean towel, "Serpent will take care of his body. The other guy didn't give us anything either. We'll give Presley the Randell's information and let them deal with it from here. We have more problems that are a little closer to home. We will take care of Trevor Ashben for his crimes against his father. According to missing ear guy, Ashben had nothing to do with the women."

We passed Serpent in the hallway. He is a big fucker,

CHAPTER TEN: ACE

standing at 6'8 with muscles on top of his muscles. His tattooed black eyes followed our movements, glancing briefly at the bodies still dripping blood. Serpent nodded to us, waiting for his orders.

"Two bodies, do what you must with them. We don't want to know." I told him, nodding my head towards the door. It was better to not ask questions and just trust the larger man.

Serpent tipped his head and went into the torture room. I shook my head as Cayden looked at me. We both knew that as long as we kept him well fed (two bodies would be enough for the next few weeks) that he would be on our side.

My phone buzzed to display Ryker's name. He sent a simple message that conveyed our girl woke up. Showing Cayden, we made our way to the car.

The sun rose as we drove home. It was going to be a long day.

11

Chapter Eleven: EMBER

"Are you okay like this?" Cayden asked me. I had stiffened when he put an arm around my waist. We were laying in his bed for the first time. His room was large with a bed in the middle. The walls were black with dark gray trim and two large windows with gray curtains. There were two dark wood tables with lamps on both sides of the bed and a large matching wardrobe.

Cayden felt I deserved a reward for being good these past few days. It has been four days since my spanking, and I have been perfectly behaved. He said that I needed to get out of that basement. Ace, Ryker, and Cayden all made it clear that my ass would be toast if I tried to run away. With that fear in the back of my mind, I was placed in his bed.

I nodded my head and relaxed against him. He then sighed, "Princess, I need words. What color?"

I swallowed, "Yellow." I feel safe with these guys but am still hesitant to get too comfortable. With the small talk over, I settled in for the night. I slept fitfully at first, but soon fell into a deeper sleep.

CHAPTER ELEVEN: EMBER

* * *

He is hard. He is huge. He is pressing into my back. "Princess," shit, he knows I'm awake. "Can I try something? If you tell me to stop, I will." I nodded nervously. "Verbal, love," he whispers gently.

"Yes, sir," I murmur anxiously.

Cayden's hand moved the hair from my neck. I tense as his lips connected with the sensitive flesh at the base of my neck. I bit my lip at the feeling. I've never been with a man like this before. His mouth felt so good as he moved until he found the sensitive spot on my neck.

His hands worked their way to the hem of my tank top. My breath caught as he tugged at it. "Can I take this off?" His words danced in my ear. "I don't care about your scars, sweet firestorm." His hand snaked up my back, tracing one of the many large scars.

I shivered, "promise?" At his confirmation, I agreed.

That was all he needed to pull my shirt up. I sat up a little to help him, however he quickly pushed me back down. Cayden slowly climbed on top of me, he kissed down my neck. His lips danced across my collarbone until he came to my boobs. A moan was forced from me when he wrapped his mouth around my nipple. I hurriedly put my hand over my mouth. Cayden growled and took my hands, placing them above me.

"Keep them there. Never," he whispered harshly, "hide from us!" My lips parted and I let out a breathy groan at his words.

He switched to my other nipple. I fought to suppress the involuntary sounds. His hands continued to tweak and pinch my hard pink nipple that he was previously sucking on. He scraped his teeth about the sensitive peak, and I couldn't keep quiet any longer. I felt his smile against my skin. My eyes were shut tightly, I could only feel his mouth kissing down my stomach, his fingers flicking my nipples. The bed creaking and our combined panting breaths swarmed my senses. My senses were heightened and dulled at the same time. My hips bucked as Cayden reached the top of my panties.

"Open your eyes, beautiful girl. I want to see me as I play with your pretty nipples. Watch as I tease and suck on you until you are shaking with need." His dark voice commanded. I slowly opened my eyes to see his signature smirk.

I reached out to touch him, my hand finding his soft hair. Cayden grabbed my hand. He forced it above my head, crawling back up my body. With his hand holding my wrists together, he hovered his mouth over mine. "What did I say about your hands?" I gasped at his closeness, at his knee in between my thighs, pushing against the thin material covering my pussy. His lips grazed mine before he got up. "Do you trust me?"

"Yes," I breathed, not wanting him to stop.

My eyes never left his as Cayden reached over to a drawer in the side table. He withdrew a pair of leather cuffs, "Choose a safe word, princess."

My eyes widened as his darkened. He watched me closely, his knee still against my covered clit. After a moment of silence, he knelt down next to me. I felt Cayden's thumb brush some hair from my face. His smirk softened to a gentle smile which encouraged me to speak, "Thunder?"

"Why thunder, princess?" I hated that he wanted an explanation. My throbbing clit begged him to get on with the fun. He slowly moved his knee away from my pussy before rocking it back against it. I started to grind against

CHAPTER ELEVEN: EMBER

him, matching his movements.

His knee moved outside of my thigh, not giving me the satisfaction I craved. "No, no, sweet firestorm. Tell me you would like thunder as your safe word. Be a good girl for me and I'll give you what you need." His hand patted my pussy, "So wet and hot for me, aren't you. You want me to stick my finger into your needy cunt. Use your words, princess."

My face heated up at his words, "Thunder is loud and commanding. It forces you to pay attention to it."

He hummed and slid a hand under the waistband of my panties. "Thunder it is. You can say this at any point, and I will stop everything immediately. What is your color?"

"Yellow."

He stood, removing his hand and rubbed my wrists soothingly before the leather cuffs closed around them. Tattooed hands worked their way down my body. His fingers flicked my nipples causing a moan to escape me. They continued until they reached my panties. In one swift motion, my only covering was on the floor.

I desperately wanted to cover myself. The cool air on my exposed pussy made me shiver. Cayden chuckled as he started kissing the sensitive flesh on my left thigh. His deep growl stopped me from closing my trembling legs. His fingers dug into my skin as he forced my legs wide. He nibbled his way down my left thigh and up my right. I was shaking and biting my lip so hard I thought it would bleed.

He put his hands under my ass and lifted me to his lips. My hips bucked as he held me down. His breath was warm as he laughed. Cayden placed a gentle kiss on my clit. My breath hitched as the sensation. He lifted his head and gave me a wicked smile. "So needy, sweet firestorm. So, fucking needy."

An ungodly sound left my lips. "Normally I would have you beg, but I just can't wait."

With that his tongue attacked my pussy. I screamed as he nipped and sucked and teased my most sensitive area. I pulled against my bonds, whimpering in frustration. Cayden's hands wrapped around my waist and held me down. His tongue danced over my clit, building an overwhelming feeling deep inside me.

"Please!" I screamed. That seemed to encourage him as his fingers entered me. First one, then a second one. He pushed them knuckle deep before pulling them out and shoving them into me again. His teeth grazed my clit, and I screamed as he kept pumping his hand. Cayden's hand squeezed my ass as he sucked my clit and fucked me with his fingers. I opened my mouth to scream again, but no sound came out. Then I was floating in ecstasy.

Cayden slowed down, leaving teasing kisses up and down my body. I didn't know why I was shaking, but Cayden's soft lips on mine calmed me. I tasted myself on him, the taste was unlike anything I've ever tasted. I was unsure if it was bad that I liked it on his lips. My eyes fluttered open as he hovered above me. He made sure I watched as he cleaned his fingers and licked his lips.

"Good girl," he murmured huskily into my ear. "Color?"

"Green," I said breathlessly.

I heard clapping. At first, I thought I was imagining it, but Cayden moved to show Ace and Ryker standing by the door. I felt my already red face turn crimson. "You put on a good show, little flame." Ryker purred.

"Beautiful, baby blaze, beautiful." Ace walked over to me with a towel. I watched as he put it gently on my pussy. I

CHAPTER ELEVEN: EMBER

sighed at its warmth and the feeling on my sensitive area. Trying to move away from the towel only made Ace chuckle and hold my legs. Cayden uncuffed me and rubbed my wrists to relieve any soreness. Ryker was not in the room, but I heard the water running in the bathroom. They were all taking care of me.

Ace picked me up, carrying me out of the room. "I'm sweaty and disgusting," I whined. His only response was to hold me tighter, making me sigh. I laid my head against his chest allowing Ace to carry me to the bathroom.

He placed me down in the warm water and Ryker took his place next to me. I sighed as the water eased my sore muscles. "You did so good, little flame. I'm so proud of you! We all are!" I wondered what they were proud of me for. I only laid there and let Cayden do all the work.

Ryker grabbed a cup from the sink and dumped water on my head, carefully avoiding my eyes. He grabbed a bottle from the edge of the tub and poured some liquid onto his hand. Ryker massaged the shampoo into my hair expertly. I let out a sound of appreciation as he washed my hair, even remembering to leave the conditioner in for a few minutes.

We held easy conversation while he cleaned me up. I blushed as he used a soapy washcloth on every part of my body. He grinned when I wriggled as the washcloth ran over my pussy. He did it again and shook his head. "Still needy?" He breathed into my ear. I looked at the wall, unable to meet his gaze. "Be a good little flame and you'll get rewarded. On your knees so I can wash your sexy ass."

"R-Ryker, I can't." I tried to reason with him, but he shook his head and gestured for me to rise. I slowly rose and allowed him to run the washcloth over my ass. I fought the urge to smack him as cleaned my tight back hole.

He winked as Cayden walked in with a warm towel. I moved to lean back on my knees. "Have a good bath, princess?" He asked as Ryker helped me out of the bathtub. I nodded, embarrassed at their constant attention and the humiliation of being bathed.

Cayden dried me off, running the towel over my hard nipples and sensitive clit. I moaned and he smirked, "Just drying ya off!"

Cayden picked me up and once again I was being carried. "I can walk you know!"

"I want to carry you." He said simply.

I worried about the scars on my back, but nobody said anything or acknowledged them. Ryker kept his eyes on mine and my back was away from them the entire time, even during the bath my back was never the focus. Maybe they really didn't notice.

I groaned but gave a small smile when he squeezed my ass. It was a reminder to both of us. A reminder of his ownership and my duty to obey his commands.

12

Chapter Twelve: CAYDEN

Ember is the most beautiful thing to ever enter our house. Getting to feast of her perfect pussy was the perfect way to start the day. After Ryker gave her a bath and we got her dressed, the three of us fed her breakfast. It killed me when she looked to us for approval before she ate.

Over the past four days we have been trying to get her to understand that food is important to survival. Ember was by no means ugly or too big. She was perfect for us; we loved a girl with love handles. Skinny girls that ate like birds and were obsessed with their looks had no personality.

Ace was watching over our curvy firestorm while Ryker and I worked with Austin to hunt down Trevor Ashben. He wasn't in his warehouse and the assholes we caught didn't know anything about his whereabouts. Austin and Ryker were keeping tabs on Ashben's known locations, but nothing stood out.

"I'm sorry man, nothing on him. He's gone off the grid. We destroyed the last drug trade and save those girls. That must have scared him into hiding." Austin looked at me over the top of his computer screen.

"Fuck!" I shout, punching a mirror. The glass cut my hand and fell all around me. I barley felt it, it wasn't until I felt warm liquid flowing down my arm that I knew I cut it.

Ryker stood from the desk he sat at and walked cautiously over to me. He took off the black sweatshirt he wore and wrapped it around my bleeding hand. I fought the urge to tell him to fuck off, instead nodding a thank you.

"Cayd, why don't we clean up your hand and go home. I think you needs some time with Ace and our girl." Ryker's hand kept pressure on mine as we went to the bathroom down the hall.

Austin knew our dynamic, he was a Dom himself. I heard him called down the hall to us, "Go home! I'll call you with any updates."

I allowed Ryker to clean up my hand. He ran my hand under water and grabbed the first aid kit. I hissed when he used rubbing alcohol to clean the wound.

"You're lucky you don't need stiches," Ryker commented as he finished wrapping my hand in gauze. "You're also lucky I don't beat your ass for not controlling your temper."

I looked down, Ryker rarely showed his dominant side without Ember around. "I'm sorry, Ryk. My emotions are high with everything going on. I just want to find the fucker."

Ryker nodded in agreement as we walked to the car. I had him drive us home. There wasn't any use to us being there. Sitting around wouldn't help Austin or our men.

The truck wasn't in park before I jump out and rush inside. Ryker shouted after me, but Ember was the only thing that I needed right now. Ember was the only thing I could think about during the ride. I wanted to hug her, spank her, fuck

CHAPTER TWELVE: CAYDEN

her, and do whatever the fuck I please to her.

"EMBER!" My voice echoed down the hall. Ember's beautiful face peaked out from behind the kitchen door. She had a nervous expression on her face as her eyes darted between my hand and my face. I lifted my good hand and made the 'come here' gesture with my middle and ring finger.

Her hesitant steps made me frown, "Are you scared of me?" I demand. She jumped slightly but shook her head. "Do not lie to me!"

"I'm not, sir! I-I just had a bad day. I'm sorry." She mumbled, twisting a strand of her hair. She stood a few feet from me, refusing to look up.

Sighing I opened my arms, "You have nothing to be sorry for. Sweet firestorm, come give me a hug. I think we both need one."

The relief I felt when she came running to me. We stayed holding each other for a while before I scooped her up. Settling her on my hip, I carried her into the kitchen where Ryker was debriefing with Ace.

Ace looked up at us and smiled. "Looks like both of you had rough days. Baby blaze, why don't you and Cayd put on pjs. Here is your lighter, you can go burn paper outside." As curious as I was about Ember's day, that could wait.

He handed Ember the green lighter that she used when she was feeling anxious. Ember has a strict set of rules when it comes to fire. We noticed that burning things seems calm her. The motel footage showed that clearly. The past three days consisted of taking fire breaks. She had no fear when it came to the flames which concerned me a little. However, she was under careful supervision and was given a few items to burn.

I could feel how fast her heart was beating as she nodded

and fidgeted with the lighter. None of us pushed her to speak, instead I carried her up to my room. Ember sat quietly on my bed as I pulled out comfy clothes for both of us. A hint of curiosity flashed in her eyes before the shield came back up. It was rare that she was wearing more than one of our t-shirts and a pair of shorts.

I gestured for her to stand and helped her into a pair of sweatpants and one of my shirts. Despite never seeing her unclothed back, I knew there was some wicked scars. She begged us to let her keep that part hidden. We may be assholes, but we respected that wish when we heard the fear in her voice. As I got her changed, I kept my eyes on hers and made sure she was facing me.

Stripping out of my jeans and dress shirt, I got dressed in a matching outfit to my girl's. Giving her a smile, I took her free hand and squeezed it. Her blush told me that she enjoyed watching me change.

Both of us headed to the back patio. As soon as we exited the house, she flicked the lighter on. For a few moments she watched the flame dance in the slight breeze before letting it extinguish.

I watched her for the next hour. Her blond and red hair was braided back giving me a full view of her pale neck. Her curves made my mouth water. I loved her soft body and how it contrasted her three men's hard bodies. I smiled when I thought about her bear hugs and how she clings to us when upset.

Our girl is perfect for us, she balances out our dark side with her bright flame. The light in the dark abyss that Ace, Ryker, and I are.

13

Chapter Thirteen: EMBER

The next few days flew by. They were filled with smiles, laughs and training. We fell into a comfortable routine throughout the day. I would be woken up, if I wasn't already awake, around eight. We would have breakfast and I would be taken back downstairs.

Ace has said that they "just don't want to worry about your safety. We know you are safe during the day if you are in your room." I knew that meant they still didn't trust me. If I were them, I wouldn't trust me either.

Ryker would let me out when he came home on his lunch break. We would have lunch before I was brought back to my prison. I was given books and a tablet with limited access to keep me busy. It didn't serve me well to complain no matter how boring the basement was.

When they were home, I was able to have a lighter. Some nights they even let me set paper or grass on fire if I was having a mentally rough day. Lucas never understood my fixation on fire, but the flames were always so beautiful and comforting when they danced. Ace, Cayden, and Ryker seemed to know that I like fire. I was never brave enough to ask if that's why they called me the pet names they do. I made a mental note to grow a pair and ask them.

My nightly schedule goes like this. Ace comes home first and lets me out. I help him with dinner, which always ends with a mess that Cayden and Ryker have to clean up. The two men would make me pay for it during our evening workouts and training sessions.

I was being taught how to incorporate simple workouts into my in-ring training, as well as self-defense tips. I was running the ropes and learning to take bumps. My back killed me and I'm sure it is bruised from the ropes. We spent three hours training, split between in ring and in the gym. The men had built a ring in their backyard and a gym in the basement.

After this we took turns taking showers and sat on the couch. As much as I would love to shower with one or all of the men, I wasn't there yet. They understood that and never pressured me.

We would have ice cream and watch TV. They bought cookie dough ice cream for me and three different streaming services for the shows and movies I liked to watch. I would typically be on someone's lap or cuddled into someone's side after we finished eating. It was as if they would die if they weren't touching me. I didn't mind though.

Today was different from the few previous days. Today was Friday.

Today was an event day.

Ace came home like usual and came into my room. I gave him a hug as he stepped in and closed the door. He scooped me up like I weighed nothing and sat me down on his lap. It is amazing how much I have come to like him in the short week

CHAPTER THIRTEEN: EMBER

that I've been here. How much I like all of them.

"Hi, baby girl!" His pet names make me melt every time.

I smiled shyly, "Hi."

"I have something to give to you, along with the rules for tonight." He started, reaching into pocket. He pulled out a charm bracelet. It was a shiny silver with four different charms.

The first was a red and orange flame that fit my love of fire. The second was a flat piece of silver metal with the initials RD carved into it. The second was a piece of gold metal with the initials AC engraved in it. The final charm was a piece of smooth black metal with the initials CR written on it. Ryker Dolton, Ace Calloway, and Cayden Reed are giving me a charm bracelet.

"I love it!" I wrapped my arms around his neck.

"I'm glad! It is important that you never take it off. You can shower with it, sleep with it, have sex with it, whatever you need to do. Taking it off with result in a severe punishment, one where you won't sit for a month. Ember, promise me that you will never take it off." Ace demanded.

I blushed, still not used to the threat of being spanked, despite how often he says it. I nod, "Yes, sir. I will never take it off."

"Good, now put it on." I shook my head and grinned before handing it back to Ace. He looked confused until I held out my left wrist. He put it on me and we took a moment to admire it. Finally, he said, "They really wanted to be here to give you them, but they got held up at work." They often had to work later or one of them would be late for dinner, so I was used to it. They still wouldn't tell me what they did besides wrestling, but right now I didn't need to know.

Ace rested his chin on my shoulder, "I'll tell you the rules for tonight during your spanking. Stand up." I begged them to let me go with them. I felt isolated and wanted to be with my friends. It took three days of begging and the promise that I will be given a warning spanking before the show.

I stood up and allowed him to pull down the panties that I wore. He tugged me over his lap and rubbed my bottom in soothing circles. I knew I wasn't in trouble, but my stomach still filled with butterflies at my position.

"Good girl. First, you must tell us where you are at all times. We will let you go with Ramero or our other friends Kai and Grant, but we must know about it." Ace's hand rained down on my defenseless ass several times. He targeted every inch of my butt from the top of my cheeks to the middle of my thighs.

"Two, you may not have any contact with Lucas. If he comes up to you, you walk away. Three is that you should never be alone." I squirmed as his hand started to feel like wood. He never stopped; I knew that my butt had to be a dark pink by now. Tears filled my eyes and I hoped that he was almost done with the rules.

"You know I am spanking you to make sure that you behave tonight. You are not in trouble; I love you very much. Let's finish this." He started spanking faster, but my brain was wrapping around his statement instead of the pain. He loves me?

"Four, you join our group in front of the audience. You whack Lucas's head with the chair or whatever we give you. You stand proudly with us." He gave four more smacks to the area where my ass met my thighs, "Understand?"

"Yes sir," I mumbled, trying to collect my thoughts and my throbbing bottom. Lucas is my brother, my twin. I can't hurt

CHAPTER THIRTEEN: EMBER

him. I want to hurt him though. Ace loves me, I need to do this for him. I don't want to get spanked again. "Gray," I whimper, my thoughts getting the better of me.

Ace sat me on his lap, grabbed my head and put it to his chest. "Follow my breathing, love. It's okay, you're safe. That's it. Deep breath in," he paused, "and out. Do this again, in. And out." We sat like this for a few minutes as I calmed down. Ace wiped my tears and kissed the side of my head. He then asked, "What color, baby blaze?"

"Yellow," I told him after a moment. He nodded and we sat in silence for a few more minutes. I shifted, trying to find a comfortable position. Having a freshly spanked ass made sitting difficult.

Soon he announced that it was time to get ready and that he had the perfect outfit. He placed my feet on the floor and stood. I followed him silently to his bedroom which held a large closet. "I'm going to try a new command with you, okay?"

"Yes, sir."

"When I say 'kneel' you are going to drop to your knees with your hands in your lap. Now, kneel."

I fell to my knees easily and put my hands in my lap. Ace moved towards me and pushed my head down, gently. He then pushed my shoulders back to straighten my spine. Ace stepped back to study me. "Very good, now stay like this."

I did as I was told, even as Ace went into the giant closet, not daring to move. I kept my breathing steady, focusing on the sounds that the tattooed man made. He was a constant comfort and reassured me with a few words when he was out of sight. Ace's footsteps approached me and after a moment, his work boots appeared.

I looked up at him. He was holding a pair of black jeans and a black blouse with a skull on it. Ace frowned, "Did I tell you to look at me?" I shook my head, eyes wide as I lowered them to the ground. "I'm gonna give you a pass because you are learning. I love looking at your eyes, but when I say not to move, you do not move. Next time you disobey me, you get punished, understand?"

I went to respond but paused. Am I allowed to speak? He only wants verbal answers, but he never gave me permission to speak. Was I going to get in trouble for speaking? I could get in trouble for nodding. Ace could probably sense my panic; he lifted my chin. "Baby girl, you can answer. When I ask a question or if you feel your safety is at risk, you may speak."

I breathed out a sigh of relief, "Yes, sir. I understand."

He then helped me up and told me to get changed. He watched carefully as I put on the jeans. I wasn't wearing pants as my t-shirt went to my mid-thigh. After the jeans were on, I paused at the hem of my shirt. "Sir?" I asked, hesitantly. He nodded for me to continue, "Can-can you turn around?"

"No," he said plainly. When I made no effort to change my shirt, he walked over to me. "We are going to be late." He grabbed the shirt. I placed my hands over his. The men have seen my stomach before, but today I was feeling more self-conscious. I had so many scars covering my stomach and back.

"Please! I promise I'll change, please don't!" I cried out. When he pulled my shirt up, I attempted to jump back. "Blue!"

He stepped away and sighed. Now, I've pissed him off. He hates me. My breathing picked up and I had backed myself into a corner. I apologized repeatedly, doing my best not to cry. Tears were for the weak, he'll hate me more if he sees me

CHAPTER THIRTEEN: EMBER

cry. He took a step towards me holding out his hands in a non-threatening way. "You're okay, I'm not gonna hurt you. I promise."

Ace repeated the process from earlier, focusing on getting my breathing slowed. When I was calm, he asked, "Why are you embarrassed to change your shirt? You are beautiful, I don't like that you are hiding. One of your rules is to never hide from any of us. We gave you privacy before, but now you are ours. I want to see all of you."

I sniffled, "I look like a cutting board. I am littered in scars. It's ugly. I'm ugly." Besides hitting me, Lucas enjoyed using his trust pocketknife to enforce whatever lesson I was being taught. "I'm ugly," I muttered, tears welling up.

"You are beautiful, baby girl. I don't care about your scars. None of us do. They just prove you survived. You are strong and powerful." I shook at Ace's words. He really didn't care. Even as he pulled my shirt over my head, revealing the scars I've kept hidden. I kept my eyes open, despite wanting to desperately close them.

His eyes roamed over my exposed torso, and he slowly turned me around. My face grew red as he studied my back. He ran a finger over the angrier looking ones, making me bite my lip. He turned me back to face him. "Stop biting your lip." He stuck his finger in my mouth, forcing it open. "When we get home, the boys and I are going to kiss each and every scar until you are no longer embarrassed by them. Okay?" He then planted a sweet kiss on my forehead before grabbing the blouse.

I let him dress me. I failed to notice the black boots that he had placed by the bed. Ace helped me tie the laces. We then made our way to his dark blue pickup truck. He opened the door for me. What a gentleman, I thought with a laugh. He closed the door and made his way to the driver's side. Ace started the car and reached into his pocket.

"I am going to give this to you. Cayden, Ryker, and I are already programmed into it. Lucas is blocked." He said, handing me my phone. "If you prove that you can handle having it, you may get it during the day. Tonight will be a test run. We expect you to answer any messages we send immediately."

I took the phone from him and looked at it. It was fully charged with a few messages from my friends. "I understand, sir." I opened my messages and saw that someone had sent messages to my friends saying that I was taking time away from electronics. He told me he would see me tonight.

"Did you text my friends?" I asked, upset. "You shouldn't have done that! That has to be illegal!"

"Ember, I understand your upset," Ace started, but I cut him off.

"Upset? Upset! I'm more than that! You kidnap me and then tell my friends that I'm fine! You lied!" I rant. I continued to complain until I no longer felt like strangling him.

Ace to his credit let me throw my fit. When I stopped, he waited. After a moment he sighed, "Ember, I understand why you're feeling big emotions." He sounded like he was talking to a child, "However, you still need to show respect to me. I am still in control here. I can and will punish you for being disrespectful. I am sorry that this was not handled to your liking. Now, if you are done, we must be going."

Biting my lip, I looked down, he was angry. Now he hates me. He fucking hates me. Fighting tears, I said, "I'm sorry, sir."

CHAPTER THIRTEEN: EMBER

He nodded and threw the car in reverse.

14

Chapter Fourteen: EMBER

After reassuring me a thousand times that he wasn't mad, I finally stopped apologizing to Ace. It took about five minutes of silence before I began pleading for his forgiveness. What is wrong with me? Why was I so dependent on him?

We had just arrived at the building when Ramero rushed over to me. He gave me a bear hug, lifting me off my feet. "Are you okay?" He asked, eyeing Ace. "Did you fuck a duck?"

This was our code, if I was in danger I would plainly say 'no', but I answered, "No, but a duck fucked me!" It wasn't with my usual enthusiasm, but it conveyed that I was fine. We came up with it when Lucas first started getting really aggressive.

Ramero laughed and smiled. Before turning to Ace, "If you dare hurt her, I will personally kill you." He then whispered something I couldn't hear into Ace's ear. I frowned and watched as Ace whispered something back. Ramero seemed satisfied and dragged me away.

He pulled me out into the parking lot. When we stopped by a dumpster, Ramero ran a hand through his short hair. "Don't be mad. Please, don't be mad."

CHAPTER FOURTEEN: EMBER

"At what?" I asked concerned. It wasn't like him to be so nervous or visibly upset.

"Imighthaveknownaboutyougettingkidnappedandthoughti twasagoodidea!" He rushed out. I barely understood him.

"Slow down!" I demanded. I have had enough problems for one day, not being able to decipher him should not be one of them. It was hard to be mad at him, what could possibly make me so angry in his head?

He took a deep breath, "I knew about those guys kidnapping you." He looked guilty. He knew? Why didn't he stop it? "They told me about Lucas, and I believed it was for the best." I was shocked at his words. They told him and he hid it? "I also knew you liked them and hoped that you got good dick in the process."

I barked out a laugh. It sounded strange, unnatural. It morphed into maniacal, unhinged laughter. Laughter that came from deep in my belly, something that scared me. Ramero reached out a hand, nervously. I could not stop laughing. It was my last defense against the surge of emotions that I was feeling. My friend finally worked up the courage to place a hand on my shoulder. "I'm so sorry, Ember." He's sorry? It took all my effort not to turn my laughter into tears.

I gasped for breath and looked up at him. "Damn right you should be sorry." I snapped, shrugging his hand off. I looked at the dumpster studying the graffiti. Someone had written "Fuck Alex." Who is Alex? I have no idea. Another wrote "James was here." So original. "Randal is a pussy." Another Harvard level writing. I rolled my eyes and looked back at Ramero, "Someone wrote 'Josh sucks dick'," he looked at me like I was crazy. His eyes traveled to the dumpster.

Nodding slowly, "That person is right." I nodded. Josh, a

local guy, is a terrible wrestler. The only logical reason he was on the card was the exact thing that was written on the dumpster. He sucks Rival Hitting Wrestling's owner Jeremy's dick in order to get five minutes of show time. Ramero eyed me cautiously, he would probably agree with everything I say.

Grinning at him, I wanted to be angry. I wanted to tell him that I hate him, but I can't. I figured being honest was the best way to go, "I'm mad, but I understand what you were trying to do." Should I have forgiven him? No. But his friendship was important to me. He was the only one who knew everything about me. Ramero was the brother that I wished I had.

"I'm sorry, pumpkin. I should have rescued you. Do you want me to put an end to this? I know Ace is gonna take you to his place, but I can stop him."

I shrugged, "I think I'm okay. Call it Stockholm Syndrome, but I like their company. They've treated me well. I kinda miss work though."

He nodded, "As your friend I need to tell you that it is Stockholm Syndrome. But it is also my job to make sure you lose your virginity before you turn 22." I rolled my eyes. "Hey, I'm just saying, it might help. You wouldn't be such a prude."

"I am not a prude!" I exclaimed. I may be a virgin, but I am most certainly not a prude. I am definitely not innocent. My body may have not been dicked down, but my mind has been. This week has certainly proved it. I turn 22 in another few months, and he did promise this in high school.

Ramero is the only man that Lucas would let me hang out with. Surprisingly I'm allowed to because Ramero is gay. Lucas may be homophobic, but he tolerates my friend. I think it's because Ramero makes a good bodyguard and could kill

CHAPTER FOURTEEN: EMBER

Lucas if he wanted to. I looked up at the larger man and saw a smile. I gave one back and shook my head. "Em, I'll put an end to this scheme if you want. Say the word and it's over. If you wanna stay with 'em, then I won't stop you. I'm going to support you."

I nodded, "Is it bad that I'm happy with them? Like I know they kidnapped me and want to kill Lucas, but they make me feel safe. I was actually green the other day!"

He was now grinning, "I think they're good for you. I hate to say it, but Lucas is an asshole. At least you're around people who care for you and your wellbeing." I nodded along. "Don't look now, but you have two men walking towards you."

I turned to see Cayden and Ryker wandering over to me. I gave them a small smile, which they returned. I noticed Ramero moved a few steps away from me to give us space. Cayden reached me first and gave me a hug. Ryker followed suit.

"We missed you!" Cayden planted a kiss on my forehead. We spent a few minutes admiring the bracelet that Ace gave me. Ramero gave them a warning, saying I was his family. During this talk, Ramero had his arms wrapped around me protectively. Cayden and Ryker noticed but didn't comment. They nodded along with his speech, understanding his motives. Ramero said that he would kill them if they hurt me. That I had been through enough. After confirmation that they were going to keep me safe, I was allowed to go to them. They gave me a final hug and told me to be ready for tonight's event.

After they left, Ramero laughed, a deep rumbling noise. "I think you will be okay with them. They seemed to take me seriously."

I nodded, "I'm glad you approve."

"Okay, enough about your men. Guess who is making their return tonight?" Ramero said in a sing-song way.

"Who?" I asked, there had been many injuries or promotional switches that I was at a loss.

Ramero started jumping a bit, "The amazing, Paranoia Presley!"

"Oh my God! She's back?" I was now jumping with him. Presley Archer completed our trio. She had suffered a broken ankle in Philly months ago and was unsure when she would return. She could beat up any man or woman with ease. Every man wanted her, but she only had eyes for one woman, Harper Sinclair. Ramero, Presley and Harper all teamed together, led by their manager, Alyssa Holland. Together, they called themselves A Bitch and Her Gays.

After Ramero and I fangirled for a few minutes, he got a text from his tag team partner. Together, we raced to the parking lot to find Presley and Harper. I hugged both women. "You changed your hair!" I exclaimed, running my fingers through it.

"Yeah! Harp and I dyed it last night." She looked lovingly at her girlfriend. Harper blushed as Presley ran a hand down her side to grab her girl's hand. Presley's bright blue hair matched her eyes. Her ivory skin contrasted with her partner's rich tan skin. The contrast only seemed to make them a more perfect match.

"We have a few hours before the show, why don't we go find the common room?" Ramero asked, clearly seeing the need to stop the women's moment. After all, they would fuck in the parking lot if we didn't drag them inside. They've done it before and there is no doubt they would do it again.

CHAPTER FOURTEEN: EMBER

We found our way to the large common room where all the wrestlers, commentators and staff kept their things. The people on all RHW cards knew better than to try to take somebody's belongings. Some people had ribs played on them or at their expense, but nothing was ever truly damaged.

I notice my guys huddled in the corner. My guys? *My* guys. I just thought of them as mine. Are they mine?

I was pulled out my thoughts when Lucas walked through the door. He saw me and I jumped behind Ramero. My friend looked confused, but then saw the mop of blond hair walking toward us. He stood in front of me, shielding me from the view of my twin.

"Ember!" Lucas called to me as he neared. I put my head down and decided to study the bags that lined the wall in front of me. I blocked out his voice by looking at the red suitcase. It held Kai's things, which Ramero and I would use to rib him all the time. Lucas called out to me again, this time closer. I forced myself to get lost in my thoughts.

Kai went out to the ring one day and Ramero and I grabbed his sneakers. He always had a hot temper and that made it all the more fun to mess with him.

Lucas was now in front of my bodyguard, my men approached rapidly.

Kai returned to find his sneakers filled with slime. Not impossible to clean, just annoying. I would know, Ramero and I used to prank each other until we agreed Kai was more fun.

Lucas's hand was on my shoulder, Ace's angry growl filled the room.

I focus on the memory, the anger on Kai's face when he returned to his things. He knew instantly who did it but did nothing more than glare at us.

I heard my twin shout, Ramero had thrown him away. *Kai was cleaning his shoes, grumbling about what assholes we were. We wore grins for the next few hours.*

Then it was over, Ramero pulled me into a hug as I squeaked out "Blue" and my men were instantly at my side. I was shaking, Ramero was there, Ace, Cayden and Ryker were there, Alyssa, Presley and Harper were there. I was safe. I am safe.

From then on, I was not allowed to leave their sides. Ramero and my friends could come talk to me, but I wasn't allowed to go anywhere without them. Although I wouldn't tell them, the idea of leaving them had me shaking.

Finally it was show time. I watched from behind the curtain, my men at my side, as Presley made her big return. She saved Harper and Ramero's asses from a three on two assault. She got a big pop and the crowd erupted into chants for her. Ace kept me tucked into his side until it was our segment. Soon, it was my turn.

Lucas went out to the ring to call out my men. Ace, Cayden and Ryker told me to go, answer his call. They had my back. Lucas would do nothing in front of an audience. He kept all of his punishments and his painful hand behind closed doors. Hesitantly, I wandered out to the ring. The crowd cheered as I walked down to the ring, if only they knew. He held the ropes open and gave me a huge hug as I entered. I stiffened, wanting to be back in the arms of my men.

"Last week after the show, the Bloody Wolves decided to kidnap my sister." The crowd booed. He never addressed why they just let me walk down to the ring. Lucas wrapped an arm around my shoulders, and I felt sick. "Nobody gets away with hurting my family!" Except you, I thought, fighting the urge

CHAPTER FOURTEEN: EMBER

to roll my eyes.

Loud music played over the speakers and the Bloody Wolves appeared. I sighed in relief as they made their way towards us. My men looked pissed, maybe because Lucas touched me. Lucas shoved me behind him and stood ready to fight. The men circled the ring. They each took a side other than the one I was on. "Did we kidnap her?" Ace teased, "Or did she come with us willingly?"

"She would never," Lucas screamed at Ace. Cayden slid me a kendo stick. I silently bent down and grabbed it. Praying Lucas didn't turn back, I lifted it and took a deep breath.

Ace lifted his microphone once more, "Are you sure about that?"

SMASH! Lucas was on the ground. I smiled, kendo stick in hand. The crowd went silent for a moment before erupting into hateful boos. Lucas may be an asshole, but he is a babyface in the promotion. At Cayden's instruction, I hit him again. And again. And a fourth time before they were satisfied. The familiar feeling of fear crept in, but when Cayden's arm snaked around my hips it dissipated. We posed over my twin's body, then made our way up the aisle.

The segment only lasted two or three minutes, but it felt like it took the entire night. The backlash would be harsh, but I can handle it. At least I hoped I could. We were packing our things when Lucas came flying into the locker room ready to kill. His eyes were set on me as he stormed my way. I shrunk back, pulling on Ace's arm. I felt like a child, but at that moment I didn't care. My heart was pounding out of my chest and my breathing became rapid.

"How could you, you whore?" He demanded as I flinched at his words. My men quickly stood in front of me. Presley,

Harper and Ramero joined them. Alyssa pulled my arm, dragging me outside and over to Ace's truck. When the cool air hit me, I felt like I could breathe again. I let out a whimper when we sank back against the tire.

Alyssa drew gentle circles on my back in a calming gesture. We stayed in silence for a few moments. "Ember? You are so brave." She whispered to me. She didn't have to whisper, there was no reason to. I think she didn't want to scare me. It was the right thing to do.

I shook my head in disagreement, "I should have fought back. I should have never let him hurt me."

"You survived his abuse; you are fighting back now. You just needed the right support. You are a survivor, love." Alyssa reassured and went back to silence. A comfortable, calming, relaxing silence.

"Ember!" Ace's bellow echoed across the quiet parking lot. I have no idea how much time had passed, but Ace was coming for me. My men were coming for me. Alyssa was the one that responded, and footsteps ran to us. She got up and moved to the side so my men could see me. They were covered in blood and sweat. I took note of their bruised knuckles and messy hair. There had been a brawl.

Ramero was also bloody, but he gave me a smile. "I'll see you later!" Presley, Harper, and Alyssa echoed this, leaving me alone with my guys.

Ryker picked me up. He was doing his best to avoid getting me bloody. "Let's get you home, little flame."

15

Chapter Fifteen: EMBER

I sat on the couch staring blankly at the TV. There was nothing playing, just a black screen that reflected myself back at me. All three men split themselves between the three bathrooms. Ryker was in my shower downstairs; Cayden was in the one on the first floor and Ace was upstairs. It was a quiet car ride; Ryker kept a firm hand on my thigh the entire time. He released me when we pulled into the driveway, leaving me missing the warmth. I silently followed them inside.

"Stay here, baby girl." Ace said, pointing to the couch. I did as I was told, still trying to process the night, not having the energy to disobey. My brain just didn't seem able to comprehend everything. I just stared into the dark TV, having too many thoughts and none at all. I could do nothing but sit and stare. Sit and stare until my men get back.

I didn't hear Cayden come into the room. Didn't notice him until he blocked the TV, until he blocked my reflection. He looked concerned, his brows were furrowed, and his head tilted to the side. "Princess?" He asked cautiously. I couldn't bring myself to meet his eye. I kept my eyes staring at the black boots that Ace gave me. His footsteps came closer.

Soon he knelt in front of me, using two fingers to force my head up. When I was staring at his concerned eyes, he said, "Sweet firestorm, I know tonight was hard. Do you want to talk about it?" I shook my head. "Okay. What can we do to help you?" My shoulder shrugged, truly unsure. I didn't want to speak, that seemed like too much at the moment.

"Can I sit with you?" I nodded and squealed when he picked me up.

Placing me on his lap, I settled against his chest watching us through the black screen of the TV. Cayden traced shapes and words on my thigh. He would murmur the words or things he drew to me. "Beautiful, the sun, triangle, brave, strong, amazing." It went on like this for a while. Cayden didn't stop when Ryker and Ace joined us on the couch. It was as if they knew I needed this.

The silence was both unsettling and comforting. All eyes were on me, frowns were on all their faces. I hated that they were upset, but I was too numb to reassure them. I was almost certain my reassurance would mean nothing anyway. My men, especially Cayden, knew when I wasn't sincere.

Finally, Ace cleared his throat, "I told you we were going to do something after the show. Do you remember what that was?"

I thought for a moment, but nothing came to mind. It had been a long night and I struggled to get my thoughts together. "I'm sorry," I whisper, too embarrassed to look at him.

"You have nothing to be sorry for, you went through a lot today." Ace paused and gave me a smile, "I said that we are going to kiss every scar and insecurity that you have. Are you still okay with that?"

CHAPTER FIFTEEN: EMBER

I looked at them with wide eyes. Are they going to hate me or think I'm ugly? Ryker broke me out of my head, "We won't judge you, little flame. You survived; you are strong."

I let out a shaky breath, "What do you want me to do?"

"Do you have to use the bathroom, love?" I blushed at the direct question. Cayden was still drawing shapes on me while Ace smiled, "We want to know everything, using the bathroom shouldn't be embarrassing. Come on, why don't you pee and then we can go from there. Cayden will go with you; we don't want you to be alone right now."

After an embarrassing couple minutes, Cayden walked me back into the living room. He had to turn on the water and turn around before I could pee. He gave me a sympathetic smile and said, "We are first going to bring you to your room."

I nodded and Ryker picked me up off of Cayden's lap. He carried me down the stairs to the room that was my prison cell. It now felt safe and like a home. He placed me down on the bed as the other men filed in. Cayden picked up where Ace left off, "Ace says you have the most scars on your back, can you take your shirt off?"

I licked my lips, "Ar-are you sure?"

"If you're comfortable, then we're sure, my sweet firestorm." The two other men all confirmed Cayden's statement with a nod. "Would it help if we turned around until you are ready?" This time it was my turn to nod.

They turned around in unison and I gave a small sigh. Hesitating, I knew this was the only way to get over my insecurities. The only way to move on from Lucas's abuse. I'm probably going to need therapy and professional help, but right now this is what I need. I pulled the shirt over my head and put my back to my men. I quietly said, "You can turn around."

I heard a mix of reactions. Ace had already seen my scars; however, he reacted the same as earlier in the day. Ryker's reaction scared me the most, he was angry. His growl was enough for me to grab the shirt that I had thrown on the bed. Cayden stopped me, gently taking the shirt from my shaking hands. He guided me to turn around and face them. I could see Ryker's fists balled so tightly that his knuckles were turning white. Out of instinct, I shrunk back. He is going to hit me. He is going to hit me hard. He's much stronger than Lucas, he will hurt me. Ryker looked at me in shock. I tensed as he came over and wrapped me in a hug.

He apologized to me, before pushing me gently onto the bed. "Can you roll over, little flame? We want you to lay on your stomach." I obliged, exposing my back. I felt somebody's fingers unclasp my bra. My breath hitched as the area that embarrassed me the most was exposed.

"He carved that into you?" Cayden asked, disgusted.

My face was now wet with tears of shame and embarrassment. "I'm sorry." I wailed, now realizing it was a mistake to have trusted them. They think I'm gross, ugly, unattractive, hideous! My tears now fell like a rainstorm.

A soothing hand was now rubbing circles on my exposed back. "Shh, baby girl, shh. You're okay. I promise, you're okay." Ace whispered in my ear. He turned my face so that we were eye to eye. He was kneeling to make sure that he could see me. He wiped my tears from my face and smiled, "Thank you for trusting us with this. I know it's hard."

I nodded and he stood up. "Now, if you want us to stop, just say your safe word. Understand?"

"Yes, sir." I mumbled.

CHAPTER FIFTEEN: EMBER

"What's your safe word and color, princess?"

Taking a breath I said, "Thunder and yellow."

After a chorus of praise for verbally responding, they got right to work. I shivered as I felt the first pair of lips on a smaller, older, and less traumatic scar. These men are good at keeping promises. They slowly took their time going up and down my back, kissing each and every insecurity of mine.

They all avoided the one I hated the most, however. Their lips felt smooth and comforting as they took turns kissing my back. A few times a tongue joined the mix and traced the scars. I sighed when they all moved to the ugliest patch of skin I have.

Taking turns, they kissed it. Again and again and again. Tracing the letters with their tongue, kissing it until I could think of nothing but their lips and tongues there. Until I forgot that Lucas craved the word 'WHORE' into my back. I smiled to myself; they really did care. Once they deemed that it was enough, they rolled me over.

I held my bra tightly to my chest, trying to hide myself. They moved my hands away from my chest and pulled my bra off. Ace held my arms to the side as they admired me. My pick nipples hardened as the cool air touched them. I grew goosebumps at all the eyes staring at me. Despite the blush on my cheeks, I liked the attention.

Ryker tugged at my jeans, "May we?" He asked politely. I looked at him, they had already seen most of me. Why not?

"Yes, sir." I said, giving my consent, the honorific rolling naturally off my tongue.

Ryker made quick work of getting my jeans off, I lifted my hips to help him. My face grew an even deeper shade red when he growled, "Beautiful," as he pulled off my panties.

Ace chuckled, "Soaked, baby girl? I'm glad we have that effect on you." My face had to be crimson as I fought him to cover my face. "No, no, no, stop fighting."

I stilled but turned my head to face the wall. Somebody kissed my inner thigh and I jumped. They repeated the process and soon I realized they were taking turns. Each kiss, lick, and bite closer to my pussy. Closer to the place I needed them to touch most. I let out an embarrassingly loud moan as someone bit and sucked on my left thigh. I squeezed my eyes shut and unconsciously bucked my hips.

"Princess," Cayden teased, "open your eyes." I shook my head. "Open your eyes and we will give you what you want." I shook my head again.

A thought occurred to me and now I couldn't let them know. They would stop, they would laugh at me, they would hate me. Lucas would kill me. At the thought of my brother, I screamed, "Stop!"

They did, immediately. It wasn't my safeword, but they seemed to notice that I was uncomfortable. All hands and lips left my body and I quickly covered myself with a blanket. I played gently with the end of the blankets, avoiding the looks of the men in front of me.

"Ember?" I cringed when Ace said my name. I have grown addicted to their pet names. I've become too close with them. Me and my stupid heart. Always getting me in trouble. Is it too late to beg for Lucas's forgiveness? To pledge my loyalty to him? Ace had somehow appeared directly in front of me.

"Are you okay? Did we go too far?" This is Ace, I had to remind myself. This is one of the men who took me away from my shitty brother. This is the man who spanked me for being a naughty girl. He is the man that could have hurt

CHAPTER FIFTEEN: EMBER

me but chose not to because that is not what good people do. That is not how people should treat each other. He taught me the difference between discipline and abuse. Ace is one of the most patient people I've ever met. This is Ace, he would never laugh at you. Ace kissed and licked my scars as a reminder that he doesn't think I'm ugly.

"Please don't hate me," I started. Taking a deep breath, I muttered, "I'm a virgin."

The room was silent before Ace spoke again, "We understand. We will wait until you're ready."

I froze, they will wait until I'm ready? They don't hate me or want me out? Instead, they will wait, make sure I am certain with my decision. I was about to respond when the doorbell rang. Cayden and Ryker went to answer it, leaving me with Ace.

"I'm sorry that I am such a burden, I hate that this is not just simple!" I exhale sharply, frustrated with myself.

"Stop this, you are not a bur-" Ace was cut off by Cayden yelling for us to get upstairs. I quickly put my clothes back on. I held his hand as we went up the stairs to meet the other two. We were met by a tied up and beat up Lucas. He was screaming at me to help him. I pushed myself into Ace's side, staring at the person before me.

"Fucking whore!" He spat, "Get me out of this!"

I was pushed behind Cayden and Ace as Ryker punched my twin in the face. I looked away as I heard the loud crack of his nose being broken. Despite being exposed to violence, I didn't like to see it. I was surprised it was not broken in the earlier fight. Ryker smiled, clearly satisfied with their work. "You do not call our woman such horrible names!" he shouted.

Lucas groaned and Cayden turned to Ace. He whispered

something in his friend's ear and both grinned. Ace went to fill Ryker in on their plan and Cayden turned to me. "Alright princess, does that asshole know you're a virgin?" I nod. Cayden chuckled, "We have an idea. Do you trust us?"

16

Chapter Sixteen: CAYDEN

"Who the hell is knocking on our door? It's past eleven." I grumble as Ryker and I headed up the stairs. "If it is a fucking salesman or some shit, I'll kill them!" This was the last thing we needed. Our girl was having a breakdown because she had a bad day. She was a fucking virgin. A terrified virgin.

I was already in a bad fucking mood because we weren't there to give Ember our bracelet and then Lucas attacked. On top of that, we lost our lead on Trevor Ashben.

Seeing Ember's scars made me want to torture and kill the son of a bitch. Who carves 'whore' into his own sister's body? My girl is terrified by her brother, but now, she has three big bad wolves to protect her.

Ryker looked out the window and let out a growl. I tilted my head to the side, but immediately took the gun that Ryk took out of the safe. I glanced at the cameras that were displayed on a tablet by the safe.

"Open the door," I demand of Ryker as I took the safety off my gun. Complying, he swung the door open to reveal Lucas.

He charged in like a bat out of hell, right into my gun. He

was already beaten from the earlier encounter. I grabbed his scrawny ass and put the gun against his ear. Ryker kept his gun trained on the other man's chest.

"Lucas Stokes, what do we owe this displeasure?" I spit, wishing to kill this prick already.

"Give me my sister back. If you want her, you can pay me for that whore."

My blood boiled at his words. Ryker stormed over to him and punched him square on the jaw. Holding the bastard as he went slack, I nodded for my partner to continue. Usually, Ryker wasn't the violent one. He was blunt, but not violent. The assault went on for another minute or so before I dragged him to a chair.

Tying him down quickly, we called for Ace and Ember to join us. Keeping our eyes and guns trained on Lucas, we devised a plan. Ember needed to agree, but this would fuck Lucas up.

As much as we wanted to kill him, we had to be more discreet than in our house. I already called Ramero to come get him. Ramero will bring him back to headquarters where we will make him suffer even more. Tomorrow he will be all ours, maybe we'll even let Ember kill him.

17

Chapter Seventeen: EMBER

I was kneeling at Cayden's feet, head bowed, hands in my lap. I made sure to kneel exactly like Ace taught me, not wanting to be corrected in front of Lucas. Ryker and Ace tied their long hair up into buns and moved towards me. Why did tying their hair up get me wet? They looked so good with their hair pulled back. "Now little flame, let's give our guest a show."

I was overcome with nerves but had to trust that my men knew what they were doing. Ace moved to pat my head and run a hand down my back. I shivered in response, and he laughed, "so responsive." He then guided me to my feet and whispered, "Say thunder and we will stop, baby girl." After that he moved me behind the kitchen table. I breathed out, leaning into Ace's comforting hand.

He passed me off to Cayden who bent me over the kitchen table. "Now Lucas, we are going to take turns fucking your sister. I'll let you choose who gets the honor of taking her v-card first." I blushed and Cayden moved to Lucas who was now screaming. "Who gets to take that sweet pussy, Lucas? Do you think she'll bleed?" Cayden whispered in his ear.

I looked down as Ryker pulled down my jeans and panties. He made sure the table covered everything so that Lucas couldn't see below my waist. The cold air felt weird against my now exposed pussy. I whimpered as he bit up my thighs, licking at the bites he and my men left earlier. I knew it was wrong, knew it felt wrong, but I loved every second of it. His lips danced on my skin, creating patterns that I never thought would feel so good.

"Mmm, so wet for us," Ryker hummed, rubbing my ass. I jumped when he slapped it and then sighed as he went back to rubbing it.

Ace smiled, "Shall we draw straws?"

Cayden put a washcloth in Lucas's mouth as Ace broke bamboo sticks. He handed them to me, "Mix them up, baby girl." I did so and held them out for my men. "Yes!" Ace cheered; he drew the biggest straw.

He moved to stand behind me. Leaning down to whisper to me, "Are you ready baby blaze? I'll be gentle." Cayden came over and handed his friend a packet and a tube. I heard him open the packet, a condom, I realized. He then poured liquid from the tube on his hand. His fingers were cold as they entered my pussy. The lube helped his fingers slide into me. I moaned as he spent a minute stretching my tight hole. He added a third finger, preparing me for his cock. I whimpered, trying to move away.

Ryker started playing with my clit, whispering, "Relax, little flame. We got you. Focus on my hand, on me." I forced myself to relax, focusing on all the new feelings. I closed my eyes and groaned as Ace pulled his fingers out. Ryker didn't stop, even as Ace lined himself up. I gasped as his cock entered me. He went slow, painfully slow, allowing me to adjust to his size.

CHAPTER SEVENTEEN: EMBER

He growled, breathing out, "So tight. So, fucking tight." I gasped in pain; he was so big. All my senses seemed to dull. I registered Cayden talking to Lucas, Ace pushing in deeper, and Ryker praising me. Everything seemed so distant. When Ace was fully in, he paused. I knew he was giving me time to adjust, however he decided to taunt Lucas, "Are you ready to watch me fuck your sister's tight cunt?" I tensed, but kept my eyes shut.

I pushed back a little, signaling I wanted him to move. He chuckled and slowly started to move. My breathing picked up, I could hear nothing but our breath and the sound of skin hitting skin. I moaned as he picked up the pace. I allowed my mind to focus on the pleasure.

"Such a tight fuck! You feel so good, baby! Keep pushing back to me, you like this, don't you? So pretty. You're gonna come so hard around my thick cock!" Ace spoke as he picked up his pace, slamming my body into the table.

All of my senses seemed to come alive, I could smell the sweat and arousal coming from both of our bodies. I could feel Ace's fingers digging deep into my hips. My breath was now more of a gasp, and I felt immense pleasure. "Don't stop!" I moaned, "Oh God! Please!" I felt Ryker pinch my clit and I was sent over the edge. I screamed, Ace groaned, and I fell limp on the table. Ace stayed inside me for another moment, before pulling out.

"Good girl." He whispered to me. Ace then looked at Lucas, "You said she was a whore. Carved it into her skin. What you failed to realize is that whore, isn't an insult. It just means that she fucks more often than you. It means that she can get anyone she wants while you jack off in the back of your car."

Lucas tried to yell at him. Cayden punched him again.

Cayden chuckled, "Ryker, ya wanna give our girl some attention?"

I looked at him and he winked. "Please!" I begged. I felt so needy, still desiring to be filled.

"Whatever my little flame wants, my little flame shall get." Ryker said and rolled a condom on. I gasped as something cold rubbed against my lips. "You like the metal, love?" I moaned in response. He's pierced.

He did the same thing Ace did, started slow. His piercing toyed with my sensitive area, making me shiver and let out small noises. When he made it all the way in, I rocked my hips. I needed him to move, I needed to be fucked. Lucas didn't matter at that moment. For the first time I felt I had control over my brother.

Ryker groaned and snapped his hips. He pulled out, almost all the way and slammed back into me hard. Cayden pulled my hair a little as his friend roughly fucked me. My head followed my hair which made me look Lucas in the eye. I whimpered, as he gave me a look of pure hatred. My cheeks flushed and I looked away. Cayden got the hint and let me go. My heart melted as he let me go. He knew my limits and wouldn't go further.

I soon forgot about my brother, about the situation, about everything as Ryker pushed me further onto the table giving himself more access. His body pressed over mine, protecting me from the watching eyes. I let out another embarrassing moan as he circled my swollen clit and bit down on my neck. "Come for me, little flame." Ryker panted and I gave a loud shout. Once again collapsing on the table, I realized I had one more person to go.

Cayden.

CHAPTER SEVENTEEN: EMBER

I was exhausted. My pussy was sore and felt thoroughly fucked. I wondered just how much more I could take. Cayden patted Lucas on the head and said, "I'm gonna fuck ya sister until the only name she could think of is mine. Until she forgets you even exist." I love when his city accent comes out and he is less proper. He spoke like this in the ring or when he was really passionate about something. My body turned to mush for him.

His words themselves made me blush and somehow made me even wetter. I needed him, I ached for him. "Cayden," I moaned, reaching out to him.

Cayden smirked and walked over to me. "Is my sweet firestorm needy? Does she want my cock inside her?"

I let out a choked sound at his words as he put a condom on. Instead of going slow like his friends, he rammed into me, pausing until I moved against him. I screamed at his action, a mix of pain and pleasure washing over me. I pushed against him, and Cayden didn't hesitate. His rough thrusts shoved me against the table, giving a new sensation to my nipples.

I whimpered, begging for him to keep going. Ace moved to my still throbbing clit, giving it some much desired attention. "Don't come yet," Cayden choked out as I squeezed around his cock. I needed to come, how dare he not let me come! He twisted his hand in my hair , using it to guide me to look at my pissed off twin. "Look at the asshole who hurt you, what is his name?"

Cayden rammed into my harder, I was in so much pleasure that I couldn't formulate sentences. I let out a noise, but it was unintelligible. "Exactly, princess. Now, scream my name as you come!" He pulled my hair and bit the sensitive spot on my neck as Ace pressed down on my clit.

"CAYDEN!" I screamed. I was now limp, only being held up by a hand in my hair. Closing my eyes, I was pulled back into his muscular body. A hand quickly fixed my jeans causing me to whine at the sensation.

"No whining," Cayden's deep voice whispered as I met his shiny blue eyes.

He smiled and asked, "Color?"

I sighed and lightly murmured, "Yellow." I was so tired, but still slightly on edge because of Lucas's presence.

"Lucas, it looks like we took your sis's v-card. You wanna see my dick covered in her blood?" I hid my face in Cayden's chest at his words but had no energy to be embarrassed.

Someone wrapped me in a blanket and carried me back downstairs. Sleep called to me, but Ace gently shook me awake, "Not yet, baby girl. Soon, I promise. I'm going to put you on the toilet, can you pee? We can't have you getting a UTI."

I gave a small smile against his chest. He really did care about me and my health. I did as I was told, not feeling embarrassed by him watching me. By now he has seen everything. Cayden had really hyped up the bleeding. Surprisingly, I wasn't really bleeding, just sore. I stumbled as my legs decided not to work.

"You're gonna feel this for a while, baby." Ace murmured and carried me over to the bed. He laid me down gently and walked over the wardrobe. I watched sleepily as he pulled out one of the t-shirts and walked over. "Arms up." I put my arms up half-heartedly.

"Aww, is someone sleepy?" Ryker cooed and Cayden echoed him. They both entered the room as Ace had finished putting the shirt on me.

CHAPTER SEVENTEEN: EMBER

"Lucas is gone. You did so good today. We are so proud of you!" Ace murmured, laying on the bed.

Cayden picked me up and put me on top of Ace, "You were amazing! Thank you for trusting us!" He laid on the side of the bed against the wall and threw an arm over me.

Ryker turned off the light, "You are such a good girl, little flame. Such a good girl!" He laid on the other side of the bed and threw his arm over me.

I was now boxed in, warm and cozy as Ryker pulled the comforter over us. I knew I was going to be sore and embarrassed tomorrow, but that was an issue for tomorrow.

An issue for tomorrow.

Chapter Eighteen: EMBER

I winced as I shifted. I felt disoriented for a moment. A rush of panic hit as I was unable to move. A hand started rubbing my back in slow circles. It was soothing and familiar. I settled down and allowed the person to calm me. My eyes didn't want to open, the warmth was so inviting.

"We've got you, little flame." Ryker whispered into my ear. He was on my left side, and I slowly remembered that Cayden was on my right and Ace was underneath me.

The other two stirred, both staring at me. I blushed when I realized three pairs of eyes were looking at me. I buried my head in Ace's chest, wondering what they saw. My messy blonde hair, my red cheeks, bruises, and hickeys covered my neck and shoulders. I could only hope my morning breath wasn't as bad as I thought. "Aww, princess, ya being shy?"

Ace kissed my hair, "Look at us baby blaze. We don't like when you hide from us." I felt a hand slide up my neck and into my hair. It pulled gently, forcing my head to go with it. I was now looking Ace in his eyes, unable to look away.

Ace tucked some stray hair behind my ear. Judging from

CHAPTER EIGHTEEN: EMBER

where the hand in my hair was, it was Cayden who had control. He held my head up, whispering, "How sore are you?"

I thought of the ache between my legs, how nervous I was to move. I knew I was going to be limping. I knew I was going to be in pain. I welcomed it, needed it. "Very, sir."

"Good." Cayden tightened his grip, pulling slightly and I let out an involuntary moan. My face must have been crimson as they all laughed. Why was this so embarrassing?

Ryker ran a hand down my spine. I shivered, cursing my reactions to these men. "So fucking responsive." I felt his deep voice rumble in my ear. I gasped as someone's hand cupped my pussy. "Don't move."

Ryker disappeared from my side. Cayden held me still as Ace wrapped his arms around me in a bear hug. His fingers ran from my neck to my tailbone in a slow zigzag pattern. Ace's morning wood pushing against my thigh. There was a light kiss placed on my aching, needy clit. I jumped and bucked my hips, wanting more.

I felt Cayden hold my hips as Ryker started in with long licks. He teased and traced his tongue over my pussy, always missing the spot where I needed him the most. I moaned and whimpered and whined, "Please sir!"

"Needy girl." Ace breathed into my ear. "Does someone like Ryker's tongue? You like the way he's reliving the pain?"

"Yes, sir," I moaned.

Ryker teased me some more before blowing on my clit. I gasped as he did this again. Cayden dug his fingers into my hips, "Tell us you're beautiful." His tone of voice told me that following his commands was the only way to get what I wanted.

"I-I'm beautiful."

Cayden placed his lips at my ear. "Ryker needs detail, princess."

"Um, I, um," I was cut off.

"You really think Ryk can hear you? Speak loud and confident!" He encouraged me.

I thought for a moment, "I have nice hair." Ryker licked my clit twice before stopping. "I have pretty eyes." He kept going and I moaned, "I have nice boobs and, and a nice ass." That seemed to be enough as Ryker sucked and licked my pussy. He targeted my clit and shoved two fingers into me. I let out a breathless scream as I came hard.

My men leapt into action after to clean me up and get me into a bath. Cayden sat with me in the bathroom. It hurts to move. I was so sore. So sore in a good way. He gently washed my hair, taking care to leave the conditioner in longer.

"Cayd?" I asked as he rinsed the last of the conditioner from my hair. He grunted an acknowledgement. I said, "Thank you."

"For what?"

I laughed, what do I say when there is so much. I decided to go with, "Leaving the conditioner in, it's a bitch to detangle."

He shook his head and moved to wash my body. "I would do anything for you." He used a washcloth and some coconut smelling soap to clean me up. I smiled as he took care in washing my pussy. The cloth went up and down my arms in slow movements. He dragged it over the scars on my back and over the marks that my men left. After the bath, he wrapped me in a warm towel that Ace had taken from the dryer and carried me to the bed.

Ryker took over and dressed me. He carried me upstairs and put me on the couch. "Stay here, little flame." I did as he

CHAPTER EIGHTEEN: EMBER

said and attempted to get up when he asked me to come to him.

I limped to the kitchen, never feeling pain like that before. It was a blissful pain. I winced as I sat on Ryker's lap. He chuckled, "I like seeing what we did to you. It just means that we fucked you properly."

The rest of the day went on with them having me walk short distances to see their work. They also had me only wear a thong and a blue matching bra to show off the marks and bruises. I smiled every time I looked in the mirror and saw their handy work. For the first time I loved what I saw in the mirror.

I fidgeted with my lighter throughout the day. Despite my men smiling and taking care of me something felt off. Ace took a phone call halfway through the day before sending me downstairs. They told me that they had to talk about work stuff and that I needed a nap. Instead of arguing, I listened and drifted off to sleep with Cayden petting my hair. No sense in arguing, I was too sore for a spanking.

Our routine changed after that day. When they went to work, I was allowed upstairs. I could watch TV and cook for myself. One rule that they had was that I had to be either naked or in only underwear at all times. I listened and was their obedient girl.

A few days after our first night I decided not to listen. I decided to be a brat. I wasn't sore anymore and felt needy. Going into the basement, I looked at my clothing options. They had bought all new things for me that ranged from sexy to comfortable.

Despite my protests, they spend thousands of dollars on clothes, books, and other things they deemed necessary. They wouldn't let me work, so I had no way of paying them back which made me feel terrible. I vowed to myself that I would pay them back somehow.

After surveying my options, I put on sweatpants and a long sleeve sweater. I wasn't cold, I just wanted their attention. I knew they could see me through the cameras installed throughout the house.

My phone rang within minutes of me changing and it was Ace.

"Baby girl, are you cold?" His deep voice asked as I walked into the kitchen.

"No, sir. Why, are you?" I asked innocently. At least I hoped it sounded innocent enough.

He growled, "Take off the clothes. You better be completely naked by the time we get home."

I laughed and hung up. Maybe not the wisest choice, but who was he to tell me what to wear? I was happy with my actions, or I was until they came home. I was surrounded by three angry men who didn't appreciate my disobedience.

"Someone's been a naughty girl." Ace shook his head. I shrunk back into the couch. "What happens when you are a brat, Ember?"

I cringed at my name, "I get punished."

"You get punished," he agreed. Before I knew it, I was on my feet and being stripped of all my clothing. They stared at my body for a moment before I was face to face with the carpet.

Ace had taken me over his knee and was rubbing my bare ass. "You will count. You miss a number, we start over. If you squirm or try to avoid me, we start over." That was the only warning I got before the first slap echoed through the room.

"One, sir." I said, at the beautiful sting.

CHAPTER EIGHTEEN: EMBER

"Two, sir!" I squeaked at the next one.

By five I was fighting to not move, the heat building in my core threatening to explode. At eight I could take no more. I moved trying to get the perfect amount of pressure on my clit.

Ace paused, "Did you just move?"

"I'm sorry, sir." I muttered, desperate for him to touch me.

Cayden spoke up, "She appears to be enjoying this. Maybe we have to make it hurt. Princess your ass is already turning into a deep pink, maybe the paddle will make you realize who you belong to."

My eyes widened. I just wanted fun, not to have my ass beat. "Not the paddle! I'm so sorry!"

He laughed and Ace bent me over the arm of the couch. I tried to fight, but he wouldn't let me up. I whined, "I was just bored! I'm sorry!"

Ryker sat in front of me and grabbed my hands. "Hold my hands, little flame. You are ours. You ask us for attention, not misbehave for it."

I apologized again and bowed my head. This was going to hurt. Ace had me count again. He told me that I was only getting ten, but he was going to make them count. By five I was crying. By seven I was begging.

"Ten, Daddy!" I screamed before I even realized what I said. The room went silent other than my sobbing.

"Baby girl, what did you just say?" Ace asked, scooping me into his strong arms. I cried into his chest for a few minutes, not just from the pain on my ass, but from the embarrassment. "Baby blaze? Did you call me Daddy?"

I blushed and hid my face. He smacked my sore ass in a warning. I sighed and mumbled, "Yes, sir. I'm sorry."

He pulled my face towards him. "Say it again." I shook my head, and he kissed me hard. "Say it!" He breathed against my lips.

"Daddy," I murmured.

He smiled and kissed me again. "Only call me Daddy from now on, understand?"

"Yes, Daddy!"

19

Chapter Nineteen: RYKER

Five days. Five fucking days since Lucas escaped. The day after we fucked Ember, Trevor Ashben's men somehow broke into our headquarters and helped Lucas break free. Now we had a solidified their connection and made Ember even more of a target. This also meant we had a rat.

Ace, Cayden, and I sat in Ace's office with Austin. We had just went through our staff and picked the ones that were known to have ties to Ashben or seem untrustworthy. Splitting the forty-two men among the four of us, we spent hours digging through their histories.

Two men popped up on our radar, only one of them was on duty the morning that Lucas disappeared.

"Fuck," Ace cursed as he looked at the person on the screen.

Alex Doviack. Fucking Doviack. He is one of our most trusted men, someone that we never thought would have ties to Ashben.

Austin turned the computer towards us to display camera footage from that morning. The footage depicted Doviack and Ashben's right hand Chase Ratton. The two were talking outside the Sinful Paragon Strip Club. It was owned by Ashben, who used it as a front for all his illegal actions.

Trevor Ashben has been a pain in the ass since day one. He grew an army using his daddy's money and turned his father's business into a mockery. George Ashben would be rolling over in his grave if he saw the way Trevor sold women. His father treated women with so much respect and kindness. The women at Sinful Paragon were treated like his daughters before he died. Now, they were treated like slaves.

George signed a peace treaty with Ace's father, Adam Calloway, and then signed one again when Ace, Cayden, and I created ACR Empires. We took over for Ace's father when he died and grew the weapons trade and hitman services larger than Mr. Calloway ever could.

Our agreement with the Ashben family involved their drug movements. We agreed to share shipments to certain clients. Mr. Calloway made this agreement with his longtime friend as their respective empires grew. When Mr. Calloway was shot, George was at his funeral and made peace with Ace.

George Ashben was gunned down by a mystery killer. One that Trevor never looked into. Ace hunted, tortured and killed his father's murderer. Trevor never looked into George's death which led us to look into it.

He was like an uncle to us; his son was one of the students that bullied me through high school. Looking into his death was the least we could do for the man who helped us grow after Mr. Calloway's death.

We gave Austin the orders to find the location of his death and see if there were any cameras. Although there were none, we learned that Trevor was the one that found him. We took one of his men that was with Trevor when George was

CHAPTER NINETEEN: RYKER

discovered. Cayden and Serpent learned that Trevor didn't just find his father. He killed him.

Now, we are after him for the murder. Somebody has to hold him accountable for George's death and the disruption of our business.

All that leads to now, the footage showed Doviack and Ratton standing outside a strip club. Nobody seems to know where Doviack is or how to reach him. We trusted the asshole; we pay him well. Why the hell is he working with Ratton and Ashben?

Cayden dragged a hand down his face, "When I get my hands on that fuc-"

"You'll kill him, torture him, we know. Cayden, we know." I let out a long sigh, "You have been saying that for an hour and a half now. This isn't helping." Cayden and I both have tempers. Mine doesn't show as often, but complaining isn't going to help us.

"Cayden, I am annoyed with you." I snapped, using the phrase that they taught me. I never learned to regulate emotions the right way. In high school I would blow up and then melt down all in a span of five minutes when I was overwhelmed. It took a while, but they taught me to use my words and remove myself from a situation when I was angry or overwhelmed with emotion.

Ace stood, "Ryk, come with me. Cayd, stay with Austin and finish going through Doviack's file. Then start to trace the car that Lucas was in."

I let out a sigh of relief, Ace taking charge always grounded me. I love Cayden and Ember, but Ace was my rock. He knew how to calm me and what I needed. Ace put a hand on my back and guided me out of the office.

We walked down the hall to my office. Each one of us had our own office, but decided Ace's was good enough for all of us. My space held a desk, chair, couch and several bookcases. Hidden among the books and in drawers was several implements that could be used to spank a sub.

In this case, me.

Ace rubbed a hand up and down my spine gently. He led me over to the couch and cuddled me next to him. "What do you need right now?" He asked in a quiet, commanding voice.

I shuddered at his tone, "I don't know. I-I just get so annoyed when Cayden complains and distracts us from getting anything done. I love him, but he is a brute and useless in the office. How can I work or track down Trevor and Lucas if he is being an asshole the entire time?"

He waited until I finished my rant before saying, "Thank you for using your words. You know Cayden means well, but like you he is frustrated and upset. He might seem like he can't do office work, but he can. Just like you, his brain works differently, and he processes things and is motivated by things in a different way."

This isn't the first time we had this talk, but it is always reassuring that Ace isn't sick of having it. He was patient and would talk me off the ledge anytime I needed it. I look around the office before getting up. I know I was angry, but I now feel guilty for snapping. We are all under a lot of stress and I just pulled Ace away from the search because of my childish actions.

Grabbing the infamous paddle from the bottom desk drawer I held it out to my Dom. "Sir, please paddle me."

Ace rose and stood in front of me. Despite the very small height difference, I still feel small. Ace's presence was always

CHAPTER NINETEEN: RYKER

large and intimidating.

He took the paddle and looked me up and down. "Why do you deserve a paddling baby boy?"

My cheeks felt hot as I mumbled, "I wasn't nice about what I said to Cayden, and I took us away from the hunt."

"As your Top I want to say that I don't think you deserve one. However, I will give it to you to alleviate your guilt. Do you still want me to spank you?"

I nodded, "I need it."

Licking his lips, he gave a sharp nod. It was rare that I knew exactly what I needed without Ace's input. "Pants down, over the desk." Ace walked over to the door and locked it. "The count will be ten. Then we will cuddle on the couch for a little while before going back and see what Cayd and Austin found."

"Yes, sir." I agree.

20

Chapter Twenty: EMBER

The few days after Lucas turned up at the house were odd. I was given more freedom, but my men were grumpier. They were more stress and punished harsher. They never hurt me, but I also couldn't get away with anything and I was definitely not allowed outside without them. My ass was aways red and sore. Their control was sometimes overwhelming, but it was also comforting to know I'm loved.

"We want you to wear these," Cayden said, handing me a pair of panties. I looked at him confused until I felt a hard piece of plastic hidden in the lace material. It was event day, and all my men were dressing me.

"Sir?" I asked, curious about his intent.

Ace came up behind me, "Put them on baby girl." I shook my head; I knew what this was, and I was not going into the ring wearing them. He slapped my ass, "You want a sore ass too? I don't mind punishing you before we leave." I gasped and moved away from him. My ass was still a little sore from the paddle.

I moved right into Ryker. "Is there a problem, little flame?"

CHAPTER TWENTY: EMBER

I took a calculated risk and ran. As I was being put over Cayden's knee when I remembered how bad I was at math. I kicked and squirmed trying to get away. The discarded panties taunted me from across the floor. "I'll put them on! I'll be your good girl! Please!"

"I'm only gonna give you twenty. Tonight will be your real punishment." Cayden told me, pulling my panties off and throwing them to the side. I went limp and groaned as he gave me my twenty. After his handprint was burned into my ass, he sat me on his lap. "Are you gonna behave?"

"Yes, sir." I mumbled embarrassed, as he wiped my tears. He rubbed my ass and patted it a few times. Ryker came over and put the panties on me. Ace showed me a remote. Pressing a button, I was overcome with pleasure. They were vibrating! Ace played with the speed until he found one that he felt would be 'comfortable'.

"Kneel," I did, placing my hands in my lap. Ace smiled, "No coming. We'll see if you earn it tonight, you have a lot to make up for."

I bowed my head, "Yes, sir."

The three men walked away, Cayden towards the closet, Ace to the bathroom and Ryker out the door. I stayed where I was. I knew better than to move. The vibrations speed up and I let out a low moan. My breathing picked up and Ace laughed.

Cayden walked out with a long black dress and a pair of black platform boots. "Alright my sweet firestorm, time to get dressed. Stand up!"

I stood up, my legs barley able to hold my weight and turned to face him. Ace stood behind me and pulled my off shirt. The cold air made my nipples hard and sent a shiver down my spine. Cayden teased me and brushed the dress over my nipples as he pulled the dress over my head. I felt strange wearing this dress without a bra, but I could not bring myself to complain. Who actually likes to wear a bra anyway?

Next, he put on my socks and boots. I felt helpless as he dressed me. I knew however that after a punishment I lost most of my independence. I didn't mind however, one word and they would back off.

Ryker walked in and whistled, "Damn, looks good!" He wrapped his arms around my waist and nipped my ear, "I can't wait for this dress to be on the floor tonight." I shuttered.

"We don't wanna be late!" Cayden said, ushering us out of the bedroom and towards the car.

***

I was now standing in the center of the ring. Cayden was holding my hand, and my other two men were standing next to us. Ace was screaming into a microphone calling out Lucas. After last week, I was not looking forward to seeing him. Ramero had kept me hidden from him when I was away from my men.

Ramero asked me many times if I was okay. I couldn't tell him that I had a vibrator in my panties, so I said that I was nervous. I didn't lie, I was nervous and would probably be shaking without the vibrator. Ramero had given me many hugs in an effort to calm me. I really don't deserve him.

Now, however, the constant vibration was a comfort in this tense moment. I stood tall, giving a smile to the audience when Lucas didn't show up. I heard a grunt from Ryker before Cayden yelled at me to get out of the ring. I stepped between

CHAPTER TWENTY: EMBER

the bottom and middle ropes. Quickly jumping to the floor, I looked up and saw Ace being thrown to the ground.

Lucas and two of his friends were attacking my men. Cayden and Ryker were down on the ground. I tried to urge them up, but to no avail. So, I did the only logical thing, I jumped into the ring.

"Luc, stop!" I shouted, throwing myself onto Ace. I closed my eyes and waited for the impact. The back of my head screamed that he wouldn't hit me. He had to keep appearances, hitting me would make him look bad.

"Ember, fucking move!" I shook my head and Lucas screamed, "You useless bitch, move your fat ass!" I heard a shout from the audience at the words Lucas spat. A few people booed my twin which made me smile.

Ace growled and commanded me to move. Cayden and Ryker jumped Lucas's two friends and Ace jumped up to attack Lucas. I moved back out of the ring and watched the action. Cayden and Ryker threw the two men out of the ring and into the guardrail. Ace was performing a series of kicks and chops to Lucas's chest and back.

My three men met in the ring and ganged up on my twin. Someone had brought a chair into the ring. Lucas's head was smashed into it over and over. The sound echoed throughout the building. Ryker flipped over Lucas giving him Canadian Destroyer onto the chair, Cayden picked my brother up and power bombed him onto the chair, finally Ace hit Lucas with a piledriver to further punish him.

I suddenly fell against the ring. The vibrations in my panties now are strong. I let out a low moan and struggled to hold myself up. Ace gave me a look and slipped the remote out of his pocket just enough for me to see. My face grew crimson at the thought of all these people seeing. Cayden lifted me up and helped me into the ring. The vibrations slowed enough for me to stand and pose with my men.

"Tonight is gonna be hell for ya, princess," Cayden whispered into my ear. His signature smirk was ever so present, and Ace and Ryker gave me a look that I knew all too well.

I am so fucked.

21

Chapter Twenty-One: EMBER

The ten-minute car ride felt like an eternity. Ace sat in the backseat next to me as Ryker drove. Cayden was in the front seat with the cursed remote. Ace's mouth was on my neck, licking, kissing, and biting at all the exposed skin. Cayden was messing with the speed causing me to squirm and beg.

"Please, please sir!" I panted. My clit throbbed, my panties soaked, probably leaving a wet spot on the seat.

Ace smiled against my skin, slowly moving down to my breasts. His mouth wrapped around my nipples, hardening them through the fabric. I let out a loud moan. "Pull down the front of your dress." Ace pulled on the thin spaghetti straps. I shivered and did as I was told. Cayden turned up the power. I was left exposed from the waist up, pressing my shaking legs together.

Ryker and I made eye contact through the rearview mirror. He gave me a cocky grin proving that he was enjoying my torment. Dropping his eyes back to the road, I was left to Ace's control. He spent the rest of the drive biting at my nipples. He slapped them and dragged his tongue over them. He fondled my breasts, making them ache. Although it was only about five minutes, this felt like forever. I tried to get away from him, however the seatbelt restricted my movement.

Ace tsked, "Nice try baby blaze." Ryker put the car into park. "It's time for your punishment."

Cayden put the vibrator on the highest setting. I had no time to react because I was pulled out of the car. Half-naked, I was carried through the back gate. I blushed at the idea of being exposed to the people in the surrounding area. Nobody was in sight, but that didn't mean they couldn't see me. None of the men seemed to mind that their neighbors could see my naked breasts.

Ace went inside, Cayden carried me to the ring in the backyard and tugged my dress fully off. Next my boots were taken off and discarded outside the ring. I was rolled into the squared circle where Ryker stood. "Kneel little flame. Be our good girl."

I did as I was told. Hanging my head low at being so exposed. The fences were high but could still be seen over from the neighboring decks. The hard wood of the ring dug into my knees as Ryker placed a hand on my neck forcing my head up. The vibrator was still humming, and I was fighting the urge to come.

"Look around, anyone can see you. So vulnerable," he whispered into one ear, "so submissive," in the other. He forcibly turned my head so I could see the neighboring houses that faced the backyard. Ace returned and Cayden joined us in the ring. He turned off the vibrator and I sighed gratefully.

Cayden dragged me over to the corner facing the neighbor's house. These neighbors were a young couple that were sitting in their kitchen. I could see them through the window, their

CHAPTER TWENTY-ONE: EMBER

backs to us. If they turned around, they would see all of me. I shuttered.

Cayden placed my arms on the top rope. Ace stood behind me and secured them with rope. He tied the rope up to my shoulder before moving to my right arm to do the same. Ryker kept busy by pulling off my panties and kissing down my thighs. He pushed my legs to the bottom ropes, stretching me out. Cayden used another length of rope to tie me there. The rope extended up my stomach and around my waist to hold my other leg in place. The night was warm, but goosebumps lined my skin. I shivered as the night air hit my pussy and exposed body.

I tested the bonds and found myself unable to move. I whined and tried harder. "Now stop that! You take your punishment like a good girl or I will extend it!" Ace told me harshly. I whimpered but stopped moving.

"What's your safe word?"

"Thunder."

Ryker nodded, "Color?"

"Green," I told them honestly.

At that, they jumped into action. They started to kiss and nip over every inch of my body. Teasing me as they skipped over the places, I needed their lips the most. I was gasping for air at the three sets of lips that roamed over me.

"How wet are you, princess?" Cayden asked, running his large hands down my chest. I whimpered and held my breath as his hands moved down my stomach. He dipped a finger into my pussy and hummed. "Looky here boys! She is absolutely soaked!"

"Mmmmm, I bet she is," Ace gave a wicked grin and fell to his knees in front of me. He gently kissed my clit. I tried to buck my hips, but I couldn't move. I was spread wide for him. I whined, "Please Daddy! Please Ace!"

"Why are you being punished?" Ryker asked, roughly shoving two fingers into my pussy. I screamed at the sudden intrusion. He laughed, "I don't think that's the answer."

Ace smacked my clit and I screamed again. "Why are you being punished?" He asked as he went back to rubbing the sensitive nerves in slow circles.

"I-I put myself in danger!" I said breathlessly. Ace and Ryker sped up and as Cayden played with my boobs. I was so close, so very close. I was moaning and writhing under their attention. Just when I was about to let go all their actions stopped. "No!" I shouted, tears filling my eyes.

"Naughty girls don't get to come, do they?" Ryker growled.

I shook my head sadly, already knowing the answer. "No sir."

Cayden started to chuckle, "Looks like we have an audience, princess. You better put on a good show!"

"No, please no!" I whimpered, as I saw the man and woman from next door sitting on their deck. I was about to protest some more when the men resumed their actions from before.

"Such a dirty girl letting our neighbors watch." My men stopped their action as I was just about to finish. They did this twice more before I started to cry. The desire was getting almost unbearable. I would never put myself in danger again if they let me come.

"I'm sorry. Please!" I sobbed, going limp against the ropes. "I'm so sorry sirs!" My tears rolled down my body to drip onto the canvas. Cayden wiped away my still falling tears gently.

"You may come. But only if you earn it." My head was tilted upwards. At this angle I could see our neighbors having

CHAPTER TWENTY-ONE: EMBER

their own moment. I could hear the woman's moans mixed with her partner's grunts as they enjoyed themselves. As they enjoyed the sight of me.

Ace jumped up to stand on the middle rope, Ryker kneeled in front of me, and Cayden grabbed my hand. Ace pulled out his cock and brushed it against my lips. "You are gonna make each of us come, if you need to stop, squeeze Cayden's hand three times. That goes for whoever is holding your hand. Understand?"

"Yes, sir!" I said as clearly as I could.

I opened my mouth wide to allow him entrance. He grabbed my hair and roughly shoved his cock deep in my mouth. I gagged and coughed around it. He began fucking my face, using my hair to guide my head. Tears leaked out of the corner of my eyes and Ryker decided that it would be the perfect moment to dip his tongue into my pussy. I screamed around Ace's dick when Ryker added three fingers fucking me roughly. Ace plunged in and out of my mouth, his hips smacking my face every thrust. Between Ace and Ryker, I was begging to come.

Ace let out a strange groan and grunted, "Swallow!" before his salty seed shot down my sore throat. I choked and did my best not to cough as he held his dick in place until I swallowed. I was then forced to clean off every bit of it. Ryker paused his motions and switched with Cayden who then switched with Ace who went in between my legs.

The process repeated again. After Cayden came, he moved to my pussy. I panted, "No more!" My voice was hoarse and barely more than a whisper.

"One more, baby girl. One more." With Ace's words, Ryker's cock entered my mouth. "We are so proud of you. You take our cocks like such a good girl."

I whimpered, his dick was large and pierced. The metal at his tip scraped against my throat as it constricted around it. Once again I gagged and tried to use my tongue to speed up the process. Cayden's mouth and fingers provided a distraction from the pain. I was so close to coming. Ryker finally shot his load down my throat and pulled out.

"Come for us, little flame. You earned it," Ryker said, composing himself.

I attempted to scream but no sound came out as I let myself go finally. I saw stars and suddenly everything was calm. I felt nothing but happiness and tranquility. I was floating. I didn't register the tears flooding down my face or the fact that I was being untied.

I've never felt so good.

22

Chapter Twenty-Two: ACE

Our girl was deep into subspace. She took her punishment beautifully. She probably never registered being untied or given a quick bath. I smiled as she looked up at me with glazed eyes, babbling incoherently. Ryker and Cayden were cleaning the ring and putting the ropes away, allowing me to cuddle Ember.

We were on my bed, her on my bare chest. Skin to skin contact is always good, so I never put her in clothes. We went over aftercare in one of our chats and she agreed that food, water, and cuddles were what she needed most. I commanded that Cayden and Ryker bring water and chocolate in when they joined us.

"Daddy?" She murmured, still dazed and not fully there.

My cock twitched; I love when she calls me that. Down boy, I silently told my dick. "I'm right here baby blaze. I'm not going anywhere."

She whimpered as I ran a hand over her spine. The door opened and Ember lifted her head to look into my eyes. My ego grew when her nervous eyes met mine. "Just Cayd and

Ryk. They brought chocolate and water. Why don't you sit up?"

"Sleep." She sort of said and nuzzled into my chest. The three of us laughed before I put a hand on her back and sat up. "No!" She whined, trying to push me down.

Cayden shook his head lightly smacking her ass, "No whining. Drink." He held a straw to her mouth. Ember wrapped her mouth around it and started sipping on the straw. She drank half the bottle before spitting the straw out and turning back to me. I signaled to Cayden that he could put down the drink with a nod of my head. Both men cuddled up beside us and fed our girl pieces of chocolate. She let out a loud yawn as we slipped under the blankets.

* * *

The next few days passed quickly. Ember behaved, Lucas went back into hiding, and Ashben was still nowhere to be found. We could have grabbed Lucas event night, but he had Ashben's men watching us. RHW didn't need bad publicity anyway. However, yesterday Doviack was caught. I watched with Ryker as Cayden and Serpent worked him over.

Doviack was one tough asshole. It took two days to break him, but we eventually got what we needed. From a mangled and bloody body croaked the last location of Trevor Ashben and Lucas Stokes.

"Greasy Chick. T-They were hiding at the bar." He could no longer open his eyes, he was missing all but one ring finger on his right hand, and he looked like a cross between a dart board and a punching bag. Serpent cut the tattoos from his skin as both a way to torture Doviack and prepare his body.

CHAPTER TWENTY-TWO: ACE

Serpent once told us, "Tattoos are like the fake cheese, all chemicals and no taste."

I shuddered at the knowledge of what he does to the bodies. I'm a sick fuck, but he's something else entirely. It's a good thing he's on our team.

Cayden slit his throat, before leaving Serpent and our clean up team to the attend the body. He was going to get cleaned up in the bathroom attached to his office before joining us.

Ryker turned to me, "Greasy Chick? That's over an hour drive. Trevor bought that a while back, right after George was killed."

I thought over the information for a few minutes. "We should hold off on swarming the place until later."

"What? I did not just spend two days breaking that prick not to use the information!" Cayden yelled as he entered the office.

I rubbed the bridge of my nose, "Cayd," I start before he cuts me off.

"No! We are going to break down the door of the Greasy Chick and kill Lucas and Trevor!" Cayden was yelling in my face by that point.

Grabbing his ear, I dragged him over to the couch in my office. "Ryker, lock the door. Cayden you are going to get your ass beat because you need to relax. It is clear that you are unable to listen to reason and need an adjustment." I started to lecture.

Ryker never benefited from a lecture, Cayden however, needed to hear the disappointment in order to feel guilt. He was a brawler and pain on its own did nothing to deter him. Ryker was used to being berated and brought down, so words didn't matter as much as actions.

I tugged down Cayden's sweats and grinned when I saw that he wasn't wearing underwear. Forcing him to bend over the couch I unbuckled my belt. Without warning I swung. I sound of leather meeting flesh echoed in the office.

"You clearly felt like you were the dominate one in this relationship. Between topping Ember and Ryker, as well as torturing Doviack, it is clear your ego is out of control." The belt snapped against his ass four more times. I continued spanking him while saying, "I am your Dom. We signed a contract. If you have something to say, you will be respectful and talk to me without being a brat. You do not yell at me or demand anything without listening to reason. Am I understood?"

"Yes, sir!" Cayden yelped as I moved the belt lower to his sit spots.

"Ryker, get a plug and ginger lube from my desk." My eyes never left Cayden's ass as my belt continued to punish him. "Baby boy, we have talked numerous times about letting your emotions come before reason. You will sit with the plug in your asshole until we leave to get Ember for RHW. In this time, I will also explain my reasoning for not going to that disgusting bar."

He groaned, "I'm sorry, sir."

I put on a glove lathered up the anal plug with the ginger lube. I also put more of the lube on his tight ring of muscle before thrusting a finger inside. He hissed as I added another and scissored my fingers. I removed my fingers and pressed the metal plug into him.

"Deep breath. My cock is twice the thickness of this." I murmur as the plug pops into his tight ass.

He lets out a whimper, "It burns, sir."

CHAPTER TWENTY-TWO: ACE

"Good. Now stand up straight and put your hands on your head." He looked at me fighting a disrespectful expression. "Be careful. I was just going to have you stand at attention, but now I can see you still need to be punished." He stayed silent and followed my directions.

"Ryker put on gloves." I command. This was not how I envisioned my day going. At least Ryk could listen. "Give our boy a hand job using the ginger lube. Cayden you are not allowed to come if you feel the urge."

Ryker got work and I gripped the other man's chin. "Cayden, we will not be storming Greasy Chick because we don't know if he was telling the truth. Tonight, we are going to send one of our guys to follow Lucas after the show. Rushing into things could put civilians in harm's way or lead ourselves and our men into a massacre.

"Cayden you are a badass, you are strong and smart. Sometimes your brain gets ahead of you. You are passionate about helping the people you love, which is a good thing. I love you for that. You are being punished for yelling at me, being disrespectful and not thinking about others."

Cayden was whimpering and a lone tear rolled down his face. "I-I'm sorry sir! Please, it hurts! I'm so sorry!"

Ryker looked up at me, but I shook my head. "What are you going to do differently if we are in a similar situation?"

He took a breath trying to fight the urge to come and fight the burn of the ginger. "I won't yell at you and try to lead people into harm's way. I promise to think before I act!" His breath was coming in sharp pants and his hands were starting to pull at his own hair.

"Ryker stop. Please get a wet cloth for him." I hugged Cayden and coaxed him to sit on the couch with me. Ryker returned and wiped the ginger lube from Cayd's dick before cuddling next to us.

"It's Ember's first match tonight, we need a clear head. I love all three of you, let's get our girl." I kissed both of my men's heads.

23

Chapter Twenty-Three: EMBER

It was event night. I was more confident now that I was finally going out to the ring as more than a manager. This is what I have been training for. My men prepared me for this. Tonight was a big night. I was going to make my debut as a wrestler. I was full of nerves and adrenaline.

"You got this, baby blaze." Ace told me. He was rubbing my back gently as I was trying not to puke. There were only fifty people in attendance, none of them cared about me or my performance.

I was surrounded by my men who did their best to comfort me. They had come home early from work to go over our plan for the night and distract me from my nerves. It worked until we had to get to the building. Until Ramero reminded me of my performance.

I was wished good luck by all of my backstage friends as my music started. We had spent the past few weeks preparing for my first match. We had also spent time building up the storyline for me to wrestle Harper. Harper had assured me that she would help me if I struggled. I trusted her completely and felt confident that the match would not be terrible. I was used to the painful bumps and knew how to perform basic wrestling maneuvers.

I took a deep breath and went through the curtain to my men's music. They followed me and together we made our way to the ring. Ace held the ropes open for me and Cayden led me to our corner. I jumped nervously from foot to foot. My men left the ring as Harper approached. Ramero, Alyssa and Presley joined her making me feel more comfortable. My favorite people were ringside for my debut.

Ryker called out words of encouragement. Ricky, the ref, asked if I was ready and I gave him a small nod. Harper gave an enthusiastic yes and he signaled for the bell to ring.

She ran at me, and I dodged. I elbowed her in the back and started a beat down on her. Harper rolled out of the ring, and I followed. I was bigger than her, but she Harper had strength that no person her size should. She took advantage of the second it took me to slide out of the ring and threw me into the guardrail. I grunted at the impact, and she picked me up and threw me again.

Harper rolled me into the ring and put me in a headlock. If I could escape Ace's headlock, Harper's wasn't a problem. We traded holds for a minute before I pushed her into the ropes. We did a traditional trip, leapfrog, dropkick before going back outside the ring. I dove onto her in a tope suicida which involved me diving between the middle and top rope on to her. I then rolled her back into the ring.

I was a heel. I needed to cheat. Needed to make the fans hate me. I need heat. I signaled Cayden to distract Ricky while Ryker threw me a pair of brass knuckles before turning to Ramero. Presley, who was cheering on Harper, was distracted

CHAPTER TWENTY-THREE: EMBER

by Ace. I hit a working punch right on Harper's jaw. She fell and I pinned her for the three count. I laughed and rolled out of the ring as Presley and Ramero ran to attack me.

My hand was raised by Ricky who followed me out of the ring. The crowd hated me, which only made the moment sweeter. My men walked me through the curtain where I was greeted by Jeremy who gave me a big hug. "Amazing job! I am so proud of you!" I blushed at his praise. Jeremey was like a father figure to me. Ramero had a crush on him, but I didn't see the appeal. He was almost twenty years older than the two of us.

Harper and Presley walked through the curtain next and hugged me. Ramero and Alyssa did the same as they retuned. They congratulated me and we walked to the locker room. I felt a stare coming from the end of the hall. I nudged Cayden who looked at me. He looked to where I was staring and saw Lucas watching us.

"Ignore him, my sweet firestorm. You did so good tonight. Don't let him take that from you." I nodded and we went to our bags.

I followed Harper into the bathroom where the women typically changed. She smiled at me, "You did amazing! That was such a fun match. I would love to wrestle you again!"

I looked at my friend, "I had fun too. I didn't hurt you too badly, did I? I wanted it to look realistic."

"You didn't! Girl, you're all good!" Harper laughed and opened a stall. "You worry too much. I'm a big girl, I can take what you throw at me. You are a natural in the ring, keep it up!"

I thanked her and locked the stall door. I took a few breaths before pulling off my sweaty red crop top and black sports bra. I put on a simple black bra and one of Ace's t-shirts. I then changed out of my red spandex shorts and into a pair of black leggings. I walked out to stand next to Harper who was taking off her makeup.

I watched her for a moment before doing the same. It was bothering me a little anyway. Harper was like a big sister to me. She was a few years older and had years of experience that she loved sharing with me. I felt like the annoying little sister who copied all her big sister's movements. Harper always just smiled and allowed me to follow her lead. Together we walked back to the locker room and split up to go to our individual partners.

"Hi, baby girl. You did so well, I think you deserve a reward when you get home." I blushed. I was sore from the match, but these guys never fail to get me in the mood. Ace smiled, "Let's get our little wrestler home!"

We all walked out of the building and headed towards the truck. I noticed we were being followed. I moved closer to Ace who also noticed what was going on. He signaled to Cayden and Ryker who split from us. I looked up at Ace confused and scared. There were three men following us and now it was just the two of us. He smiled reassuring me. I heard screams from behind us and realized they went to ambush our stalkers. I breathed out a sigh as we made it to the car.

Ace ushered me into the car. I heard a mangled grunt and quickly looked at him. He slumped over and Lucas stood behind him. Ace struggled as Lucas started punching him. They fought for a moment before a loud gunshot echoed through the parking lot. Ace fell to the ground and Lucas grabbed me.

Ace's lifeless body was beneath me.

CHAPTER TWENTY-THREE: EMBER

Ace's lifeless body lay bleeding in the parking lot.
Ace's lifeless body.
Ace is lifeless.

24

Chapter Twenty-Four: EMBER

My head throbbed. My throat was dry and aching. I slowly opened my eyes, closing them quickly when light stung them. Where was I? Ace's lifeless body flashed in my head. He was dead. Someone killed him. Lucas killed him. Swallowing the need to sob, I let out a tiny groan.

I forced my eyes open and looked around. I was in a dirty cement basement tied to a splintering wooden chair. Tears flooded my eyes as Lucas walked in holding Ace's bloody shirt. Crying won't solve anything.

He threw it at me and gave me a sadistic grin. "Ember Breelyn Stokes, you have been a very bad girl." At his words, tears started to fall. "Stop crying, you pathetic whore." I flinched and he laughed. "You will be punished, very harshly. I will break you. I will make you the perfect sister, the perfect obedient girl."

"Never," I choked out, "You murdered him." My voice cracked.

"*I* didn't kill him! *You* killed him!" Lucas screamed in my face. He shoved Ace's shirt into my mouth. "Do not blame me

CHAPTER TWENTY-FOUR: EMBER

for your lack of loyalty. For your disobedience. This could have easily been avoided if you never went with them!"

He shook his head and walked away from me. I watched him through tear blurred eyes as he went to a table at the side of the room. He grabbed a knife and a bottle. Lucas walked over to me and put the knife against my arm. "You need to be punished, sweetheart. Scream all you want but know that you deserve this. You are toxic. You turned your back on me, you got your boy toy killed. Everybody who you encounter has gotten hurt or worse. We need to release the bad. There is this medieval method called bloodletting. Bloodletting is a great way to purge the bad blood and bad toxins that make you so fucking evil."

I shook my head, trying to beg him not to cut me. I've been on the receiving end of his knife too many times. The pain is sometimes unbearable at best, now it might kill me. He rolled his eyes and sliced my arm open. I whimpered and did my best to move away. He tsked, "Stop moving Ember. You need to remove the toxic blood. If you behave, I'll let you speak again." He made several cuts, deep enough to bleed, but not enough to scar.

"We can't have you get an infection," he said and poured liquid from the bottle onto my wounds. I screamed through my lover's blood as it burned. The strong smell of rubbing alcohol attacked my nostrils. Tears streamed down my face, and I thrashed, wanting desperately to soothe the pain. Wanting my men back. Wanting Cayden and Ryker and Ace.

Ace. My beautiful, brown eyed Ace. My Ace who will never touch me again, never hold me, never call me 'baby girl' again. I couldn't breathe, couldn't focus on anything but the physical and emotional pain.

Lucas cut me again and I could no longer focus on anything, but the waves of panic that flooded me. I tried to catch my breath, but it was no use. I tried to scream "BLACK" at the top of my lungs; not that is mattered to him anyway. It never stopped; the pain continued until eventually I felt nothing.

***

Ice cold water was thrown on me, forcing me awake. My eyes shot open, and Lucas was smiling down at me with his crooked teeth. They must have been damaged by all the times his face was used as a punching bag. "I lost you for a moment, but I think you're almost cleansed."

I looked at my body. I was sitting in my underwear, bleeding from almost every part of me. Normally I would have been embarrassed at the lack of clothes, but pain was my only focus. I gasped and struggled against my bonds. Lucas poured more of the burning liquid on my cut-up legs and I screamed. I was panting, trying to push the shirt out of my mouth.

Lucas cocked his head, "Do you have something to say?" I whimpered and nodded. "Are you gonna behave?" I nodded again. "I will give you one chance. Don't fuck it up."

I coughed as he removed the gag from my mouth. My voice was hoarse as I spoke, "I'm sorry, Lucas. I messed up. Please forgive me!" I looked up into the eyes that we share. There were many times that I looked into the mirror and willed my ocean blue eyes to change color. I tested them so many times to see if they were darken sadistically like his. I hated being a twin.

Pleading with him is one of the only ways that I would probably be freed. He loved when I begged, Lucas lived for it.

CHAPTER TWENTY-FOUR: EMBER

I hated that pleading with him was the only way to stop the pain. I'm his twin sister!

I flinched as he pushed my messy hair out of my face. "Ber, I love you. And I will forgive you." He paused and walked over to the table. He grabbed a towel before wandering back over. "Eventually. You broke my trust. You have to understand that." I winced as he put the towel over one of my deeper wounds. "Now, if you want to sleep in a bed tonight you will do exactly as I say."

I swallowed my pride, my hatred for him and murmured, "Yes, sir." Would my men think of me as weak for it? I need to get back to them, more importantly I had to win back my brother's trust.

He walked out of the room, returning a few minutes later with a first aid kit. I silently watched him patch up the worser cuts and stop the bleeding. He said nothing as he brought me a cup of water and allowed me to drink deeply.

"Thank you, sir." I said, trying to get on his good side. He murdered my Ace. He murdered one of the few people that actually cared about me. That knew the real, uncensored, unfiltered me.

"You're welcome, Ber." He looked at me and untied the ropes around my legs. "When I untie you, you are not to move. Understand?" I nodded and he moved to my arms. I stayed completely still, unmoving as he turned away from me. I knew this was a test, why else would he walk away while I was untied. It wasn't like I could do anything, I doubted I could walk in my state anyway.

He turned back and smiled, "Obedient already. Being good for me like you were for him." I fought back a rebuttal. How dare he say anything about Ace. He laughed, "I guess you can sleep in a bed tonight. If you behave, I will give you food tomorrow. Your behavior will determine everything."

He guided me to a mattress near the back wall of the room. Lucas basically had to half carry, half drag me to the bed. There were chains on each of the four corners. He laid me down and put the chains around my wrists and ankles. I didn't test them, I didn't fight back, I did nothing but let Lucas do whatever he felt necessary.

"I will punish you in the morning. You will accept it, no complaints. Then I will forgive you and we can work on building trust. Okay?"

"Yes, sir." I was now nervous, what was he thinking?

Lucas kneeled down next to me and said, "I love you. I'm so happy to have you back." He kissed my forehead and got up. I watched him turn off the light, forcing the room into darkness. The door slammed shut and I was alone with my thoughts.

Ace is dead. I'm in pain. I need to get out of here. I just want my men. I would do anything right now to sit with them on the couch. To listen to Cayden's horrendous singing. Ryker's rough comments. Ace's overbearing presence.

Despite crying so much today, I sobbed again.

Ugly, wet tears.

Chapter Twenty-Five: ACE

I nursed my arm. It hurt like a bitch. Cayden is out tearing apart different leads on where Ember is. My arm was sore, my knuckles hurt from where I punched the wall. I had a mild concussion and a hell of a lot of anger. It was late, I had to clean my wound and try to get some sleep. I also needed to let out some steam, but that was not the most important thing on my mind.

A knock on the door brought me out of my pity party. "Come in!" I didn't mean for it to come out so harsh.

"Ace?" Ryker stood almost unsure at the door. I knew he wasn't handling everything too well, but comforting wasn't possible right now.

"What?" I winced at my tone. I was the rock and right now, I wasn't do a very good job.

Ryker cleared his throat, "Can I clean your graze?"

I nod, at least make him feel like he's doing something important. I decided not to talk until I could get my emotions under control. Ryker turned to get the first aid kit. He is a fucking genius but is shit at anything human. It took years for us to basically train him on social cues and how to be a functioning part of society.

It was middle school, the boy's locker room smelled like BO and preteen boy. Cayden and I walked in, complaining like usual. We kept to ourselves for the most part, not interested in the normal 6th grade bullshit. That day was different, that was Ryker's first day.

"Hey new kid! Are you staring at my dick? Are you looking to get the shit kicked out of you already?" David, the 7th grade bully interrogated the timid boy. When the boy didn't respond, David punched the kid square in the nose.

I nudged Cayden who also witnessed the event. Despite being a year younger than him, David knew better than to mess with us. My father funded the school, but he also employed the bully's dad. I fought back a grin, knowing that this was probably going to be fun.

Sauntering over I gave Ryker a look over. His clothes were dirty, he was in need of a shower and didn't belong here. This was a private school, it cost a lot of money to go here and judging by his appearance he didn't have it. Why the fuck was he here then?

"Back off David." I shoved myself in front of the trembling boy.

"He was looking at my dick, Ace!" David whined, even as a 12-year-old I knew he was a little bitch.

"Get over it, he was probably staring in shock that yours is so tiny." I snarl back and dismiss him with a wave of my hand.

Cayden had a hand on the boy's shoulder and lead him away from David. Opening my locker, I gestured for him to sit on the bench in front of us. The boy's dark hair fell in front of his face, his chocolate brown eyes cast down. He needed a haircut, but his eyes intrigued me. He held his nose, trying to stop the bleeding with his hand.

"What's your name?" Cayden asked, changing out of his gym

CHAPTER TWENTY-FIVE: ACE

clothes.

"Ryker Dolton." The boy, Ryker, mumbled. I handed him a few paper towels from the bathroom and gestured for him to hold to his nose.

"Well Ryker, were you really staring at David's dick?" I ask, trying to figure out his deal. Did he deserve the bloody nose?

He didn't answer, instead looked around. The locker room had cleared as all the boys made their way out to lunch. We were alone.

He shook his head, "I-I've never been in a locker room or seen anyone's um..." he trailed off. His face was bright red and his voice was shaky.

"Cock?" Cayden supplied.

Ryker nodded, "I don't understand why he got so upset. We both have one, you know?"

Cayden looked at me with a raised brow. I cleared my throat, "Ryk, can I call you Ryk?" He nodded consent. "Ryk, that is considered gay. Guys don't look at other guys dicks."

I took out my first aid kit cleaned the small cut that was on the bridge of his nose. "But I am gay, well bi, but still." This boy was just digging himself a deeper hole.

Cayden stifled a laugh, "Dude, us too, but don't go telling people that. Shit like that makes people uncomfortable." Being gay in a boys school was a way of getting yourself bullied, tormented, and humiliated.

"Why?" He asked as he pulled the paper towels away. His nose stopped bleeding; luckily it wasn't broken.

"Because it does!" Cayden always had an explosive temper. He didn't handle being questioned very well.

"Cayd, relax." I roll my eyes before looking back at Ryker. "Ryker, people don't like different. We are different, we like boys and girls. Liking boys makes us different. So, do both of us a favor and don't talk about gay shit to anybody but us. And don't look at other people's dicks!" He was so innocent, which made him even more attractive. I loved a good mystery.

Ryker flinched at my raised voice but nodded. The poor kid looked so scared. He looked between me and Cayden. "What are your names?" His voice came out in a quiet squeak, the fear was evident.

"I'm Ace Calloway and this is Cayden Reed. You can sit with us at lunch. Grab your stuff." I tell him. Leaving the locker room I slug an arm around his shoulder, "We are gonna protect you, Ryk."

We later found out that Ryker got a scholarship because he was gifted. He also had a 504 plan, which made him a target for bullying. Despite being a year younger, he tutored Cayden and I in exchange for our protection. We would have protected him for free, but turning away academic help would have been stupid.

Ryker walked back into the room with the first aid kit. I looked at him, wondering what would have happened if we let David kick his ass. He gently unwrapped my arm and made a face. "Look that bad, Ryk?"

"N-No Ace." He stuttered. I glanced up in the mirror and saw my face. The look on it was pure anger and hatred.

Letting out a loud sigh I pulled my arm away. "Ryk, baby boy, I'm not mad at you. Ember is gone because of me; she is enduring who knows what because of me!" I yell and throw the bottle of rubbing alcohol at the wall.

"Ace. Ace. Ace!" Ryker grabbed my arm, his face was white as a ghost. He swallowed several times, a nervous tick. "That wasn't your fault. It is only Lucas's fault, and you know it! I may be shit at being a normal person, but even I can see this ain't your fault!"

CHAPTER TWENTY-FIVE: ACE

I looked at him, listened as his voice dripped pure dominance. He never took that tone with me. Ryker picked up the bottle and walked over to me.

"I am taking this just as badly as you are. You need to get your head out of your ass before I replace it with the head of my dick."

I looked blankly at Ryker, who was this guy and when did he become so demanding. He straddled me, our dicks separated by our boxers. He cleaned my arm and put fresh gauze on the wound.

"Now, what do you need? To punish me, for me to punish you, to cuddle? What do you need?"

"I need our girl."

Chapter Twenty-Six: EMBER

Lucas threw another bucket of cold water on me. I was already shivering, so it just made things worse. My body felt like it was covered in tiny papercuts. Lucas smiled, "Wakey wakey, Ember. You've slept long enough."

My teeth chattered and I did my best not to respond. I had gotten no sleep; I was terrified to do so. He unchained me and helped me to my feet. Helped isn't the right word. Pulled me to my feet. I fought back a scream as he almost dislocated my shoulder.

He dragged me to the chair again and told me to stay. I looked at him curiously but did as I was told. Lucas spoke, "I thought long about what your punishment could be. I wondered if Ace's death was enough." He paused and turned to look at me. I secretly hoped it was, but I knew my brother better than that. "It wasn't. You left your only family a month ago. 31 days to be exact, times that by the three men you spent your time with. 93. Add the seven days in a week to get 100. Finally, an extra fifty for embarrassment. You will be getting 150 lashes with my belt to your bare back."

CHAPTER TWENTY-SIX: EMBER

"I'm sorry! Please don't! I promise that I will be good." I struggled to catch my breath. My body was already badly hurt and those lashes would only further aggravate the cuts on my back.

Lucas knelt in front of me, "Relax. Once this is done, we can move on. Okay? It will hurt, but I will take care of you after this. I will build my broken sister back up and guide you to be my perfect girl again." He gave me no chance to respond before he put a gag in my mouth. Ace's shirt. Ace's shirt was once again a gag.

He lifted me up and carried me to a pair of chains hanging from the ceiling. I noticed blood on the floor. How many people has he tortured here? How long has he hurt people? A tear slipped as he locked the chains firmly around my wrists. I was barely touching the floor as he took my bra off. My breasts were now out on display, furthering the humiliation.

"This will only hurt for a little while. Scream all you want. If you fall unconscious, I will wake you up and we will continue. Understand?" Lucas asked, but I couldn't answer. I was already crying, wishing I could be strong like my friends. Like my men.

I shrieked as the belt first cracked down on my bare skin. Its crack filled the room over and over. The swoosh of the leather though the air filled my ears, always followed by a deafening crack and a burst of pain. I moved and struggled to uncuff myself. After the first few I fell limp. He liked when I struggled, why give him the satisfaction? I could do nothing but cry and try to beg. The belt never stopped.

The whistle of the belt coming down on my bloody back made me flinch every time. I don't know how many he landed before he stopped. It felt like a thousand lashes before it stopped. I was panting, tears streaming down my face, my breath coming in pants that I could never catch up with.

Then everything stopped. I heard a loud commotion behind me but didn't have the energy to react. Lucas shouted and then nothing. I did everything I could to disassociate from the pain. I wept as hands were placed on my face. I saw a familiar face. Surely, I must be imagining it. I haven't eaten or really drank anything. I was in severe pain and fighting with my anxiety.

"My sweet firestorm, stay with me. I got ya." The chains were being fidgeted with as my eyes slid shut. Whatever I was seeing was not real. I was delusional and exhausted. I just needed sleep. I needed to escape. I needed to get out of this horrible world.

* * *

"Please wake up little flame." I heard in my ear. I felt a pressure on my hand. Everything felt so heavy, so painful. It hurts to try to open my eyes, my back hurts, my body hurts. Everything hurts. Whatever sick game Lucas was playing, I wasn't going to have.

I whimpered in pain and heard shouting. "I think she's up!" I recognized Ryker's voice. Footsteps rushed into the room. I tried to open my eyes, but the light burned too much.

"You're safe, my sweet firestorm. I promise." Cayden ran a hand through my hair. I sighed at his touch and did my best to lean into it. It felt so good after Lucas's violent hand. "Can you open your eyes, beautiful?"

"Too bright!" I whined and they were quick to dim the lights. I slowly opened my eyes and looked at Cayd with teary eyes,

CHAPTER TWENTY-SIX: EMBER

pushing my injured body up to hug him. He held me for a moment before I was passed to Ryker's arms.

"I missed you, little flame. I am so sorry this happened to you." Ryk murmured in my ear.

I nodded and nuzzled into his neck. I heard another pair of footsteps enter the room. I turned in Ryker's arms. A sheepish looking Ace was standing there. I started bawling.

"ACE!" I screamed. I leapt out of the other man's arms and practically fell into Ace. The pain never registered as all I could think about was my man being alive. I cried into his chest and heard him start to cry. His breakdown only made me cry harder. Cayden came over and carried me to the bed before laying me down on top of Ace. "H-how?" I sniffled. "Y-You were dead!"

He shook his head, and I breathed in his scent. "Baby girl, I was never dead. He knocked me unconscious and shot at me. Dickface is a shit shot. He just grazed my arm." I grasped him tightly, before hearing him wince. I noticed that my hand was on top of a bandage and quickly let go. "Did he say I was dead? Did you think I was dead?"

I nodded, "I'm so sorry!" I was ugly crying. Snot dripped from my nose onto his shirt and my face must have been tomato red. "I'm sorry, Daddy!" I cried into him. My nose was all stuffy, I must have looked like shit. I couldn't stop crying or apologizing to him.

"Shh, baby. I know. You have nothing to be sorry for, I should have been better." Ace told me, his voice cracking. "I should have protected you better. I should have been a better boyfriend." Now we were both crying. My always strong Ace was crying. I was happy to be back and happy to know he was comfortable enough sharing his emotions. It felt wrong to see him cry though, especially at something that he had no blame in.

"Stop!" I practically shouted. I really didn't need him thinking it was his fault. It was an ambush and he needed to know I didn't blame him. However, I knew he was beating himself up. He was punishing himself for letting me get taken, for letting me get hurt. I was punishing myself too. "Please don't blame yourself, I don't. You found me. I'm safe."

"But," Ace tried, I shook my head.

"You want to make yourself feel better? Take care of me. Lord knows I need it! I just need your love and support. I promise that we can talk and work through your self-blame after I feel better." Saying that felt selfish, but I knew that he needed to take care of me. Our connection was strong enough to know what he needed from me. My stomach growled, "And after I get food in my system. I'm hungry!" I fought back a laugh as I went from sobbing to starving.

He nodded and gave me a small smile. "Okay, baby. Let's go get food. If you do blame me, you would tell me, right?"

I nodded, "Yes, Daddy."

I wrapped my arms around his neck, "To food!" Ace announced and carried me with one arm off to the kitchen.

27

Chapter Twenty-Seven: EMBER

My men would not answer or ask any questions until after I got food in my stomach. Dinner was quiet, I ate, and they watched. I wouldn't let go of Ace, so Cayden had to cook. He made boxed mac and cheese, unhealthy, but quick. I was so hungry that I wolfed down the food. Ace had to remind me to breathe and chew. I felt a bit bad that I held onto Ace, but my other men seemed to understand that I needed him.

"Baby girl, it's not going anywhere. I promise. Slow down, pretty girl." Ace said, playing gently with my hair. I slowed, not much, but enough to satisfy my men. Normally I would be embarrassed at how much I ate, but right now, nothing seemed to phase me.

Ryker took my bowl as Ace brought me into his bedroom. Cayden met us there with a first aid kit. He took off the t-shirt I was put in and laid me down on my stomach. When they brought me home, they must have cleaned the belt marks on my back. I winced and whimpered as he took the bandages off.

"I know, sweet firestorm. I know it hurts. Hold Ace's hands

for me, okay?" Cayden said softly. I did as I was told, but quickly tried to get up when I heard a bottle open.

"No! Please don't! I-I-I," I suddenly couldn't breathe. I tried to suck in air and scramble away from Cayden. The pain was almost unbearable, but I couldn't let him hurt me like Lucas did.

Ace sat me up and placed my hand on his chest, "Follow my breathing. You're okay. You are safe, I promise!" Once I calmed down, he grasped my chin gently. "What happened, baby? What scared you so bad? All Cayd did was take off the gauzes."

I sniveled, "L-Lucas hurt me w-with t-that!" I pointed fearfully at the bottle of rubbing alcohol that Cayden held.

Cayden put it down and held up his hands. "Princess, I promise that I just need to clean the lacerations. You know me. You know that I would never hurt you. Do you trust me?"

Ryker walked into the room and looked curiously at Ace. Ace shook his head and continued to hold me. I looked at Ryker and Ace before nodding. "I trust you."

He gave me a kind smile and helped me lay back down. Ryker moved to my right side and Ace stayed on my left. I gasped as I felt burning on my already painful back. "My brave girl," Cayden said as he continued to dab at my back. He went as quickly as he could without dumping the bottle on me.

I squirmed but did my best to stay still. My men whispered words of comfort and told me how good I was being. I bit my lip as Cayden finished his work. He put bacitracin and gauze on the deep cuts. When he was done, he kissed the base of my neck and told me I was his "good girl".

I move to Ace still feeling a little guilty for gravitating towards him. He smiled down at me, "Baby blaze, I need

CHAPTER TWENTY-SEVEN: EMBER

to pee." I looked up at him and reluctantly moved off his lap. He tapped my ass, ushering me to Ryker who sat across from me. I crawled into Ryker's lap and hugged him.

I watched Ace walk out the door towards the bathroom. How did he survive? I was sure he died in that parking lot. Could it have been stress? I let out a long, drawn-out sigh.

"What's wrong, little flame?" Ryker asked. "You're safe now."

I shook my head, "How did he survive?"

"What?"

"How did Ace survive? I was sure he was dead." I mumbled, more to myself than to him.

Ryker rubbed my thigh, "That asshole made you think he was dead. It was his way of manipulating you."

I nodded, "I guess so."

He kissed my neck, I tilted to give him more access. Ryker picked me up. None of my men seemed content to let me walk. I didn't really mind though. He sat me down on the couch and took a step back. I watch, missing his hands already.

"Princess," Cayden started. All my men sat in front of me, watching carefully. "Can we talk about the past two days?" I nodded, biting my lip. Cayden shifted and put his finger in my mouth. "No biting your lip. They are ours, Em. Only we can bite them."

"Yes, sir." I attempt to say around his finger. He removes his finger and kisses me gently. I melted into him, into his lips on mine.

He broke away and smiled, "You don't have to tell us anything, but we want to know what he did to you. Take your time, sweet firestorm. Whenever you're ready." He placed a hand on my leg as I looked at the others.

I fidgeted with my hands, "Um, I saw A-Ace die." Ace looked

away, growing red. I reached out to my man, and Ryker nudged him. Ace walked over to me, and I pulled him down next to me. I then gestured to Ryker to move in front of me. He knelt down and I launched into a shorten version of the past events.

My men never stopped touching me. They hugged me when I broke down because Lucas blamed everything on me. They did their best to reassure me that I wasn't toxic or a horrible person. I told Ace nothing was his fault. Although it took convincing on both sides, we agreed there was no blame on either of us.

Ace explained, "I was hit with something, I think it was a rock and I fell. When I fell, I hit my head on the side of the car." His cheeks reddened, "Not the most heroic story." I fought back a giggle, my graceful and dominate Ace hit his head when he fell.

Cayden picked up where Ace left off, "We heard a gunshot and ran to you both. Em, you were gone, and Ace was on the ground without a shirt. That asshole was a horrendous shot and only grazed A's arm. Why did he take Ace's shirt?" I thought he was homophobic, did he really want to see Ace's chest that badly?

I made a pained noise, "L-Lucas gagged me with it. Psychological torture or some shit. It was the gag in my mouth when you found me. Speaking of which, how did you find me?"

They all explained how they questioned everybody and did some bad things that I didn't need to know about. Cayden made it into the basement first and I blacked out before I could see Ace. They saved some of the gory details and refused to tell me about how they found my location. Somehow, I knew it was illegal and would probably get them into serious trouble.

CHAPTER TWENTY-SEVEN: EMBER

Now wasn't the time to ask anyway.

"What happened to Lucas?" I asked, nervously.

They looked at each other and back at me. Another answer I wasn't going to get. I looked away from them, upset. Ryker cleared his throat, "Why don't we talk about this another day. I wanna spend time with you."

I knew that this was their way of avoiding the question. I knew I should pry. But I was so tired. So, I let the question go. They'll tell me one day, I hope.

We had all shifted to sit on the couch to watch a movie. I laid down across their laps, being careful with my back. We spent a few hours on the couch relaxing and enjoying being back together. After the third movie, Cayden got up awkwardly. He was in the middle and tried to get up without making me get up.

It caused many laughs as he struggled to climb over me. I finally got up against his wishes. He smacked my ass, not hard, but in a joking way. I smiled and he complained, "I could have climbed over you."

I shook my head and hugged him, "No. No, you really couldn't."

"Brat." He rolled his eyes and squeezed my ass. I gasped and tried to move away. "Where ya trying to go?" I gave him an innocent look. He cooed, "Princess, you're lucky you're cute."

Cayd kissed my forehead and walked towards the bathroom. Ace gripped my hips and pulled me into him carefully. Cayden came back with hot chocolate and chocolate chip cookies. I sighed; everything was right in the world once again.

28

Chapter Twenty-Eight: EMBER

I was surrounded by my men. Ryker and Cayden stood on my sides and Ace stood in front of me. All of them had worried looks on their faces and seemed conflicted. Ace reached out and I flinched away from his hand. This nightmare was worse than the others. After Lucas kidnapped me, my nightmares returned full force. Less than two minutes ago I was screaming bloody murder and trying to escape Cayden's arms. I apologized over and over again, unable to think or hear anything but their anger. These men had to be angry I woke them, right?

"Baby Blaze?" Ace murmured quietly. He sat down on the edge of the bed and slowly grabbed my hand. I flinched, but he held a firm yet gentle grasp. "Breathe with me. You are having a panic attack; you need to breathe with me." He put my hand against his bare chest. "In. Ember, breathe in now!" His voice was soft and demanding. I sucked a breath in. "And breathe out. Good girl. Again, breathe in. Hold. Now breathe out. You are being such a good girl for us." He murmured.

Once my breathing and pulse were almost back to normal, I

CHAPTER TWENTY-EIGHT: EMBER

flung myself into Ace's arms. The other two quickly swooped in and I soon found myself in the middle of a three-man hug.

"I'm sorry I woke you guys up. I-I didn't mean to." I sniffled, trying to stop the tears from falling. It seemed like all I did was cry since I was kidnapped.

Someone rubbed my back in slow circles, while another hand pet my hair. Six hands were touching me softly, all trying to eliminate the fear and negative emotions from my body.

Cayden's warm breath filled my ear, "Sweet firestorm, what's got you spooked? Tell us about your nightmare."

I shook my head, hiding deeper into Ace's chest. A hand, probably Cayden's, smacked my ass lightly. In a sick way it comforted me, he wasn't like Lucas, my Cayd would never harm me.

I squealed when the hand hit the curve where my ass meets my thighs. "I'm sorry!"

Light tsking surrounded me, all my men were tsking me. Ryker was the first to speak, "No more apologizing for things that aren't your fault. We won't force you to tell us, but we want to share the burden that you are carrying."

I looked between the three men. They all had a mixture of concern and anger written on their face. Somehow, I knew the anger was not directed towards me. It was the instinctual trust I had with my men, they loved me. Taking several large breaths, I nodded. They just want to listen to me, make me feel less alone.

"Um, I-I dreamt about Lucas again. There were several different time periods in this dream. I-I guess it would be easier to tell you about when I was a kid." My throat was suddenly dry, and my chest tightened.

"Drink," Ryker gave me a bottle of water.

I gratefully took a sip and wiped my face. "Our father left before we were born. When Lucas and I were nine our mother threw us out. She was a drug addict and often had men come over at all hours. That bitch threw us out when a man promised her the world if she didn't have children. Lucas protected me, he found us food and shelter, he hid us from child services. Told me that if I got into any trouble or anything I would be taken from him. The police and child services would separate us.

"Lucas started working and training when we were sixteen. He was always protective and sometimes mean, but never to the extent he is now. I've never seen him so vicious. Like, when we were sixteen, he started hitting me. It started with a smack to the face when he deemed I misbehaved. Then it turned into kicking and a few punches her or there. As I got older, he thought I was ugly because I gained weight. I didn't try too, I just kept getting bigger no matter how little I ate."

Cayden shook his head, "That bastard. You are beautiful."

The sincerity in his voice made me choke up. Taking several breaths I continued, "It all changed when he caught me lighting paper on fire. Something about fire drew me in. I never burned buildings or living things, just paper or wood. He thought I was hiding something, so he took the lighter. He tied my hands and screamed at me. Then, then, then," I broke into sobs.

"Shh, baby, we got you." Ace soothed. The three of them calmed me down and focused my breathing. They let me cry and wiped away my snot despite my protests. "You don't have to finish if you don't want to."

"I need too," I whimpered, "please let me finish." They

CHAPTER TWENTY-EIGHT: EMBER

nodded. "He put the lighter to my bare feet and screamed at me. He demanded what I was hiding, demanded to know why I was burning the paper." Tears fell and didn't both to wipe them away, "Lucas burned my feet. It hurt to walk for days. I wasn't hiding anything.

"I loved Lucas, but his temper grew as we got older. He continued to get more violent and added knives and boxcutters to the mix. I relied on him for everything. Hiding the lighter was my only options, the flames still calmed me. I guess like most abusers, he had good moments too. During thunderstorms he would lay with me and comfort me. It's like he actually cared about me, you know? I never saw it as abuse until you pointed it out."

We sat in silence for a few minutes, I could feel the tension in the room. Cayden was almost vibrating with anger. I slide out of Ace's lap and into Cayden's. Hugging him tightly, we sat embraced. I heard sniffling and lifted my head to realize he was crying.

"Cayd, darling, why are you crying?" I asked as his arms tightened.

He shuddered, "You survived so much. What you told us probably wasn't even the half of it. You are the strongest person I know; I wish we protected you sooner. You are too good of a person to have to deal with that."

"You're here now. That's all that matters. I love you guys."

Instead of going to sleep, my guys stripped away my clothes and laid me down on the bed. Their lips trailed over my body, hands aways touching me. I gasped at their touch and smiled. They're distracting me but showing me that they love me at the same time. Several orgasms later, we collapsed in each other's arms.

I wouldn't trade anything because now I have my men.

29

Chapter Twenty-Nine: CAYDEN

Eight days! It has been eight fucking days since we got Ember back and still no sign of Lucas. I feel bad for our girl. She's back having nightmares and wakes up crying. I want to kill Lucas for what he did, I'm not ashamed to admit that I cried as she told her story. The poor girl went through hell.

She is also once again stuck in her room. We hated taking away her small freedom, but her safety is top priority. We have two of our guys watching the house and cameras watching Ember. She had a few tantrums causing us to take away her tablet or phone.

Soon she will probably do something extreme knowing her. I just hope it isn't stupid like sneaking out of the house or large-scale damage. I hate that we have to treat her like a dog, letting her out only when we are home, but we have too.

Every day her and I go outside and burn things. She fidgets with her lighter during the day, but at night she gets to play. We have been burning larger and larger things in the firepit. Last night we burned the newspaper and several folders of documents that ACR no longer needs.

I rubbed my hands down my face as I watched the cameras. Ace kicked me out of his office when he saw my temper start to rise. Finding Ember was both difficult and easy. She was in the Greasy Chick's basement. We knew about that hideout, but we couldn't get in right away when Ace was shot.

Ace somehow remained the voice of reason, telling us to make sure she was there before rescuing our beautiful damsel. He didn't want to spook them into killing her. It pained me to wait, but we all needed to keep our anger down.

We were talking about where Lucas could have gone and where Trevor was when I snapped. I had gotten Ember out, but Lucas disappeared before anyone could retrieve him. He was knocked out, so where could he have gone? The pain on Ember's face flashed through my head every time they mentioned Lucas. I rubbed my forehead, willing my headache to go away.

The door to my office opened. I looked up briefly to see Ace and Ryker walk in before drawing my gaze back to the cameras. They sat in the two chairs across from me.

"Anything new with Ember?" Ryker asked quietly.

I shook my head painfully, "No, she's playing with her lighter. She's probably bored from lack of stimulation." We haven't fucked her or done other than eat her pussy since before she was kidnapped. I agreed with not scaring her or doing anything extreme, but fuck my balls hurt. "Maybe if we gave her some more pleasure she wouldn't act out as much."

Ace licked his lips, "Is it too soon? I know Lucas didn't rape her or anything, but would we scare her? Our mouths are one thing, but fucking her could do more harm than good."

I looked at Ember, "Maybe she wants her ass beat. She's been testing us. We made everything official and yet we

CHAPTER TWENTY-NINE: CAYDEN

haven't done anything but take away her only sources of entertainment. It's like we are punishing her for getting kidnapped or having a dickwad for a brother."

"We aren't! She knows that! Right? She knows that, right?" Ryker looked so vulnerable in that moment. He is still working on learning about his emotions and social cues. Ryk loves with all of his being. The man just learned to open up to us a few years ago. I should have realized that he would get upset about my comment.

"I'm sure she does," I try to sooth. "She knows it's for her safety. Just saying that I don't like locking her up."

"Cayd is right. Ryk, you make it a point to do her hair at night and tell that you love her. She knows she is well loved and not being punished for getting kidnapped. We are just overprotective assholes that don't want to see our girl hurt again."

Ryker nodded. Ace always knew what to say. He was good with words and patient enough to deal with our asses.

"Any news on anything?" I asked already knowing the answer.

Both men shook their heads. Ace cleared his throat, "Lucas is missing, and Trevor hasn't surfaced. We did come up with a new plan. Remember the girl Lucas went out with when we brought Ember home?" I nodded. "She has been seen with him a few more times, so we are tracking her. Austin is tracking her phone looking for patterns. He's also looking into her background. If we see her again at RHW we'll put a tag on her."

It was a good plan. If this girl is still with Lucas, we can use her without ever going near her. We don't hurt women or children but using them to get to a target isn't that harmful.

"That's a-" I pause as my eyes widened. "What the fuck is Ember doing?" I turned the screen, and we watched as she attempted to pick the lock.

"I'm going to call her." Ace growled.

"She needs her ass beat," I mutter as Ace selected her contact.

"Hello?" She answered innocently.

"What the fuck are you doing?" Ace demanded.

"Nothing, Daddy. I'm just reading a book." Her response almost made me laugh.

It made Ace laugh however, "What are you reading?"

"Some shitty romance novel. I better finish it. Bye Daddy!"

"She fucking hung up on me!" Ace's jaw hung open in shock. He quickly recovered and called her back. We watched as she dropped the phone on the bed and went back to the door.

I stood and grabbed my keys. "Let's go. I'm driving."

30

Chapter Thirty: EMBER

I stared up at the ceiling. Ever since Lucas kidnapped me they have been so protective. I finally had freedom to move about the house and now I am back trapped in the small bedroom. I had begged them not to put me back here. Ace told me it was for my protection. Cayden told me he couldn't bear to lose me again. Ryker told me he would make sure I would have everything taken away if I kept arguing. To save my sanity, I obediently sit in my room.

I have a phone, a tablet, and books, but I didn't want any of them. I wanted to roam the house, go outside, do something outside of this prison. However, something good did come from Lucas kidnapping me. We made it official. They are my Doms and I am their sub. I can now call them my boyfriends and they can call me their girlfriend.

I was fighting the urge to be a brat. I was angry and upset for being locked away. My men let me get away with a lot of things the past few days. It seemed that they were almost scared to punish me. Cayden changed the bandages on my back three times a day. Although there will be bad scars, they are healing nicely.

I bit my lip; I need them to be my Doms. To stop being scared to punish me. As much as I didn't want to be in trouble, I wanted life to go back to normal. It has been over a week; they wouldn't let me go to RHW or see my friends. I loved spending time with them, but I'm lonely. I miss Ramero. I tried to convince them to let me see him, phone calls and text messages weren't enough. I was shot down. I tried throwing a tantrum and ended up getting my tablet taken away for a day.

I glanced up at the camera and wondered what I could do to push their buttons. I rolled out of bed and walked over to the door. I knew it was locked, but I tried the knob anyway. I wandered around the room until I found a bobby pin in the bathroom. I was lucky Ryker kept hair stuff in the bathroom for me.

I looked directly into the camera and moved to pick the lock. Presley had taught me a few years back when Lucas threatened to lock me away. I laughed to myself; Lucas wasn't the one locking me in a room. I loved my men, but hated this room.

My phone rang and glanced at it. Ace was calling. I finished picking the lock and walked over to the phone. "Hello?"

"What the fuck are you doing?" Ace demanded.

I flinched at his tone, "Nothing, Daddy. I'm just reading a book." I knew that he was watching, but I hoped using his preferred name would lighten his anger.

He laughed a dark chuckle, "Yeah? What are you reading?" The disbelief was apparent in his voice.

I gulped, "Some shitty romance novel. I better finish it. Bye Daddy!" I hung up. He called back immediately, but I put

CHAPTER THIRTY: EMBER

the phone on the bed. Ignoring the warnings in my head, I walked out. How much trouble did I want to get into? Should I leave the house?

I decided against it, instead going to the kitchen to get food. Outside was too daring and would probably get me locked up for the rest of my life. My men weren't supposed to be home for another two hours. I hope they don't come home early, if so, I would be in more trouble. I walked into the living room and turned on the TV. I ate some fruit from the fridge and watched *The Simpsons* until I heard three car doors slam. I jumped and ran back downstairs, neglecting the remainder of the fruit.

"EMBER!" I heard Ryker bellow as I closed the bedroom door. I closed my eyes and dove under the blankets. The door flew open, and I began to regret my choices. I cowered as my only protection was pulled away.

"Ember!" Ace growled, pulling me to my feet. His grip was tight, but not painful. "You know you are in deep shit, right?" I nodded, unable to look at him. "Look at me!"

I looked up at him, "I'm sorry, sir. C-Can we please get this over with?"

Cayden sighed and with a thick accent said, "You aren't tellin' us somethin'." I froze. Cayden always knows. Always fucking knows. I squeezed my thighs together, my panties ruined by his accent alone. "Tell us, Ember."

I shook my head, feeling my cheeks heat up. I felt Ace grab my chin. I looked at him and he lifted his eyebrow. I licked my lips, "Y-You refuse to punish me. I-I just want things to go back to normal. I don't want to be locked up or given a pass on something. I was j-just trying to piss you off, get things back to normal. Whenever I try to talk about it, you take away things and don't listen. I'm frustrated!" Angry tears flowed from my eyes; no amount of willpower would stop them.

Ace let go of me and stepped away. I looked at my feet, do they think I'm stupid? Ace gently put a hand on my shoulder and brought me into his chest, "Baby girl, I'm sorry. Why didn't you say that sooner? I guess we didn't realize we weren't listening to you."

I felt dumb, I should have said something earlier. It was the obvious choice, but I guess I have to do things the hard way. "I don't know." I mumble.

Ace sat me on his lap, facing me towards Cayden and Ryker. "Princess, we need to talk." I nodded and braced myself for all the horrible things Cayden was about to say. He cleared his throat, "We made the decision not to have any impact play until you are fully healed and mentally stable."

I snorted, "I don't think I've ever been stable."

They all gave me a look. Ace rolled his eyes, "Mentally okay. None of us are mentally stable, baby blaze. Anyway, we waited until you aren't in physical pain and we don't want you to get flashbacks while over our knees."

Ryker nodded in agreement, "We hate seeing you in pain. We also know you are already hurting. I'm sorry that we didn't listen to your concern."

"Do you understand why we haven't spanked you?" Ace asked. I nodded and he nudged me. Did they think I was weird for wanting to be hit after everything Lucas did? I was my own women, if I wanted to be spanked, I should be allowed to ask.

"Yes, sir." I sighed, deciding to express my concern. "Am I stupid for wanting to be hit after everything? Like I should be scared of you guys. The thought of you laying your hands on

CHAPTER THIRTY: EMBER

me in any capacity should be terrifying. You guys spanking me has always gave me a release and I don't want that to change. What is wrong with me?"

Ace wiped tears that I didn't even know fell. "You aren't stupid. This is your last pass; you do not talk bad about yourself. Nothing is wrong with you. We showed you that we love you through our words and actions. Discipline and spanking are part of our actions; just like hugs and kisses." He kissed my forehead as I willed my tears to stop.

"Okay. I just want everything back to a semblance of normalcy. If you every think I'm weird or dumb you would tell me, right?" They all growled, and I quickly said, "Never mind. I know you're probably angry, but I don't wanna be locked in here anymore. I feel like a prisoner. I'm a captive here just like I was with Lucas."

Cayden looked between my other two lovers, "We don't wasn't to be like Lucas, I don't like you comparing us to that piece of shit. Then you cannot leave the house. We will give you chores to do to keep busy. Do you two agree?" His voice had lost some of his thick accent, but it was just as intimating.

I felt Ace nod and Ryker tilted his head in agreement. I smiled, "Thank you!" I jumped up and kissed Cayden. I moaned into the kiss as he grabbed my ass.

"Break it up lovebirds!" Ryker pulled me away. "You still need to be punished for breaking the rules."

I bit my lip. Ryker carried me to a door down the hall. Opening the door, I saw a sadistic looking playroom. The walls were lined with whips, crops, paddles, and all sorts of other implements. I gaped at the room as I was brought over to a bed in the center of the right wall. I looked at my men in shock.

"Close your mouth or I'll stick something in it." Ryker said, gruffly. I snapped my mouth shut. Cayden laughed and opened a drawer from the nightstand across from the bed.

Ace forced me to my knees at the end of the bed, "Safe word and color?"

"Thunder and green, sir."

Cayden grabbed something from the drawer and smiled, "Sweet firestorm, you gotta stop biting your lip. I think I have somethin' that will help you." He squeezed my cheeks forcing my mouth into an "O" shape. I felt something being stuck in my mouth. I had a ball gag between my lips. "If you need to stop or say your safe word, tap the bed three times." I forced myself to calm down. I wasn't gagged with a bloody shirt, I still had my safe word.

Ace brought me to bed and stripped me naked. I whimpered around the gag as he cuffed my legs to each of the bed posts. I looked at Ace. These were my men; they will not hurt me. I fought the memory of Lucas tying me down. Ace must have noticed my panic, "It's us, baby girl. You're okay!" He kissed my forehead and moved to stand by Ryker.

Cayden was in charge of this scene. I recognized it immediately and decided to watch him carefully. I saw a hot pink rabbit vibrator in his hand as well as a black wand. I squirmed in anticipation for what's about to happen.

"You are not allowed to come. Each time you do, you get five minutes extra. Am I understood?" Cayden stuck a finger inside of me as I tried to tell him I understand. I moaned as two fingers pumped in and out of me. I whimpered as he added a third finger.

"That's a good girl, you're enjoying Ace and Ryker watch

CHAPTER THIRTY: EMBER

my fingers go in and out of your tight pussy." He said it as a statement, showing how well he knew me and my body.

I attempted to beg him, but with the gag it came out gibberish. I felt something cold at my entrance before the rabbit entered me. I cried out as it was turned to the highest setting. Cayden took a step back and smiled at my writhing body.

"Remember, no coming!" Cayden walked over to my other men who were jacking off. Knowing they were touching themselves while watching me made me feel hotter. It made me wetter. Sweat coated my body, whimpers and cries broke through the gag.

I was fighting my first orgasm. I bucked my hips and pulled against the bonds. Cayden shoved the vibrator in and out of me in rhythm to his other hand moving on his dick. The extension rubbing against my clit causing me to cry out. The grunts from my men are driving insane. I heard Ryker's breath catching and he came all over my stomach. Ace and Cayden soon followed. I almost lost control. Ryker dipped his fingers into the cum and rubbed it all over my nipples. The added stimulation broke me. I was now crying at how much it hurt. I was drooling everywhere, which made me feel gross.

I tried to close my legs, free my hands, anything to get this torture to stop. I tried to plead with Cayden, but they were lost to the ball gag. I squeezed my eyes shut and tried to ignore all the stimulation.

I failed.

I came hard, screaming as loud as I could. Cayden tsked and shook his head. "We'll be back in five minutes. Come as much as you want." Ace removed the gag and I tried to beg them not to leave, but they walked out. I came five more before they walked back into the room.

"All done, baby girl. You did so good!" Ace commented, releasing my hands. He rubbed my sore wrists as Cayden stopped the vibrator and removed it. Ryker rubbed my ankles after uncuffing me. My pussy was sore and swollen from the constant stimulation. The throat was raw from screaming and my limbs hurt from pulling on the bonds.

"Good girl!" Cayden praised and wiped my tears. He lifted my limp, naked body off the bed. He carried me up the stairs and into the shower. I was so sensitive. He quickly washed my body and brought me into his room. "Nap time, princess. Do you want me to stay with you?"

I nodded, "Yes, please. Can I have some water?"

Ace and Ryker walked in. Ace held a bottle of water; they knew me so well. I drank more than half the bottle before letting out a content sigh. Joining Cayden and I, my other two men curled up with the us. I sunk into their bodies, smiling.

"I love you guys," I murmur.

I hear a chorus of my men saying, "I love you too!" as I nuzzled into Cayden's chest.

Hours later I was shaken awake, never seeming to remember falling asleep. Ace woke me up for dinner. I whined and pulled the blanket over my head. His deep chuckle caused a shiver. The blanket was taken away and I was in the air. I squealed, but soon stopped when he kissed me.

Ace took me downstairs to the kitchen. I noticed my favorite cheese pizza from the pizzeria down the street and a two liter of soda on the table. I leapt out of Ace's arms and ran to the table.

"It's just pizza! You left me for pizza!" Ace examined, grabbed at his chest.

CHAPTER THIRTY: EMBER

I gasped, "It is not just pizza! It is cheesy goodness that is full of deliciousness! It is the best thing in the world!"

Ace laughed. Cayden walked in with plates and cups. Ryker followed with napkins and sat down. I sat across from him, Cayden nest to me and Ace sat at the head of the table. I smiled as I took a piece of pizza.

"Good?" Cayden asked as I took a large bite of the greasy pizza.

"Best thing ever!"

31

Chapter Thirty-One: RYKER

The punishment and pizza seemed to cheer our girl up. All Ember wanted was her freedom back. She never had it as a kid and now we took it away from her again. The three of us decided that keeping guards around the property would allow her some freedom. We also gave her a set of chores to do. Simple things like clean up the kitchen or vacuum.

I like watching her. I always did, but something about knowing I can go home and sink my cock into her makes it so much more special. I watched her through the camera with Ace and Cayden.

"She's so fucking hot." Cayden groaned stroking his dick.

Ace leaned over and grabbed his hand. "No touching yourself." Cayden went to protest but stopped at Ace's glare. "You too Ryker. If either one of you touches yourself, I will spank you ass and your dick bright red, understand?"

We nodded; Ace wasn't in a good mood. None of us were. Trevor and Lucas were still missing, and Ember was having nightmares every night. Half of the nightmares involved Ace dying.

CHAPTER THIRTY-ONE: RYKER

Lately Ace has stopped sleeping, he just watches Ember. He spanked her for the first time yesterday morning after she refused to honor his title and was disrespectful to all of us. We all watched as his handprint was engraved in her ass. We also monitored her reactions and listened for her safe word. Ember cried. As much as I hate seeing her cry, I fucking love it. All three of us are sadistic in the best ways.

Ace is getting grumpy and mean the longer he goes without sleep. He punished me yesterday when I talked back. I objected to him not sleeping and tried pushing the issue. Now Ember and I both squirm when we sit. Ace was much harsher on me, which is understandable and expected.

On top of all of this, Ember is sick. She seemed to have the start of a bad cold last night. Ace called her this morning and she sounded horrible. One of us is going to go stay with her and have our doctor take a look at her.

To say the least, we were all stressed. The girl Lucas was seeing was looking like a dead end. Just as I was about to try my luck with Ace again when Austin burst through the door.

"Guys! Maureen's cell phone just pinged for the tenth time at the same building. The team we sent confirmed that Chase Ratton is there!" Austin's energy was unmatched. He just officially made Alyssa his girl after she was drugged by some asshole in a bar a couple of weeks before Ember was kidnapped. Austin was happy and his work always was phenomenal when he was happy.

"Cayden and I will take a team. Ryk, I need you to look after Ember. This could be a set up and I want a person with our girl. Austin, you're on coms. Let's go!" Ace barked out orders.

I stood and grabbed the keys off of Ace's desk. He looked at me, "Unfortunately this is going to be all hands-on deck. If she's really bad take her to urgent care. We are going to need Jacob to tend to the badly wounded."

I nodded. Jacob was our doctor. As angry as I was that he wouldn't be looking after her, I understood. A few years ago, I wouldn't have, but now it makes sense. "Got it. I'll have the two guards follow us."

"Make sure they aren't seen." With that Ace walked out.

Ember still hasn't asked about what we do for work. We don't want her involved. Besides, the rumors and things we do would probably scare her. She had enough on her mind, finding out that her boyfriends are killers and criminals shouldn't be added. If she went to the feds, we would be fucked.

Getting into my truck I called the two guards to let them know I was coming home. I also told them that we were probably going out and they needed to follow at a distance. I hope Ember doesn't need the urgent care.

Chapter Thirty-Two: EMBER

I woke up congested and more tired than I originally had been. Ace's suggestion to take a nap only made me feel worse. This morning started with me having a stuffy nose and pounding headache. I had rolled out of bed to find out that I looked like a disaster. None of my men would agree, but I really do look like shit. Who actually looks good while they're sick?

I sighed and took a hot shower. It helped a little, but not enough to make me feel better. I went through the medicine cabinets and found no medicine. Where the fuck are they keeping the cold medication? I went through every cabinet and drawer in the kitchen and all the bathrooms. Nothing. Who doesn't have medicine in the house? Frustrated, sick and hating the world, I called Ace.

"Hey babygirl!" He said cheerfully.

"Hi. I don't feel good." I mutter into the phone. Sniffling, I grabbed a tissue and blew my nose.

"You don't sound it. What are you feeling?" Ace asked, concerned.

"Gee, thanks! That's what every woman wants to hear." I

rolled my eyes.

He chuckled, "Just because you are sick doesn't mean I won't punish you." He said it playfully, but it didn't make it any less of a threat.

I bit my lip, "Sorry, Daddy. I just have a headache and feel congested. Do you have any medicine in the house?" I started coughing and choking on nothing.

"We don't at the moment. I'm sorry. Why don't you eat something and lay back down. Maybe take a nap and sleep it off. Ryker will get you stuff at lunch. Okay?" Sleep it off? How the fuck am I supposed to sleep off a cold? Was Ace ever sick in his life?

I fought back a retort, instead choosing to nod, before realizing he couldn't see me. "Okay, d-do I have to eat? I'm not really hungry."

Ace didn't say anything for a moment, "Baby blaze, can you try to eat toast or something light? It might make you feel somewhat better." Despite it being framed like a question, I knew it wasn't. He was being lenient on the rules, but I didn't want to push my luck.

I let out a small sigh and agreed. I was too tired for a spanking. My body was achy already and having a red bottom would probably be my breaking point. All I wanted to do was cuddle in my men's strong arms and burrow into their warmth.

After hanging up with him, I went to the kitchen and made some toast. It took a few minutes, but I was able to eat it. I glanced at the camera and showed my empty plate. A few seconds later my phone chimed, and it was Ace. He texted me that I was a good girl and would be rewarded later. As happy as his praise made me, I didn't feel well enough to enjoy it.

CHAPTER THIRTY-TWO: EMBER

I wandered into my bedroom and collapsed on the bed. I had one last coughing fit before finally drifting off to sleep.

Now, I am awake and feeling worse. My head pounded, my throat felt like I drank lighter fluid, and my body was too sore to even life. I got up, groaned and laid back down.

I heard the front door open, and Ryker called out. "Little Flame? Where are you?" He sounded like he was at the top of the stairs. I debated for a second between yelling out to him or letting him find me. Verbal answers were expected by all my men.

"Downstairs," I weakly stated. My voice sounded weird, like it wasn't my own. It sounded ugly; I hated it. After Ace's comment, I felt more self-conscious.

Ryker came in and walked over to the bed. I pushed myself away from him. He reached for me, and I shook my head. "Come here, love. You're okay!" I shook my head again. "Why won't you let me touch you?"

I didn't want to speak because my voice is ugly, but I also didn't want him to come near me. Bad enough I was sick, he doesn't have to be. I grabbed my phone from the table and wrote in my notes. He took the phone and read my message before yanking me into his chest. I fought his arms for a split second before his hand collided in a deafening smack on my ass.

"I don't care that you're sick. If I get sick, we can be sick together. As for your voice, I don't care about that either. However, this is considered talking bad about yourself, isn't it?"

I buried my head in his shirt, "I'm sorry, sir." His warmth surrounded me, engulfing me in his cedarwood scent.

He kissed the crown of my head, "I'm gonna give you a pass.

Besides, your voice isn't that bad. You sound sick. I took the rest of the day off to spend with you. Let's get some food and meds into you and cuddle, yeah?"

I nodded and hugged him, "Are you sure? I don't want you sick. I know that you have issues with germs." Ryker was constantly washing his hands and would make faces when one of my men coughed or sneezed.

"Little flame, I would get sick for you. I love you more than you even realize. It doesn't matter that I'm sick because you need me more."

I blushed and smiled, "I love you enough to get you sick."

He chuckled and picked me up. Instead of responding, he brought me into the kitchen. He sat me on the counter, grabbed tissues and a blanket before coming back to me. I hugged the tissue box and clutched the warm blanket as he made me eggs.

I watched as his muscular figure scrambled eggs and put them into the sizzling fry pan. I started coughing again, fighting to stop the attack. Ryk got a water bottle from the fridge and passed it to me. He patted my back, forcing the coughs out.

When I stopped coughing, he put some bread in the toaster and moved the eggs around in the pan. I shivered slightly, breathing heavily out of my nose. I drank from the bottle, pausing only when I absolutely could not breath.

"Slow down, little flame. There is plenty of water." He put the food on a plate and set it down on the table. He then carried me to the table and sat me on his lap. "I'm gonna feed us. I want you to eat as much as you can, okay?"

"Okay." I muttered. We ate silently. He gave me a bite and then took one for himself. We continued this trend until I

CHAPTER THIRTY-TWO: EMBER

shook my head. "I'm full, Ryk."

He nodded, "Just one more bite. Then I promise we can cuddle, okay?" I shook my head, but he lifted the fork to my mouth, "Please? For me?" His puppy dog eyes worked on me every single time. I hesitantly opened my mouth and he placed the eggs on my tongue. I chewed as he finished the food on the plate.

"I am so proud of you! Come on, let's take medicine and get you back to bed!" I nodded, not having the energy to actually speak.

Ryker sat back on the counter, grabbed my half-finished water bottle and two boxes. I watched carefully as he took two pills out of the first box and one out of the second. "Take these, baby." I did as I was told. "Finish the water and then we can get some sleep."

I didn't fight him, finishing the water quickly. He lifted me off the counter and kissed my head. He then brought me into his room and laid us down on the bed. "Go to sleep, little flame. I got you."

I was woken up less than an hour later by the sudden urge to throw up. I fought my way out of Ryker's arms and ran down the hall. I fell onto my knees in front of the toilet as lunch came back up. Ryker came running in and held up my hair. He rubbed my back gently, trying to sooth me.

When I finished, I coughed a few times and shakily stood. Ryk held onto me, helping me rinse my mouth with mouthwash. We then made our way back into the bedroom to sit on the bed.

"How are you feeling, little flame?" He asked as I leaned against him. I shrugged, still breathing kind of heavy. "Talk to me, love."

I took a second to take a deep breath, "Not good. I-I'm tired, but I'm scared to lay down. I feel more sick when I lay down." I took his hand and played with his fingers to distract myself from what I was feeling.

Ryker kissed my forehead, "I'm sorry, if I could take your sickness away, I would. However, we should go to the urgent care. Make sure you are really okay."

I shook my head, "N-No! No doctors!" Ryker went to try to convince me, but I wouldn't let him. "I don't like them! I'm not going!"

"I know, Em, but we need to-"

"I said no!"

Ryker growled, "Do not interrupt me!" He spoke harshly, making me quiet quickly. "Ember, I understand you don't like doctors; however, you need to get better. I will be with you the entire time, I promise. If you continue fighting, you will be at the urgent care with a sore ass. Maybe I'll even ask the doctor to do a full exam, just so they can see you red bottom."

"I'm sorry, sir." I muttered, pushing my face into his neck. My cheeks were bright red at the thought of a doctor seeing my throbbing, red ass. The humiliation of the idea had me pushing my thighs together in shameful arousal.

He held me for a moment, petting my hair. "You are forgiven, baby. I think you like that idea though. Changing into a gown and have the doctor exam of inch of you after a spanking. I wonder what they would think of the naughty girl they're looking at. Fantasy for another time, even though I can smell your delicious scent. Let's go get you changed."

I shuddered at the idea. Imagining Ryker spank me before having Ace exam me and calling Cayden in for backup had me dripping. No matter how sick I was, they somehow always

CHAPTER THIRTY-TWO: EMBER

made me so needy.

After a few minutes of struggling and several warning spanks, I was dressed and placed in the car. I leaned my face against the cool window, closing my eyes. The ride was short, and Ryker was determined to get me into the doctor's office.

"Ember, I will not hesitate to spank you in the office if you fight. I don't care if it's in front of the doctor, nurse, or the entire fucking waiting room. Understand?" I grew beet red and nodded. "Be my good girl."

"Yes sir," I sighed.

The office wasn't crowded, only a girl and her father were in the waiting room. I held on tightly to Ryker anyway and he held me back.

Lucas took me to the doctor once when I was fifteen and caught pneumonia. He also called me stupid for getting sick and almost getting us caught. The doctor had been really handsy and he made me uncomfortable from the start. Lucas said I deserved it because I was a fat woman and was lucky for someone to touch me. From then on, he got me antibiotics illegally.

My man talked to the person at the front desk and filled out the necessary paperwork, asking questions he was unsure of. I gave him my social security number and told him the birth control I was on. He started struggling to fill out the forms when he needed medical history.

"Let me, darling." I said, taking the clipboard and filling out the rest of my information. Ryker was reluctant, wanting to do everything for me, but allowed me to finish the documents.

I handed the clipboard back to him. He nodded and left me sitting in a chair while he returned the chart to the receptionist. The nurse called out for the girl and her dad to go see the doctor. The girl hesitantly stood up allowing her dad to lift her up and bring her though the door.

I pulled Ryker into me when he came back. I missed him in the twenty seconds he was gone. He rubbed my back as I laid my head on his shoulder. After a few minutes a nurse came into the room, "Ember?"

I looked at Ryker who stood. He held out his hand and I nervously took it. We were led into a small exam room. Ryker lifted me onto the table and held my hand. I nervously fidgeted with his fingers. I refused to look anywhere that wasn't him. Looking around would only make me more nervous.

The door opened, "Hi Ember! My name is Ruby, I'm going to take your blood pressure and your temperature. Can you tell me about your symptoms?" I looked up and saw a woman with short green hair, covered with tattoos. She smiled sweetly and spoke gently while preparing a thermometer.

"I-I'm congested, I'm tired and I have a headache. I also threw up earlier, but I haven't felt the need to since." Ember responded.

Ruby nodded and took her temperature. "You have a fever and elevated blood pressure. However, you seem stressed, so that might be the cause of the blood pressure." She smiled and wrote something on a piece of paper. "Doctor Brittney will be in shortly."

I nodded and thanked her. Ryker turned to me, "Good girl. That wasn't so bad, right?" I made a small sound of disagreement and hugged him. He chuckled, "We will be done soon."

A knock on the door broke our hug and an older woman with kind eyes walked in the room. She smiled and looked at me. "Hi Ember, I'm Doctor Brittney. Can you tell me what

CHAPTER THIRTY-TWO: EMBER

you are feeling?"

I repeated what I told Ruby and she nodded. I was quickly examined and had a swab forced up my nose. She left the room to test the swab.

A few minutes later she frowned, her gentle eyes looked up from her clipboard. "Unfortunately, you have the flu, dear." She turned to Ryker, "You will probably get it too from being so close with her. Does anyone else live in your home?"

"Yes ma'am," Ryker responded politely.

She nodded, "I would recommend you two quarantine and stay away from them for the next five to seven days to prevent them from getting sick or at least until you stop showing symptoms."

He nodded and I sighed. Ryker rubbed my back as she gave me a prescription to help lessen my symptoms. We thanked the doctor and she left. Ryker hugged me and together we walked out the door. In the car, he called Ace and Cayden.

"Hey Ryk," Ace said through the phone. It was on speaker in the car. "How's our baby?"

He glanced at me, "She has the flu. The doc recommended we quarantine so you don't get sick."

"Hell no!" Cayden and Ace yelled at the same time. I flinched and my man placed a hand on my thigh.

I licked my lips and said gently, "It's to keep you safe."

"Not happening, don't argue." Cayden said, almost threateningly.

"It's up to you." Ryker muttered, " On your way home can you pick up her prescription?"

Ace and Cayden agreed to bring home my prescription and food. After concluding the call, we drove in silence. His hand never left my leg as he made one handed turns. I sighed as we pulled into the driveway, I dreamed of putting on my pajamas and cuddling with Ryker.

"Stay." Ryk muttered as he parked the car and got out. I looked at him confused but had no energy to argue. I unbuckled my seatbelt and waited. He walked around the front of the car and opened my door. One of his strong arms went under my legs and the other around my waist as he lifted me up. I leaned my head against his chest and wrapped my arms around his tattooed neck.

He brought me into the kitchen and sat me on the counter. "How are you feeling, little flame?" He handed me a bottle of water, commanding me to drink.

I drank a little before looking at him, "I don't feel good." I felt like crying. I hated being sick, it always made me feel like a child. Even though as a child, I wasn't allowed to be sick. He pulled me into him and rubbed my back as I whimpered.

"I got you, love. I promise." He murmured over and over again. My man lifted me off the counter and carried me into the room in the basement. I laid on his chest, closing my eyes. Another nap might do me some good.

33

Chapter Thirty-Three: ACE

By some dumb luck Ryker and Ember were the only two to get the flu. Cayden was out of the house often because he was extracting information from Trevor's men. I was in and out of the house constantly working with Austin. The day that Ryker took Ember to urgent care, we raided one of Trevor's safe houses. We now have Chase Ratton.

Two of our men were shot in the struggle, however Cayden and I were okay. We had met Ramero there before he debriefed us on who was in the building. His spy work is incredible.

"There are ten men inside the house. One of them is Ratton. Lucas and Trevor are not. There is also two women that are being passed around between the men. The brunette seems willing, the other red head doesn't." Ramero cleared his throat. "They are sitting around a table drinking in the main room. If we have one team go through the front door and another through the back, we should be fine. Although it's up to you, I would keep a team surrounding the house in case someone tries to escape."

I nodded and Cayden bounced from foot to foot. He loved this *shit and was ready to attack. In fact, he was getting impatient. I put a hand on Cayden's shoulder to steady him.*

"Thank you Ramero. You take a team of five through the back door, Cayden take five though the front. I'll hang out here for damage control." Cayden and Ramero loved the battle. They were good at fighting. This part was exciting, but I didn't care about the men in the room. Ramero will be the one to stay behind when we get our hands on Lucas and Trevor.

The two nodded and put their earpieces in. After a quick test of the coms, we split off. I had ten men and women on my team. I sent them in teams of two to surround the house and keep watch. I paired myself with Gianna.

Gianna was a badass woman who was smart and former United States Marines. She was covered in tattoos and dark makeup that made her look both terrifying and awesome. I have no interest in her, just admiration for all she has done. I respected all my staff, but Gianna has earned all the respect I can give and more. She's like a little sister who has our back.

"Ramero, you ready?" Cayden's voice came through the earpiece.

"Hell yeah!" Ramero responded.

"Three, two, one!" Cayden counted down before they teams entered the house.

Together Gianna and I watched the house as Cayden's team enter the house. He busted down the front door on the already dilapidated house. It looked like it would fall down with one strong gust of wind. The broken rocking chairs littered the front porch. It did look like a place that criminals would hide out in movies.

Gunshots and screams echoed in the quiet woods around the house. We agreed not to kill Ratton and at least one of the other men. It was also agreed upon not to hurt or kill the women. We don't hurt women.

CHAPTER THIRTY-THREE: ACE

My thoughts drifted to Ember. The poor girl was sick, and our dumbasses didn't keep medicine in the house for her. I have to get better at stocking up on basic needs for her. We had anything we needed at the office, but she was at the house all the time. Much to her dismay we have ten different types of pads and tampons for her. Her embarrassment wasn't warranted, but we wanted to make sure we were prepared. Somehow, we overlooked her getting sick and bought nothing to help her. We rarely got ill and never needed medication that wasn't prescribed by Jacob.

Suddenly Gianna jumped up and ran from my side. I jogged after her. She chased and tackled down a man twice her size. They both grunted as she turned and punched him square in the jaw. There was sickening crack as his jaw shattered under her fist.

Gianna shook out her hand before taking the zip ties from the pocket of her tactical gear. Tying his hands behind the man's back, Gianna rose and smiled at me. Her red lipstick contrasted her dark smoky eye look. She winked and gave the body a hard kick.

"You need to stop daydreaming about that pretty girl you got. It's slowing you up." *She said playfully. It was true, daydreaming could get me killed.*

I glared at her. I may be her boss, but she knew that I wouldn't be angry. I allowed my staff to banter with me, as long as it was respectful. Gianna sometimes walked on the line of disrespectful, but she was right too often.

"That's what I have you for. I pay you to have my back." *I said, keeping my tone light.*

"And do all the work." *She retorts with a laugh.*

I shook my head and looked down at the guy on the ground. He was groaning with pain, withering on the ground. "You broke his jaw." *I observed.* "You are one scary woman. I think I owe you a beer for this."

"Damn right." She gave the man another hard kick to the face. The man fell silent.

I glanced at her hand, "Your hand okay? Let me see it." I went into big brother mode without meaning to.

"I'm fine Ace. I know you think I'm like your sister, but I'm not. I don't need protecting." She shoved her hand into her pocket and turned back to the unconscious man.

That hurt, but I couldn't let it show. I haven't allowed myself to think about her in years. I met Gianna right after my little sister died. My sister, Scarlett died by suicide. Her depression won. Gianna reminded me of Scarlett's toughness and made me want to protect the badass.

"Sorry, just please let Jacob look at it." I lifted the man from the ground and walked with Gianna silently through the woods. We got back to the house as Cayden and Ramero exited the front door.

"Gianna got one!" I threw the man down at Cayden's feet.

His grin widened, "You break his jaw?"

She nodded with a smirk and turned to look at the girls being led from the house. The brunette was fighting the large man escorting her, while the red head was crying.

Gianna's smirk turned to a frown, "I'll take the redhead girl to the truck and calm her. I think Micky is scaring her."

I nod and watch as she takes the young woman from Micky and help her to the car. Gianna was just as good at calming victims as she was killing men. She had a calming nature, that I rarely got to see.

"How did it go?" I asked the men in front of me.

Cayden gave me a toothy grin, "Killed all but Ratton, the girls and an ugly rat looking guy. Matt and Nick were shot, but it was just flesh wounds. Nobody was badly hurt."

I nodded, "Have a team go through the house and have our

CHAPTER THIRTY-THREE: ACE

cleaners take care of everything after." Ramero agreed before leaving Cayden and me.

"What's wrong, A?" Cayd asked, noticing something was bothering me.

I shook my head, "I just miss Scarlett. Long story. Let's get home to Ember."

Ember and Ryker are better, Cayden and Serpent are with Ratton and I am currently in my home office. There was a knock on the door and I knew it was Ember. Ryker was at the store and Ember was supposed to be napping.

"Ace?" She asked, approaching the desk that I sat at. "Why are you crying?"

I wiped at my eyes, "I'm sorry baby blaze. I don't mean to cry in front of you."

"You can cry all you want, I do. Who is she?" Ember asked pointing to the picture I was staring at. There was a hint of jealously that made me hold back a smile. I sniffled and wrapped my arms around Ember, enjoying the feeling of her body against mine.

Sighing I picked up the framed photo, "This is my sister Scarlett. She killed herself about six years ago. She was eighteen. I was talking with a friend of mine the other day and Scarlett came up. I've been thinking about her a lot lately."

"I'm sorry, Ace. Suicide is a tough thing on the loved ones." She said in such a way that it felt she knew what I was feeling.

"Baby? Have you lost someone too?" I ask before regretting it, "If it's too difficult you don't need to tell me."

She gave a tilt of the head. "Lucas bullied my girlfriend, April, when we were in high school. She killed herself because she couldn't take his relentless words and actions. She was the love of my life. I love you and the others, but she was my first love." The pain was evident in her eyes and her voice shook slightly. "Ace, I'm sorry about Scarlett. If she was here, I would tell her that her brother is an amazing person. I didn't know her, but she would be proud of you."

My eyes were teary, how could this girl tell me about losing the love of her life and still comfort me? Ember climbed into my lap and sat facing me. She looped an arm around my neck pulling me into her chest. We both sat crying for our losses and the losses that the other felt.

Men don't cry. That is a bullshit standard and everyone knows it. It scares me that I can let my guard down around Ember. I love her, just like Cayden and Ryker. We aren't normal, but we work for us. We cry for and with each other.

Chapter Thirty-Four: EMBER

After Ace and I had a heartfelt moment in his office, we made plans for me to be out of the basement during the day. When they first let me out, I got sick and couldn't really do much in terms of chores. I was no longer trapped in that room and I was healthy. Now, I was doing often meaningless chores that had been assigned to me. I did them to avoid punishment, scared that I would be locked up again. I was currently in the kitchen, cleaning the already clean oven.

They seemed to run out of things and had me clean the oven twice this week. We haven't even used it since I last cleaned it. I looked up and noticed a camera pointed at me. I smiled and shook my head. The camera focused on my kneeling, almost naked body.

I took extra time finishing cleaning, really showing my body when I stretched to reach the back of the oven. I made a show of pushing my ass back when standing up. My phone buzzed and I laughed when Ace demanded I stopped being a tease.

Turning to face the camera, I ran my hands down my body. I pretend to drop my towel behind me. I bent at the waist, shaking my ass a bit as I picked it up. My phone started ringing. Ace.

"Hi, Daddy." I said with fake shyness.

He chuckled, "Don't play innocent now. You will do as I say, understand?"

I took a breath, "Yes, sir."

"Good girl," he growled. "Take off everything. I want you naked, now!" I glanced at the window. Nobody would see me unless they were in the backyard. After I had pulled off my underwear, Ace continued, "Spread your legs wide for me. Now play with your pussy. Make yourself feel really good, but do not come!" His demands made me wet.

I reached down with one hand and circled my clit. I let out a shaky breath. Ace encouraged me closer and closer to orgasm. I was panting, pumping two fingers in and out of me. I jumped when the back door opened. I stopped, turned my head and stood up.

Cayden walked in, "Why did you stop, sweet firestorm?" My eyes widened and I hesitated. He walked over to me and grabbed my hand. He licked my juices off my fingers and smiled. "I heard you have been a bad girl this morning," he whispered in my ear. He pulled me off the counter and bent me over it. "Ask permission before you come. Ace is in charge."

He smacked my ass, and I heard his belt buckle jingle. I tensed, ever since Lucas kidnapped me, the sound of a belt made me nervous. Cayden noticed, "Relax beautiful. Color and safe word?"

"Green and thunder, sir."

He spanked my ass again and spread my legs. His hands teased my sensitive area. Pinching my clit, pushing three

CHAPTER THIRTY-FOUR: EMBER

fingers into my pussy. I moaned and he pulled his fingers out. I whined and he spanked me a third time. "You do not whine!"

"Sorry, sir!" I whimpered.

His dick rubbed against my entrance. He pushed in slowly, giving me time to adjust. Once he was fully in, he pulled out almost all the way and slammed back into me. He repeated this, speeding up until his harsh thrusts were pushing me against the counter. His other hand was tasked with turning my ass red. It repeated smack and slapped my bottom, each slap sent left a stinging pain in its wake. I screamed at his harshness.

I was so close, "Please let me come! Please sir!"

Ace pretended to think about it, "Are you going to be a good girl? Are you going to stop being a tease?"

"Yes, Daddy!" I panted, barely able to hang on as Cayden came. Cayden didn't stop, the sound of his skin slapping against mine was deafening.

Ace chuckled, "Okay, baby girl, come for Daddy!"

I didn't need any more encouragement and screamed as I came on Cayden's dick. Cayden groaned as he came with me. I fell limp on the counter, laying my face on the cold countertop. I shivered as Cayden pulled out and picked me up. He cradled me to his chest and grabbed the phone.

"Ace, I'm gonna give her aftercare and put her down for a nap." Cayden said, talking about me as if I wasn't there.

Ace said something, but I focused solely on Cayd's warm chest and the smell of his cologne. He rocked me gently and brought me down to that prison-like room. I tried to fight him, but he gave me a solid smack on my thigh. I whimpered and let him hold me. He carried me to the bathroom, not wanting me to get an infection.

"Sweet firestorm, I'm gonna stay with you until you fall asleep and then I need to go back to work." He told me. I went to protest, but he cut me off, "No Ember, time for a nap."

He laid us down and cuddled me close to his chest. I slowly allowed myself to slip from consciousness.

* * *

I woke up, sore and still tired. I yawned and cursed as I realized that I was alone. With shaky legs, I walked over to the bathroom. The sight I saw in the mirror was scary and ugly. I did my best to fix my appearance, hoping that I would look okay when someone entered the room. My men always think I'm beautiful, but I still feel like they are lying about my after-nap look.

I limped back to the bed and curled up under the covers. I grabbed my phone and realized that nobody would be home for another hour or two. I made myself comfy, before jumping when my phone rang.

"Hi, Daddy!" I said, answering Ace's call.

Ace responded, "Hi baby blaze! Glad to see you awake. Hang tight for another hours. I'm coming home early, so be a good girl."

"Okay. Can I put on sweatpants? I'm cold."

"Sure, baby. Get under the covers and watch something on Netflix. The tablet is on the table."

I got up and went over to the dresser that had a pair of gray sweatpants. Tugging them on, I carefully walked back to the bed and laid down. Pulling the sheets over me, I picked up the phone again. "When will you be home?"

I heard Ace sigh, "Soon baby, soon. Put on a movie for me."

CHAPTER THIRTY-FOUR: EMBER

I grabbed the tablet and turned on a random cartoon movie. Ace told me he loved me and hung up as I settled in to watch the movie. I dozed off halfway through, only to be woken up by Ace. He climbed into the bed and pulled me into his chest. I whimpered as he kissed my neck.

It wasn't until I was more awake that I realized he was naked. I blushed and tried to move away from him. The more I squirmed, the harder his dick grew. Ace's hand snaked up to my throat, "Stop moving, babygirl." I froze and his deep chuckle filled my ear.

"Now, I believe I owe your teasing ass a punishment." I felt Ace's grin on my neck.

I was fucked.

35

Chapter Thirty-Five: EMBER

I limped my way into the kitchen. When Ace said he was going to punish me, he meant it. He fucked me with no mercy, hard and fast. By the end I was begging for him to stop. He kept going until I lost count of how many times I finished. I don't know if I loved or hated it.

Ace forced me into the bathroom, saying that he wanted to fuck me again and that he couldn't do that if I had a UTI. We then cuddled, having a sweet moment where we just enjoyed each other's presence. Ryker and Cayden had come home by that point, and we were called up for dinner.

Now, I was limping to get a bottle of water. Ace told me to drink water before I get my ass beat. I brought the water to my seat and joined my men at the table. Ryker smirked, "How was your day little flame?"

I glared at him, "It was tiring."

They all laughed, and I rolled my eyes, "I'm glad, love."

We ate in silence, my men glancing at me every so often. I was praised when I finished my bottle of water. I was getting frustrated and annoyed at their constant stares. It

CHAPTER THIRTY-FIVE: EMBER

was embarrassing. "Can you stop looking at me!" I snapped towards the end of the meal.

"Nope!" Cayden popped the 'p' in the word. "You are ours; we can stare at you as long as we want."

I huffed and went to get up. A hand landed on my thigh, I yelped. It didn't hurt or anything, it was merely a warning smack. I froze, refusing to move. "You do not walk away from us, Ember." Ryker growled.

I looked down, "Yes sir."

They exchanged looks, "We have the perfect punishment for you." My eyes widened at Ace's words. "Stand up." I did, not wanting to disobey. "Strip, now!"

I jumped into action, fearing what they had already thought of. When I was fully naked, I looked at them for further instructions. Cayden licked his lips and got up. He walked over to me and forced me to sit on one of the bar stools that lined our breakfast bar. He spread my legs wide, showing every part of me to the men at the table. I flinched when Ryker slid a rope around my legs. Ryker and Cayden worked together to tie me spread open to the stool.

"Raise your arms." I did as Ryker said. He tied my hands above my head, wrapping the rope over the hanging light fixture above me. I whimpered at the uncomfortable position I was in. "Shut it."

"Color and safe word?" Ace asked from across the room. He had sat back and watched me get tied to the stool.

My voice shook slightly as I responded, "Green and thunder, Daddy."

They stepped back and stared at me. "Now you will sit there while we finish eating." Cayden and Ryker went and sat back down. I squirmed under their roaming eyes. My men took their time to eat and really study every part of me. Cayden's eyes darkened when he focused on my now dripping pussy.

"Do you enjoy this? Do you enjoy being spread wide for our liking?" Ace sneered. He stood and walked over to me, "You like our eyes seeing every part of you. You're our good little girl, aren't you?"

My breath caught as he ran a finger from my knee up to the top of my thigh. I whimpered when his touch left me. I screamed when his hand clapped my clit. "I asked you a question, little girl."

My face was a deep red as I answered, "Yes Daddy."

"Yes Daddy what?"

"Y-yes Daddy! I-I'm your good l-little girl!" I cried as his hand smacked my clit a second time.

He fingers traced slow, agonizing circles around my throbbing clit. I attempted to buck my hips but being tied to the stool made me unable to move. I whimpered and whined, needy for more. His hand never stopped its torture as he placed feather light kisses on my neck and face. As painful as it was, I cried out when all touches stopped. I felt a chill at the sudden loss of warmth.

"Ace!" I choked out, trying to move my hands towards him.

"What did you just call me?" His hand gripped my throat, squeezing gently.

My wide eyes were forced to meet his dark ones, "D-Daddy!" His hand gave another squeeze making my pussy weep.

His dangerous smirk made me shudder. He took a step back and looked my body up and down. "You look stunning with our marks covering you. I think you need more. What do you boys think?"

Cayden and Ryker got up and stalked towards me. Cayden

CHAPTER THIRTY-FIVE: EMBER

looked at me hungrily, "Just a few more."

"Cover her body." Ryker's deep growl made me shake with need.

Taking a shaky breath I begged, "P-Please! I-I n-n-need you!"

There was a mixture of laughs and groans before three pairs of hands were on me. These hands were soon followed by three mouths, expertly kissing and sucking on my most sensitive areas. I could do nothing but moan, beg, and whimper as they left marks everywhere. I watched Cayden's mop of blond hair move in between my legs. Teeth grazed my clit before they bit down.

"CAYDEN!" I screamed in pain, but pleasure quickly overrode it. His grin said it all, he was pleased with himself.

"Aww did that hurt my little fire?" Ace taunted. I made a small squeak in response, and they laughed. With two or three final marks, they stepped back a few steps. I was left a crying, whimpering mess as they all walked back to the table. Ryker took a sip of his soda and moved behind me.

He brought out a tub of ice cream and a bowl and spoon. Ace took it and scooped out some into the bowl. Cayden then brought the bowl over to me. "Open." I blushed even redder than before. He was not going to feed me. I shook my head. "Are ya really gonna argue?" His hand went up to my jaw and forced it open. He shoved a spoonful of ice cream into my mouth.

"Here's the deal, Cay is going to feed you. Ryker is going to eat you. I am going to watch every move you make. You will not come or be released until that ice cream is finished." Ace smiled and moved a stool in front of me. He sat down and held eye contact. He laughed as I flinched when Ryker put his mouth on me.

For the next ten minutes I was forced to eat ice cream and hold back my need to finish. It was embarrassing and degrading to have Ace watch. His eyes drifted from my eyes to Ryker's head between my thighs. I almost lost my control, twice, both times resulting with ice cream running down my chin. It was left to drip down my chest causing me further embarrassment.

"P-Please let me come!" I cried to no one in particular.

Ace glanced at Cayden, "Did she finish her dessert?"

"Nope. She has about three scoops left. So no, princess, you cannot come."

I sighed in frustration as he put more ice cream in my mouth. At that moment Ryker decided to nip at my clit and I choked. Ice cream dripped from my mouth. Ace chuckled, "Slow down, you don't need to eat in such a hurry! I promise it isn't going anywhere."

I wanted to curse him out. I wanted to yell at him and tell him to fuck off. But he's in control and I am his good little sub. I'm being punished and I need to take it like a good girl. The humiliation was the worst part of the entire scene, which I realized was the point. Two spoonfuls later I was done. I was allowed to come all over Ryker's face. My men helped me ride out the intense orgasm.

I tried to slump against my bonds. My arms were killing me, and I wanted nothing more than to sleep. "Good girl, Ember. We are so proud of you!" Ryker said, kissing me softly.

They spent the next few minutes untying me and slowly bringing down my arms. They wanted to make sure I wouldn't hurt myself by rushing blood flow to my fingers. They had me drink water and carried me into Cayden's bedroom. Ryker

CHAPTER THIRTY-FIVE: EMBER

rubbed more shoulders, giving me the best massage of my life.

When he finished, my men stripped naked and jumped into bed, placing me on top of someone's chest. My eyes were shut, and they weren't going to open until I woke up. "I love you." I whispered and smiled as they echoed how much they loved me too.

Chapter Thirty-Six: Cayden

Chase Ratton said nothing. The past few days consisted of Serpent and I beating, skinning, and threatening Ratton. Right now, he's missing four fingers, all of his toes, and his left ear. I stared at the bloody and beaten man who sat in front of me. I'm not going to kill him. It has now become a mission to break the son of a bitch.

Giving him a final slap to the face, I walked out. I went into the bathroom down the hall and washed my hands. We decided to let him wallow in his own piss and shit for a few days and then break him.

Serpent is going to monitor him and make sure he doesn't die. In the meantime, I'm going to meet with Ramero and see if anything new developed with Lucas. The other guy knew nothing. He was low level and was there to move girls.

Ramero had the unpleasant task of talking to the brunette that was with Lucas and at the house. Poor bastard.

I nodded to Serpent who let me use the bathroom in his apartment to clean up. We provided a place in the basement for easier transport of the bodies. We supplied his food too,

CHAPTER THIRTY-SIX: CAYDEN

apparently, he has a thing for barbequed human with the amount of barbeque sauce he goes through.

I took my time going to my office. Ramero was always early to everything. Letting him wait won't kill him. I liked annoying him, it was one of my favorite pastimes. His eyes scrunch together, and he gets all huffy. He is the coolest person in a dangerous situation but be ten seconds late and he goes crazy.

"Took you fucking long enough!" Romaro exclaimed as I approached my office door.

I let out a loud laugh, "I'm what, ten minutes late? I've been with our friend Ratton."

He let out a loud breath, "One o'clock means one o'clock. Be here on time next time!"

"Yeah, yeah, yeah." I laughed, opening the door to my office. "You could have gone in." I keep the office unlocked. There isn't anything in there anyway, Ryker and my offices are just for show. Everything is kept in Ace's office.

"It's not my office, I have no right to enter when you aren't here."

I rolled my eyes, "My blessing isn't enough?"

"Nope," he grinned, "you aren't here, I'm not entering."

"Sit." I mutter, "You can come in and relax before we have a meeting."

Ramero sat in a chair across from my desk. The chairs were meant to hold bigger men, however it still looked small compared to Ramero. He was a large fucker with a hear of gold. Our best man to gain intel in the field.

"What did you find?" I held the best connection with him and often met with him to relay information back to Ace and Ryker. The two of us enjoyed a good fight and loved beer and nachos.

He rolled his shoulders and cracked his neck with a satisfying pop. Coughing once he finally said, "Nothing. The house was full of paperwork from the elderly couple that they killed. It seems like they killed the man when they took over the place and kept the old woman to be a housemaid, more like slave for them. She kept a diary that detailed everything, it wasn't pretty. The woman was killed a few months before we got there. We found both buried in the backyard like animals. I had Micky and Dave give them a proper burial together."

I shook my head, "What is wrong with those motherfuckers?" I picked up a pen and started spinning it. "So, nothing that could help us find their locations. But more on the reasons they should die. Do you have anything useful Ramero?"

I already knew he didn't. "I'm sorry man, there isn't shit in that house. I don't even think either of them were ever there. That was just a stop for trafficking according to the old woman's diary. The red head was one of the girls. Only sixteen."

"Fuck!" I exclaim. We don't deal with the skin trade, and we don't hurt women. "What about the brunette?"

"Maureen? She's fucking useless. Apparently, she willingly had sex with men. Basically sold herself for materialistic things. The night she went with Lucas, it was just for sex and free food. Trevor approached them at the bar and offered her the world in exchange for sex and keeping his men occupied in between girls. She looked young enough to pass for a girl. She doesn't know where they are now. What do you want me to do with her?"

As much as I wanted to say, 'kill her', I shrugged. "Put

CHAPTER THIRTY-SIX: CAYDEN

her under surveillance, put a tracking device in her. Figure something out."

He nodded, "Yes, sir!" Romero stood and held out a hand. I rose and clasped it. He pulled me into a hug and whispered, "On time, next time. Don't be late."

That smug asshole.

Chapter Thirty-Seven: EMBER

"Ember!" Alyssa gave me a huge hug.

Despite being healthy and fit to leave the house, I was kept home for another two weeks. Finally, my men agreed to take me to the show. I was given many rules. I knew this was because Lucas still wasn't caught. I still didn't know what my men did, but I figured it they were government people or something. One of these rules was to stay with one of them or Ramero at all times. Currently Ramero was trying to pull Alyssa off of me.

"Ramero, let me say hi to my friend!" Alyssa tried shooing him away. I laughed, allowing her to continue hugging me. She finally let go and looked me up and down. "Honey, you look amazing! Keep up whatever or whoever you are doing! Let's get food, you could use some more meat on your bones."

I blushed and she wrapped an arm around my shoulder. Food was still an insecurity of mine, despite my men proving to me otherwise. I had gained weight in muscle from training with them. My men also spanked me often because I refused to eat to make up for the weight I gained. Knowing arguing

CHAPTER THIRTY-SEVEN: EMBER

was futile, I allowed Alyssa to lead me down the street.

Even with Ramero's long legs, he struggled to keep up with Alyssa. My friend was now on a mission. She dragged me down the street to the nearby fast-food place. I pulled out my phone to text my men where I was. Last thing I needed was them panicking.

"You are a scary woman!" Ramero panted. "How are you so fucking fast? And how the hell do you keep up?" He looked at me with a confused look.

I shrugged and Alyssa gave a bright smile, "I have things to do, no time to waste." She turned to me, "Order, hon, I'm paying."

"I can pa-"

I was cut off with Alyssa shaking her head, "It's on me! Now order!"

At her command, I held up my hands in surrender, "Yes, ma'am!" I ordered a burger, to which Alyssa added fries to. I rolled my eyes and looked helplessly at Ramero. He just rolled his eyes too and went to sit at a nearby booth.

My phone buzzed and I looked down to see a message from Ace. Please don't be mad, I thought. To my surprise, it read:

Be safe, stay with Ramero. If it wasn't Alyssa, I would be mad. But Alyssa is Alyssa. I feel bad for Austin. I love you, baby blaze!

I started laughing hysterically. Austin is her boyfriend; he works with my men. He also wrestles, having a feud with A Bitch and Her Gays while I was out. Austin was new to the ring and was working up to eventually join my men as part of the bloody wolves.

Ramero grabbed the phone and smiled. Alyssa gave us a weird look as she carried the food back to the table. "How do you get everybody to like you?" I wondered and handed her the phone.

Her face lit up and she giggled, "Ace is just one person!" My phone buzzed in her hand, "Okay, Ace and Ryker are just two people."

I gaped at her. "What did Ryk say?"

Ramero looked over at the phone, "Ryker wrote 'I agree, Alyssa is too difficult to argue with. She is the only one allowed to drag you places.'"

"Motherfucker. Alyssa! They are never this lenient, are you some kind of witch?"

"No, no!" She said between fits of laughter. "I'm not a witch!" My phone buzzed again. "Cayden just texted you."

I took the phone and read the message out loud, "Doesn't surprise me. Alyssa could make the crowd love a heel. Enjoy!"

Our table erupted into laughter. We got looks from the tables around us, but we couldn't control ourselves. Alyssa flashed an apologetic look towards the other diners who all looked away. The only conclusion I had come to was that Alyssa was a witch and she had placed a spell on the entire world.

We sat enjoying each other's company. I made a face as Alyssa dumped way too much mayo on her chicken sandwich and began dipping the fries into the mayo. I love her, but that is fucking gross. Alyssa made a sound of frustration as she got mayo on her shirt. I watched as she dabbed the stain with a napkin. She can never keep her clothes clean; it must cost her a fortune doing laundry.

We finished our meal in time for the doors to open. Our walk back was almost uneventful. Alyssa had tripped twice, almost taking me down with her. I caught her both times.

CHAPTER THIRTY-SEVEN: EMBER

Ramero finally ended up carrying Alyssa because he was second on the card tonight.

We parted ways when Ace found us and led me to the other two. Apparently, Lucas had not shown up, so my men were on high alert. Tonight, I was to go to the ring with them and look pretty. It was planned that I would jump up on the apron and distract the ref. It was straight forward and should be an easy night.

Presley and Harper came over and gave me a hug. They told me I looked great. I looked at the black skirt that Ryker forced me to put on along with a black blouse.

I looked cute, but the skirt was really short. I was lucky that I hadn't been spanked recently because my marks would definitely be showing. However, Ryker did threaten to spank me with the 'brat' paddle. A hard wooden paddle with the word "brat" carved into it. I quickly told him that I was a good girl and that I would do anything to avoid it. He smiled and told me to get on my knees. My throat is sore, but my ass is not and that is a win in my book.

I watched them get changed. I still could not get over how lucky I was, they had the bodies of gods and still treated me like a queen. I watched as they shed their jeans for trunks and shirts for a simple jacket. The jackets were left unopened, which caused me to stare at their exposed skin. Ace laughed and walked over to the bench where I was sitting.

"Close your mouth, baby blaze." He pushed his nose into my neck and murmured, "If we didn't have a match, I would fuck you right now with the way you are staring."

I blushed and looked around. Nobody seemed to notice the conversation. I could only imagine the reaction of the rest of the locker room. "Ace!" I whined, as he stuck a finger against my now wet panties. He hummed and withdrew his hand.

"If you don't behave, I'll bend you over that table and fuck you until you pass out. I don't care who is watching. Now be a good girl and let's get to the curtain." He whispered, before standing and extending a hand.

I gasped, my cheeks now extremely red. He wouldn't. Would he? I knew the answer. He wanted everyone to know who I belonged to. He would do everything he just said. I shuddered and took his hand. I was going to be good. I don't think I could take that embarrassment.

I walked alongside my men down the ramp and to the ring. Cayden lifted me up and Ryker held open the ropes. Even as heels they respect me, I thought happily.

The match went well, my men won. I had helped by distracting Ricky who yelled at me to get down. I laughed at him and shook my head. When Ace gave me the all clear, I leapt down and pointed in the ring. Ricky had turned and counted to three. The crowd went ballistic screaming their hatred for us.

I raised my men's hands and then we made our way to the back. I waited patiently for them to change before saying our goodbyes. Ace gave me a smile and lifted my chin to kiss me. I let him. Then we went to the car. I was good. I was their good girl. I was not going to be fucked in front of my peers.

38

Chapter Thirty-Eight: EMBER

"Harder!" Ace demanded. I was panting, dripping sweat, but forced myself to punch harder. We were in the gym that was in their basement working on my defense skills. We had been going over kicking, punching and any other thing Ace deemed necessary for the past three hours.

"Aaaacccceeee!" I whined, after this last set. "Are we done? We've been here for hours!" I was still sore from the night before where they all took turns fucking me and just wanted to shower.

A hand smacked my ass hard. I yelped and jumped to see Cayden behind me, "No whining."

I looked down, "Sorry Cayd."

Cayden nodded and turned to Ace, "She's been working hard, I think you should call it a day."

Ace smiled, "Run a mile on the treadmill and you're done." I huffed and Cayden smacked my ass again. I jumped and mumbled a quiet sorry before rushing to the treadmill.

After the mile I practically collapsed into Ryker. Ryker had come down while Ace went to shower and Cayden went to answer a phone call. The entire time I ran, his brown eyes were glued to my bouncing boobs. I felt like covering them but decided against it after the incident at dinner the other night.

"Ryk?" I asked, my head against his chest. He had lifted me up and carried me to the room in the basement. "Are you gonna lock me in here again?"

We went into the bathroom and Ryker set me down on the counter by the sink. He cupped my face, "Why would we do that little flame?"

I shrugged, "I'm not really sure. I just haven't really been down here lately, unless you locked me in here."

Instead of replying, he wrapped his hand around the back of my head and kissed me. It was rough, but reassuring. He tasted like mint when he forced his tongue into my mouth. We fought for dominance, him ultimately winning. We broke apart, chests heaving, and lips swollen.

"Little flame," He paused and kissed my cheek, "You need a shower. You stink."

My jaw dropped and I hit his chest. "That's mean!" He grabbed my wrist and pulled me off the counter.

"Is it really?" He teased. "Strip." Ryker turned and started the shower. The hiss of the water filled the room before he turned back to see me still clothed. "What did I just say?" He growled.

I quickly peeled my sweaty clothes from my body. My man's eyes followed my movements. I watched him lean against the door as he pointed to the shower. I stepped under the warm water and groaned. Ryker's eyes darkened at the sound, but he didn't move from his spot. The water felt amazing on my sore muscles.

CHAPTER THIRTY-EIGHT: EMBER

I went to close the curtain, but a deep growl stopped me. "If you close that curtain, I will make it my personal mission to make sure you can't sit for a month."

I blushed at his words and clenched my thighs. Am I supposed to be aroused by this? His eyes watched as I washed my hair. My body extended as I dramatically lifted my arms to massage my scalp. I noticed his dick strained against his jeans. I licked my lips and grabbed the soap. In slow motions I poured the soap on a washcloth and moved it all over my body. I started at my shoulders and made cautious movements to rub it over my nipples. I let out a quiet moan but kept going until I got to my needy pussy. I made a show of washing my legs and thighs, tracing the marks that were left over. I took my time, really putting on a show for him. I rubbed the cloth against my heat, holding eye contact with Ryker.

When I finished, I shut off the water and grabbed the towel from the rack. Ryker clapped his hands slowly. "That was quite a performance, little flame. On your knees." I fell gracefully to kneel in front of him. He took the towel from me, and I shivered at the cold tile. "Cold, my little flame?" He quickly lifted me and slid the towel on the floor. My knees were grateful to him.

He unzipped his jeans and took his cock out. I opened my mouth to welcome it. I wanted nothing more to please him. "For teasing I'm going to fuck your hot mouth. Then we are going to pretend nothing happened. Understand?"

I breathlessly , "Yes, sir!"

His dick entered my mouth roughly. He wasn't kidding when he said he was going to fuck my face. I wanted to scream around it, but I couldn't. I gagged and choked on it, tears flooding my eyes. Ryker's sadistic grin and loud groans encouraged me to squeeze his balls. My pussy was dripping down my thighs. He let out a loud moan and came. I tried to swallow it all, but the intensity made some drip from my mouth.

"Good girl," he panted as he pulled out. He used a washcloth to wipe my chin and the tears that leaked out. He lifted me up and kissed my cheek before gently drying my body and hair. It was so gentle I could have been convinced he was a different person than the man who fucked my mouth.

When I was dressed in his t-shirt and a pair of panties we went upstairs. Ace had made grilled cheese for us for lunch. I did as Ryker had said and pretended that I didn't just suck his dick ten minutes ago. I ate the sandwich quickly and asked for another one. In all the excitement I didn't realize how hungry I was. My men were happy that I wanted more food, and I was glad they didn't judge me.

"So baby blaze, we are going to go to the mall this afternoon. We have a few rules." Ace said as we ate. I looked up from my food and nodded for him to continue. "First, you will be with one of us at all times. Either hold our hands or stick close to us. Second, listen to us. If we say to get something or put something back, do it. If we say to hold our hands, you do so with a smile. Don't talk back or be a brat. Understand?"

I nodded, "Yes Daddy."

After lunch, I changed into appropriate clothes to leave. They didn't seem happy that I was covered up. "We're choosing your clothes next time." Cayden mumbled as we walked to his truck.

Ace sat in the back with me, his hand on my upper thigh the entire drive. I shifted and his hand tightened. "I was just shifting, love. I'm not trying to shake your hand." His

CHAPTER THIRTY-EIGHT: EMBER

eyes locked onto mine, almost searching to find the lie in that statement. I placed my hand on his and gave him a small smile.

At the mall I held his hand as Cayden and Ryker walked next to us. I was surrounded by three bodyguards. I blushed as we got odd looks and glances. We walked into a lingerie store, and they started picking out things for me. Everything was lace or see though or revealing in some way.

I wanted to look at a bra but was hesitant to go over without them. They told me not to leave their side, so I tapped Ryker's arm. "Can I go over there? You'll still be able to see me."

He glanced around the small store before nodding, "Don't leave the store and stay in sight."

I nodded and moved to the edge of the store to look at the bra. I really liked it, but it wasn't as revealing as what they were picking out. I found my size and hesitantly walked over to Ace. He looked at me and smiled as he noticed that I was holding something.

"What's that baby girl?" He asked. My face had to be crimson as I held up the baby blue bra that was cute, but not really sexy. It had a little lace, but nothing like they had in the basket.

"I like it. It's simple and has support." I muttered, clearly uncomfortable.

He took it from my hands and threw it into the basket, "What else did you find?" Ace seemed genuinely interested. We spent about twenty minutes adding things to the cart.

I then realized something, how was I going to pay for this? Cayden noticed my puzzled look and nudged me, "What's wrong?" I went to our basket and started going through the things I had picked and took them out. "What are you doing?" His hands stopped me, grabbing my wrists.

"I can't pay for this!" I say, fighting his hands. I kept my voice at a hushed whisper, not wanting to cause a scene.

Cayden held me tightly and Ryker was putting the stuff back in the basket. He brought it to Ace who brought it to the counter. Cayden whispered in my ear, "I will bend you over right here if you don't stop, Ember."

I froze and apologized to him. He walked me out of the store and to a nearby bench. I was nervous that he was going to punish me in the middle of the mall. That thought both scared and excited me, making me clench my thighs together. He sat us down and gave me a stern look.

"Sweet firestorm, I get that you are an independent woman. But we are gentlemen and will pay for your every need. What was one of the rules we discussed during lunch today?"

I looked at the ground, "Listen and not be a brat."

He nodded, "Were you listening in there when I told you to stop and that we were gonna pay for it?" I shook my head. "No, you didn't. That was strike one, be a good girl. We will pay for everything. You will not argue or fight us. Understand? Three strikes and you get punished."

I nodded, but he grabbed my chin, "Yes sir!" I blushed when he let go. I didn't like PDA or anything public. He kissed me quickly and we stood as the other two came out.

"Hold my hand," Ryker demanded, and I rushed over to him. Grabbing hold of his outstretched hand, I was immediately pulled to his side. "Where next little flame?"

I shrugged, "I don't know? Can we look there?" I pointed to a store that was packed with stuffed animals. They laughed as I dragged Ryker towards the store.

I spent almost forty minutes deciding on what stuffies I wanted. My men told me they would each buy me one as long as I promised to behave. I made the promise and proceeded to

CHAPTER THIRTY-EIGHT: EMBER

grab a few different animals. In the end, my men impatiently waited for me to hand them each a stuffie.

I thought about arguing but figured that would only get me another strike. I love stuffed animals, Lucas refused to let me get one, even when I got a job. He told me they were childish. I think I just craved the comfort. Now the stuffed animals could help me when my men go to work and I miss them.

I decided that Ryker would get me a blue dog wearing a red bowtie. Cayden would get me a large white unicorn and Ace would get me a green frog wearing a blue scarf. They smiled as they checked out and I laughed as they now carried the large stuffed animals around the mall.

"Hey princess, do you need a laptop?" Cayden asked. We had discussed college the other night. I wanted to register for online classes, but money was an issue. Despite them saying they would pay for me, I kept declining.

I looked at Cayden and shook my head, "No, I don't think so."

My men exchanged looks, "Love, we are willing to pay for your schooling and a laptop for it." Cayden told me, guiding me towards the nearest technology store.

I shook my head, "How can you afford all of this? Bad enough you have to support me with basic necessities, but you shouldn't have to pay for college."

Ace smiled, "We are well off, don't worry about money."

"What do you do?" I asked, this isn't the first time I questioned them. Each time I did they shut me down.

"Emb-"

I cut Ace off, "Don't lie or say it doesn't matter. Why do you have so much money?" I fought my voice from raising as the three men started to look frustrated.

Cayden tongue darted out to wet his lips, "Come on, this is not a conversation for here."

I shook my head, "You will tell me now!" I knew I sounded like a brat. I should just be grateful for them. They saved me, they showed me love and they kept me safe. I had no right to ask them anything, but I wanted, no I needed to know.

Ryker's jaw clenched, "You are in no position to make demands, little girl." He growled.

I narrowed my eyes, "What are you hiding? Tell me or I'm gone." It hurt to say I was going to leave, but I didn't want a relationship of secrets. They knew so much about me, but I knew next to nothing about them.

"No, you will not leave." Ryker challenged. So, I turned on my heel and started to walk away. "Get your ass back here." I ignored him and kept walking. I ignored the footsteps that followed.

Keeping my chin up, I went to the women's bathroom and locked myself in a stall. What were they hiding? Why won't they tell me what they do? All these questions bounced in my head. I pulled out my phone and sent a quick message to Ramero. Maybe he knows something. I heard the door swing open and I pressed myself against the wall of the stall.

"Ember, I know you're in here. Come out now before you get yourself into even more trouble." Cayden demanded.

I bit my lip and jumped when my phone buzzed. I looked down and it was a text from Ramero. I gasped and screamed when the door to the stall was kicked in.

39

Chapter Thirty-Nine: EMBER

Cayden's angry face filled my vision as he grabbed me. I shrieked and tried to escape his grasp. He pulled me into his chest and placed a calloused hand over my mouth. "Ember, calm down. It's me. It's Cayden. I won't hurt you." Despite this I struggled. "EMBER! You will stop at once. We are going to walk out of here and you are going to smile." He bent and picked up my phone. "Naughty girl."

I whimpered, "Please Cayden. I-I'm sorry."

He cupped my face, "We are going to walk to the car, you will get into the car, and you will stay silent."

With teary eyes, I nodded. "Yes, sir."

He kissed me roughly, "Good girl!" He wiped my tears and grabbed my hand. I looked at the ground as he led me out of the bathroom and to the other two who were waiting.

I got angry glances from Ace and Ryker who then smiled. I have been living with psychopaths. I kept my head down, debating if I should call out for help. I decided against it when Cayden's grip became punishing. Of course he knew what I was thinking, Cayden always knows. I winced as he pulled me out the door and into the large parking lot.

He practically shoved me into the car, I whimpered as I smacked my knee into the seat in front of me. I was pushed into the middle with Ace and Ryker son either side of me. Cayden slipped into the driver's seat and locked the doors.

We sat in silence for less than a second before I broke. "Please sirs! I'm sor-"

"Quiet!" Ace snapped. He held my phone tightly and read the message that Ramero sent out loud. "They didn't tell you? They run ACR Empires."

ACR Empires. ACR is the largest manufacturing company in the state, but nobody seems to know what they manufacture. The company is notorious for people going missing and employees being sworn to secrecy. There were rumors of murder and corruption. There were rumors that the owners were part of the mafia. That they run the mafia. ACR was run by a trio of dangerous men. And I was sleeping with the dangerous trio. I was this trio's submissive. I was at their mercy.

Ryker placed a hand on my thigh. It was once a comfort, but now it felt like a trap. "What do you know about ACR?" His tone was flat with a threatening undertone.

I shook my head, "N-Nothing!"

He growled, "Liar! What do you know?"

I was shaking and tried desperately to stop the tears that fell from my eyes. Ace grabbed my face roughly and I let out a loud cry. "You will tell us what you've heard." Cayden peeled out of the parking lot.

"Please let me go!" I begged, but Ace put a hand over my mouth.

"You have no right to speak unless it is to tell us about ACR.

CHAPTER THIRTY-NINE: EMBER

When we get home, you will go to the playroom and kneel in the corner." I shook my head, but Ryker smacked my thigh. "We are being nice; you can go to the playroom, or we can bring you somewhere you won't like."

My mind drifted to the dungeons and torture chambers from all the movies and books that I have seen and read. I tried to say "yes sir" around Ace's hand. He removed his hand, and I did my best to make myself as small as possible. The car ride was both the longest and shortest ride of my life. Cayden pulled into the driveway and Ryker pulled me from the car.

Before I knew it, I was placed in the playroom. The room that typically brought me excitement, now brought me fear. I rushed to kneel in the corner the way that they asked. What were they going to do to me? I couldn't breathe. I thought of the way they said they loved me. But it just made me more scared. By the time they entered the room I was fighting a panic attack, trying not to bring attention to myself. Tears fell and I choked out "gray" hoping they would respect the color system. To my surprise they did.

"Ember, go to your room." Ryker said and they walked out. I don't know what they had planned, but I wasn't going to find out. I rushed out of the room and down the hall.

Closing the door quickly behind me, I slumped down and let out a frustrated scream. "How could I be so stupid!" I mumbled over and over to myself. I don't know how long I sat there for, but my legs had long fallen asleep, and my eyes stung from all the tears.

I dragged myself to the bed and buried myself under the blankets. Sleep refused to come, and I laid there terrified and exhausted. I looked at the cameras that had a red blink to signify they were recording. I was being watched. It was unsurprising that I was being watched.

40

Chapter Forty: Ryker

"I think she needs to get out of the house." Ace watched Ember through the cameras. We were sitting in his office discussing what Ramero told Cayden. We didn't have much time to talk after Cayden's meeting because of the show. We also did not want to talk around Ember.

"We let her out to go to RHW yesterday." Cayden argued.

Ace rolled his eyes, "Yes, but I think she would benefit from having interaction with more than our house, the venue, and the car."

I nodded agreement, "I agree, she's getting restless."

Unfortunately, our trip out was the cause of our first large fight. Her tantrum could be seen from a mile away. Now, she was freaking out. Ember was scared of us. All we wanted to do is comfort her. However, we can't let her leave.

Fuck the phrase: "if you love her let her go." Fuck that.

I don't care if she hates us. If she hates me. She is ours. She is mine.

I love her, no matter what. I would kill for her; I would die for her. I would lock her in a room just to keep her.

Ember can't escape me; I am engulfed in her flame.

I love her.

41

Chapter Forty-One: EMBER

I'm unsure how long I laid there. It felt like hours, but it could have been minutes. I stared into nothing, too scared to close my eyes. I held my breath when there was a sharp knock on the door and the doorknob turned. I pushed myself in the far corner of the bed and watched as Ace, Cayden and Ryker entered.

"You were a very naughty girl, Ember. We told you to stop asking, but you didn't listen. Now, what have you heard about ACR?" Ace sneered, leaning against the wardrobe.

I shook my head, "N-Nothing sir!"

"Ember, Ember, Ember. You never lie this much, and you know us well enough to know how we feel about liars." Cayden stalked towards me from the door. "We can do this the easy way or the hard way."

I stayed silent. Ryker huffed, "That's it. We gave you a chance. You will talk one way or another."

He pulled me by the legs off the bed and threw me over his shoulder. I screamed and struggled and tried to fight him. "Let me go! Y-You don't have to do this!"

Ryker smacked my ass hard causing me to yelp. He brought me over to the large X that took up space in the playroom. It had moved from the wall to the center of the room. He held me in place while the other two tied me facing the X. With my back facing them, I struggled to look over my shoulder.

"Eyes forward." Cayden snapped. I turned my head forward, tears welling up at his harshness.

"W-What are you g-gonna do to me?" I hiccup as something cold was pressed into my skin. It started moving and I recognized the object as scissors that were now cutting my clothes. "S-Stop!" I yelled. But they didn't, instead another pair joined the first. Soon I was tied to the cross naked and shaking. If I say my safe word, would they listen?

Ace cleared his throat and stood in front of me. "Tell me what you know about ACR, baby girl! We just want to put this behind us. This is like a punishment; you still have your safe word and your colors. If you say your safe word, we will just switch to something different."

No matter how scared or nervous I am, I know they won't ever hurt me. Even though they are angry, they still want me to feel safe. Somehow, I'm not as scared of them as I thought I would be. They would never torture me like Lucas did. My men are dangerous, but not to me. I repeated this over and over as they finished setting up whatever they had planned.

Ace pet my hair gently. I flinched at the unexpected caress, "Please let me go!" Something hard came down on my ass. I yelped, "All I know is rumors! I don't know anything!"

"What rumors?" Cayden asked, moving into my vision holding the cane. He knows I hate it; he knows it's torture for me. I looked into his eyes and realized he wants to torture me, wants to punish me for asking the wrong questions. "We

CHAPTER FORTY-ONE: EMBER

are being nice. Talk or we can bring you to a far uglier room with toys that you would find less enticing."

Ryker gave Cayden an unsure look, clearly not liking that threat. Despite Cayden's mean streak and sadistic nature, I doubt he would ever hurt me or go through with his plan. However, that doesn't give me much comfort.

I closed my eyes and the cane landed hard on my ass again. I felt the welts form, knowing he was probably going to stripe me anyway. I hissed and sniffled, "Y-You lead the mafia. You kill people who you don't like. You kill your employees when they make the smallest of mistakes. Y-Y-You are murderers. ACR is led by bad people, dangerous people." I rushed out the little that I heard from social media and word on the street.

They all started laughing, it wasn't a sweet laugh. It was the laugh of villains, of psychos. Cayden left my view and I braced myself for the stinging strike of the cane. Instead, I was met with a hand caressing my sore ass. I tried to move away from him, but that led to him pinching the skin the welts were forming on. I was panting and trying not to squirm as he added pressure to his grip. My pussy was dripping down my thighs.

"Good girl." He praised me and went back to rubbing circles on my skin. I licked my lips and waited for him to continue with the cane.

Ace stopped laughing and put his hand on my cheek. His fingers trace my jawline in slow, gentle movements. "Baby blaze, we are dangerous people." My breath hitched. "We are murderers. We kill those who deserve it, who cross us. You would never cross us, right?"

I shook my head, fighting to breathe. "N-No!"

"Take a breath, little flame." Ryker said, placing a hand

on my shoulder. I did, not wanting to find out what would happen otherwise. "We are not part of the mafia. We are dangerous businessmen who do everything we can to hide our identities. We run other operations on the side, hurting those who deserve it. We don't hurt civilians, women, or children."

"You know who we are. You found out about us because of one of our employees. That means death for both the employee and you." Cayden's cane striped my ass with each word of the last sentence. I screamed and cried tears of fear and pain.

"Don't kill Ramero! Please don't kill him." I didn't care about myself anymore. He was just trying to help me. "I-I'll do anything! Kill me, not him!"

I was shushed by all three men. Cayden moved in front of me, "Let it out, love." I cried and begged them not to murder my friend. I finally calmed myself enough for them to untie me. "Be our good girl and don't move." I didn't, I couldn't physically move.

Ace picked me up and brought me to the bed. He sat me on his lap, making sure my butt wasn't touching anything. It hurt my thighs, but I couldn't find it in myself to complain. I wanted to push him away, run for my life, but I didn't. He rocked me like he had so many times before. This time I refused to take comfort from it, doing my best to convey that I was uncomfortable.

"We are still your Doms, your men. We promised not to hurt you, therefore, we won't." Ace murmured into my neck. His promises didn't make me feel any better, I whimpered as he kissed the base of my neck.

"Please let me go, sir. I promise I won't say anything." I

CHAPTER FORTY-ONE: EMBER

tried, pulling away from his embrace.

He pulled me close to him, "We claimed you. You ain't leaving us! Do you understand?" Ace's grip was now crushing my ribs. I nodded, gasping for air.

He slapped my thigh, "Yes sir!"

Cayden gave me a sadistic smile, "You will be punished for your stunt at the mall."

"First," Ryker started, "you need to understand who we are." He walked over to me and held out his arms. I was nudged by Ace to hug the other man. I did, but I was stiff and refused to relax against him. "Em, we are the same men that we were before. Nothing's changed, little flame."

I shook my head, "Y-You're a murderer! You are gonna kill me and Ramero! You are horrible people!" I pushed him away and he let me. I backed myself towards the door.

Did I really care if they were murderers? What was really my issue, I wondered. I love them so much, that murder wouldn't turn me away. Why was I reacting like this? I knew they weren't always doing legal shit, why was I reacting like this? Murder doesn't matter to me; they would kill to protect me. I would kill to protect them. Biting my lip, I determined that I was more mad at them for lying than anything else.

"You have two choices, either go to your room or stay here and let us tell you how the rest of your life is going to play out." Cayden took a step towards me.

I took a step back, "The rest of my life?" This is it; they are going to kill me, and nobody will ever find my body. They could pin it on Lucas, hell they could blame him for mine and Ramero's murders. My insecurities and old fears came back full force.

"Come sit on my lap or kneel at the cross, baby girl." For the first time since the mall his voice was gentle. I walked over, still naked and knelt in front of the object that I was tied to a few minutes earlier.

"Nothing has changed Ember. We are still going to treat you like the queen you are. You are our sometimes bratty sub, but we love you so fucking much, baby blaze!" Ace walked over and played with my hair. I hated how I leaned into his touch. It was completely involuntary, and I tilted my head away when I realized it. He was unfazed, his touch never leaving my head. I wanted his touch, why was I trying to pull away?

Cayden echoed this, but added, "We have been good to you. We wanted to hide the violent side in order not to scare you. We never wanted to expose this part of us to you."

Ryker pushed Ace to the side and laced a hand into my hair. It pulled, forcing my head to follow. I was now looking up at Ryker's piercing brown eyes. "Little flame," his voice was surprisingly calm, "we will never hurt you, however you will never leave us. Ember you are officially tied to us. We will give you protection, love and of course, sex. You will be our sub, our secret keeper and our good girl."

I closed my eyes, wanting to agree but too scared. They were everything to me for the past few months. These were the men that took my virginity, fucked me in front of their neighbors, saved me from my brother. These were the men that confessed their love for me, both verbally and physically.

"B-but you're gonna kill me. You just said that." I breathed, keeping my eyes shut to avoid Ryker's.

He growled, "We normally would, however, you are special. You are ours, beautiful girl. We could go to jail for a long time if someone found out who we are."

CHAPTER FORTY-ONE: EMBER

"What about Ramero?" I asked, if he died or was dead, I would never forgive them.

Ryker let go of my hair and I fought the urge to rub sore scalp. I watched him from my peripherals, "Do you want him to live?"

"Yes, sir."

Ryker nodded and pointed at the bed, "Hands and knees."

I hesitated and he snapped his fingers. Fearfully I moved to the bed and positioned myself like I have many times before.

Cayden sat in front of me. "You will do exactly as we say. Typically, we would kill him, but we are in a generous mood. He's also our best spy. I'm unsure of why he even said anything. You will be our good little girl forever and your friend will live."

I let out a shaky breath at his command. I turned my head to look at Ace who was next to me. "S-Sir?"

"Yes, beautiful girl?"

I needed to ask this before I lost the courage. "Does that mean if I'm bad or break a rule Ramero wil-will-" I couldn't finish the sentence.

Ace picked me up and I was once again cradled on his lap. "No, baby, no. Don't go telling anyone who we are or do anything like that, okay? We won't kill him if you make a mistake like forgetting a meal or something like that. Take some deep breaths for me."

I felt a tiny bit better and listened when Cayden helped me with my breathing. When I was close to being okay again, I looked at the ground. "N-No more secrets, I don't want to be blindsided again." I was scared that I was going to be yelled at for making a demand.

I was surprised when they all agreed. Cayden cupped my

face and wiped away the stray tears, "We love you so much." His words only made me cry more.

Chapter Forty-Two: EMBER

I was told to bend over the bed so they could inspect my ass. All three were scared that they caned me too much. I blush a deep red as I was completely exposed. My face burned the cool sheets as they spread my legs wider. I went through emotional hell, and I'm still turned on by their actions.

The three men surrounded my naked body but refused to touch me intimately. Instead, they made me stay in position, exposed to them. Cayden had rubbed my back and Ace patted my head, but they didn't force me to do anything. I jumped when Ryker put cooling lotion on my sore ass and thighs.

Finally, they all agreed that I needed sleep. Nodding with a yawn I asked if I could move. Ace scooped me up and took me to my room. Ryker filled the bathtub with warm water and bubbles. I was placed gently in the tub. I winced as my ass connected with the hard surface.

"Baby blaze, I love you." Ace murmured as he dragged a washcloth up my leg.

Licking my lips and my voice croaked, "I love you too. C-Can we talk tomorrow?" My thoughts were all over the place and I was too tired to think any more tonight.

"Of course, love. We will answer any and all questions. I know this was a lot for you and I'm proud of you for handling everything." Ace kissed the side of my head.

Cayden and Ryker joined us in the bathroom. Ace was kneeling next to me, Ryker sat on the toilet seat and Cayden leaned against the door. They watched as Ace bathed me. Despite feeling helpless, I allowed him to wash me.

Finally, I couldn't take the silence any longer, "Am I in trouble? I-I know I caused a scene at the mall and then lied. So, I guess I am. What will my punishment be? T-The caning isn't it, is it? I'm sorry, I just was shocked that you were murderers. Wait, that's offensive, right? I'm sorry!"

"Ember!" Cayden barked, "You're rambling."

"Sorry, sir." I blushed and looked down. Catching sight of my naked body, I looked at the wall instead.

Cayden walked closer to me and knelt next to the tub. "Sweet firestorm, we never wanted to scare you. We will talk more about everything tomorrow. Now, you can rest. Don't worry about punishments or anything. Yes, your caning was only for hiding information from us. That isn't our concern right now."

I nodded, "Yes, sir."

"You didn't offend us either. We kill those who deserve it. Little flame, we are freed by our actions. I hope you know that you will be safe with us." Ryker added.

With our conversation ending and the bath water grew cold, I was lifted from the tub and wrapped in a towel. It was warm and cozy. "Ember, do you want a shirt or to sleep naked?" Ace asked as he led me towards the bed.

"Shirt please sir." I responded. I would like to wear more.

CHAPTER FORTY-TWO: EMBER

However, being cold and tired meant that I wouldn't argue. He nodded and walked over to the wardrobe. "Thank you, sir." I murmured as he put it over my head.

"Come on babygirl, you need to sleep. You had a rough day." I shuddered and nodded in agreement.

Cayden and Ryker kissed me good night before leaving the room. I was alone with Ace, tired but unable to sleep.

He laid me on his stomach and rubbed slow circles on my back. I closed my eyes, but something wouldn't let me sleep. For the first time since they kidnapped me, I didn't feel completely safe with him. Realistically I knew I was safe. They wouldn't hurt me, but now I know the truth.

I did my best to focus my breathing and pretend to sleep. When his hand stopped moving, I realized he was asleep. I waited a few minutes before creeping out of bed and running to the door. To my surprise it was unlocked. I grabbed my lighter and slowly opened the door.

The house was dark as I walked into the living room. As much as I wanted to leave, I knew I couldn't. Instead, I change my course and head for the back door. I heard a RING camera chime and cringe. About twenty seconds later, I hear three sets of footprints. I flicked the lighter on and watched the flame for a moment. I let the heat brush my face before taking a deep breath. Turning I find three angry faces.

"You fucked up." Ace said as if I didn't already know that. "Now, you are going to come back inside. You have lost your privilege to roam free. Am I going to have to drug you or are you going to be a good girl?"

I sighed, "I'm sorry, Daddy." I hoped calling him Daddy would lessen my punishment. Judging from the look on his face I was wrong.

"Into the playroom, now!" He growled. I put my head down and scurried inside. I wanted to argue and defend myself, but his tone made me change my mind.

Ryker and Cayden joined me, Ace did not. I was tied to the bedpost of the large bed in the room. A rope was also placed over my stomach and under my breasts. Cayden is an expert at knot tying, so there is no way I am getting out on my own. The welts on my ass hurt as they rubbed against the bed. Was what I did really that bad? Did I push them too far?

Cayden gave the ropes a final tug before kissing my forehead. "Good night."

Ryker sat across the room from the bed, "Sleep, Ember."

My head shook. "I-I can't." I probably could, but my head was filled with questions and sleeping tied up wasn't very comfortable.

Ryker got up and put his face close to mine. "Why is that little flame? You always sleep well when you lay in bed with us. Is that what you need?" He taunted, "Do you need the big, bad men to lay with you? Maybe fuck you to sleep?" I shivered, hating that it turned me on. "Oh, Ember. You are dripping for me, aren't ya? But I'm not gonna fuck you. I'm not gonna touch your wet pussy. You wouldn't consent if you weren't tired and horny."

He was right, I wouldn't. "Ryker, I do trust you. I trust all of you. I wasn't going to leave, I just needed to collect my thoughts. Ryk, I'm sorry." I watched his face, there was a hint of emotion before it went blank again. "I shouldn't have left. D-do you understand why I'm scared and hurt?" This was a dangerous game. He could be angry at me for questioning him. He could tell me to lay down and shut up.

I was shocked when he replied, "Tell me why? Fill me in,

CHAPTER FORTY-TWO: EMBER

little flame."

I bit my lip. Was he being serious? "Y-You lied to me." He didn't say anything, didn't move. "You hid your job and instead of explaining it, you tied me up, hurt me and then threatened to kill me. How could I not be scared by that? I may trust you, but why wouldn't I be upset that you feel you can't trust me?"

"Little flame," his face softened, "we trust you. We just don't trust the way you handle things. What we do could send us to prison or get us killed. Take tonight to think about what we do. You don't know everything; but you know that we kill and we don't handle everything the legal way. Think about if you are comfortable with that."

Ryker moved back to the chair. He's right, am I okay with this? The answer is yes. I love them and as long as they don't kill anyone I love or myself, I could live with what they do. Who doesn't want a partner who would kill for them? I have three. I already know the answer, but this conversation wasn't going to get us anywhere now.

I looked up at the rope around my wrists. My feet had cuffs that were connected to two rings at the end of the bed. My feet were spread apart, giving easy access for the three men who kept me hostage. Am I really a hostage if I love them? I shuddered at the thought of them touching me like they used to. They were killers. They killed people. They will kill me. But why do I want their touch? I crave their love or the illusion of it. I need them. They know I need them. And they were using that to torture me.

I couldn't respond as I fought the sobs that worked their way into my throat. Lucas also tied me down when he kidnapped me. Are they going to hurt me like he did? Pulling against the ropes, and panicking when I was officially stuck, my brain went wild.

I was left on display for anyone who entered the room if they glanced over towards the bed. I wanted to tug the shirt down and cover myself, but there was no way I could move. I spent much of the night crying until I finally fell into a restless sleep.

Several hours later, someone forced me awake. "Wake up princess." A rough hand lightly shook my shoulder. I flinched back, opening my eyes. "There's those pretty blue eyes."

I whimpered. "I'm sorry!" My voice was thick, my throat was dry and all I could think of was the pain they were going to inflict. I may have fucked up by walking out, but why were they being so cold? I knew I was safe, however. Making the decision to take one step at a time, I looked up at the handsome man looking down at me.

"Drink," Cayden held a straw to my lips. I did and sighed as the cool water slid down my throat. "Why did you do that Em?" He asked, taking the straw away.

I looked away from him, "Just kill me already. Why prolong it?"

"We ain't gonna kill you. We are angry, Ryker is furious, and Ace is pissed. I'm the clear headed one, that should say something." His accent was thick and sexy Cayden cupped my cheek. "Why did you leave the house? You knew we weren't happy to begin with."

"I didn't leave to run away." I mumbled. "I just needed a minute alone to collect my thoughts. I'm overwhelmed and trying not to be scared of you."

Cayden stayed quiet. He rubbed his thumb over my jaw line, and I let out the first of many sobs. I cried tears of regret and tears of anger. I cried tears of guilt and sadness. I should have

CHAPTER FORTY-TWO: EMBER

never pushed; I should have listened when I was told to let it go. I should have just let myself live in my fantasy world. My curiosity was going to get myself and my best friend killed. I would do anything to go back in time and warn myself against prying.

"Let it out, my sweet firestorm." Cayden murmured; I needed no further encouragement. For what seemed like an eternity, the tears did not stop falling. I was at the mercy of three sadistic men, and I once again felt the same helplessness that I felt with Lucas.

I took a gasping breath, "I'm sorry, sir."

"You keep saying that beautiful girl. What are you sorry for?" He asked, forcing me to look at him.

I licked my lips, my throat once again dry. "I learned about your work and hid at the mall. I also went outside after I was already in trouble, sir."

Cayden nodded, "I'm glad you feel bad because it was wrong to hide, and it was wrong to leave the house like that. However, we aren't mad that you found out about our work. We should have come clean earlier, but we didn't want to scare you. If you need air or to alone, tell us. We don't want you to be scared of us. I'm going to untie you and then we are going to talk. We will decide your punishment for both the mall and last night together."

"Yes, sir." I mumbled. "I promise I wasn't gonna leave, I just needed air. I'm sorry."

Cayden gave me a smile. This smile was different from the ones that he gave earlier. This smile was like my old Cayden. The sweet Cayden that took care of me, that saved me from my brother. Despite being tied up by him, this was my Cayden.

He moved to the end of the bed and untied my ankles. He

rubbed them before kissing each one. Cayden did the same to my wrists before helping me sit up. I eyed the water but stayed silent. I didn't deserve it. I watched as he picked up the cup with the straw and held it to my lips.

"You're dehydrated, finish the glass and then I'll get you more upstairs." Cayden gave me a stern look.

I drank all the water. I glanced around the room for the first time in a long time. The furniture was rearranged to create an empty space in the center of the room for the cross. I really hoped they wouldn't tie me there again. That was humiliating and painful when the cane was used.

He helped me up and bent me over the bed. The shirt I wore did little to cover anything, leaving my ass open to his view. He rubbed a hand over the welts, examining them for any other injury. He patted it gently cause a light whimper to leave me.

"Let's go upstairs. We can get you fed." Giving my ass a solid slap, he grabbed my hand and moved towards the door.

43

Chapter Forty-Three: ACE

Cayden had to be the one to deal with Ember. I was angry and felt betrayed. She left me. I want to spank her ass until she can't sit without thinking of me. I want to fuck her until she can't think of anybody except me. Ryker stood next to me. He was just as upset.

"Do you want to use me?" Ryker asked quietly. He knew me so well. I did need to get some stress and anger out before talking with Ember. Deep down, I believed that she wasn't running. However, going outside didn't sit right with me. She could have been kidnapped again by Lucas or even killed.

I nodded and pointed to the stairs. He walked up and went into my room. Ryker stripped naked and bent over the bed. His ass was in the air, inviting the torture I was about inflict.

"This is going to hurt; it probably won't be pleasurable for you. I'm going to take everything I need and more." I rub my hand up his spine and squeeze the base of his neck. "Red is your safe word, use it if you need to."

That was the only warning he got before my hand connected with his ass. For the next twenty minutes I used several different implements on Ryker's ass. These ranged from my hand to my belt to a cane. I also used the heavy punishment paddle, which Ryker hated. I knew that it might have been an unconscious reason I used it.

Ryker's ass was now a deep red with the starts of bruising scattered over his cheeks. I groaned, grabbed a bottle of lube from the drawer and coated both my dick and his tight hole. I shoved my dick roughly into him.

I squirted lube onto my hand and started pumping Ryker's dick. I toyed with his piercing, making him moan and whimper. His cries echoed the room during our entire scene, but now these cries were of pleasure.

"Come for me, baby boy. You deserve it." I say through gritted teeth. He let out a loud groan that mixed with my own. I emptied into his ass as he came on my bed. "Good boy." I murmur when I catch my breath.

"Stay," I got off the bed and walked into the connected bathroom. I grabbed a towel and ran it under warm water. Ryker stayed in place and allowed me to clean him up without protest. I also reached into the drawer on my nightstand to get arnica cream for the bruising.

"I'm sorry Ryk. I went kinda hard on you." He hissed as I applied the cream. Moving to lay next to him, I frowned. He was crying, long after my torture, he was crying. That wasn't like him, after a few minutes he was typically able to calm down. I rubbed his back in slow circles, concerned about his reaction. "Are you okay baby boy?"

When Ryk didn't answer I pulled his head into my chest. We sat silently; the only noise was his sniffles as he calmed himself. I ran my fingers through his hair, after releasing it from the bun on top of his head. He took such good care of his

CHAPTER FORTY-THREE: ACE

hair. His soft brown locks fell down his shoulders as gently massaged his scalp.

"Did I push you too far, Ryk?" I felt bad, he never reacted this poorly. I also never checked in with him. Ryker didn't say his safe word, but I also didn't look out for any of his warning signs. I'm a horrible boyfriend.

"No sir." He murmured; he was clearly deep in subspace. My fingers thoroughly massaged his scalp as Ryker rested his head in my neck. We stayed like this for a while. My cute boy fell asleep quickly, but I couldn't. I thought of Ember. I love her so much it hurts. Moving Ryker's hair out of his face, my thoughts drifted to the four of us. We belonged together; we needed each other like we needed air.

Ryker's soft snores faded, and he shifted while waking up. "Ace? Are you okay?"

I nodded, "Yeah, baby boy. I'm okay."

The door creaked open and in walked Cayden with a timid Ember behind him. Cayden looked at me, a questioning look in his eye. Ember gasped when she noticed Ryker's ass, a guilty look spread across her face.

"Come sit," I say, gesturing to the bed. Ryker was still naked, but he made no motion of getting up to cover himself. We've all seen his dick more than once.

"Did you hurt him because of me?" I hated the unsure quietness of her voice. My girl should never be nervous or scared around us. I also was upset that she would think that I would harm him in any way.

"I spanked him to relive stress on both our sides. I didn't hurt him in a way that he didn't like or consent too. You know that I would never harm any of you. That includes you, Ember."

She nodded; I could practically see the wheels of her mind turning. She bit her lip before taking a deep breath. "I'm sorry for going outside. I just needed a moment to myself. It wasn't to hurt you or piss you off."

Her apology was sincere. She didn't want to hurt me or run away. I already knew this but appreciated her explanation. Licking my lips, I reach for her. "Come here baby." She hesitated before crawling away from Cayden. I sat up and settled her into my lap.

"Sir?" She asked, looking into my eyes.

I brushed hair from her face and cupped her cheek. "I accept your apology. Let's talk about what we do. I need you to understand that you are not able to leave us. You will never want for anything, and we will not bring our work home. You will always be in danger, which is part of why I was upset you left."

"Danger? F-From your enemies or you?" It was a valid question. A painfully valid question.

"Never us. We have dangerous enemies, but you will never be in danger from us." I growl. "We will do everything in our power to protect you. You have to listen to us though."

Ryker, who was still laying on his stomach chimed in. "We love you, little flame. We won't harm you." Cayden echoed Ryker's statement.

She took a shaky breath, "I feel like you guys changed. I miss the old you, the ones that don't scare me. I guess scared isn't the word, but I don't know a different one. I'm not scared, I'm hesitant? Now I'm rambling. Somebody stop me."

"Okay." Cayden's tense features softened, "Sweet firestorm, we didn't change. We owned ACR before we met you. We are the same men you fell in love with. The same men who

CHAPTER FORTY-THREE: ACE

protected you from your shit brother. We are still your men. We haven't changed!"

He's right. She just found out new information, that's all that has changed. Despite being more unhinged than normal, we haven't done anything that bad to her. The three of us are more controlling and possessive but are no more dangerous now than when Ember first met them.

"Y-You're right." She admitted nervously. "I just don't wanna be hurt again. I can't be hurt like-like-li-" Our girl started to hyperventilate. I forced her to stop talking and take a breath. Cayden rubbed her back gently.

"We will never hurt you like *he* did. Don't you ever think that!" Ryker said harshly.

She whimpered, leaning into me, "Do you still love me?"

"Yes." We all said in unison. Within a few seconds all of us were touching me. Not in a sexual way, but just with the need to be close to her. My hands were on her hair and back, each moving in a slow, comforting way.

"Baby blaze, we will love you forever. We would kill for you, we would let Ramero live for you. This is scary for us too." I whispered in her ear. She loved Ramero like the brother that she never had. I understood this, him and I were going to have a long talk. He was one of my best men and I still couldn't figure out why he said anything.

She shuddered and nodded. Cayden cleared his throat. "We haven't ever let someone in, so we are a bit nervous to do so. We do trust you, but we might be hesitant to tell you some things. Promise to be patient?"

"Yes, sir," She breathed.

I just want her to show me the affection she did before. Slowly I realized that she wanted the same thing. Her small actions said it all. She leans into our touch, lets small sighs and noises out when we touch her. Her eyes hers were reddened from crying, but they were still loving and held admiration for us. They didn't hold the fear or guilt from earlier.

"Tell us what you need to know, little flame," Ryker muttered.

She sighed, "I don't know, I'm sorry. Maybe you could tell me what you do?"

I licked his lips and nodded feeling conflicted, "Are you sure you want to know this?"

Ember gave a tight smile, "I do, sir. I think it is important to know every aspect of you."

I looked at the other two who gave curt nods, "Okay then."

44

Chapter Forty-Four: EMBER

Ace took a breath before explaining their company. He talked me though their roles and what the company actually does. ACR is a manufacturing company that manufactures weapons and tactical gear. He explained that most of their things were sold to local gun and weapon stores in the area which was Ryker's job. The reason they kept this hidden and stayed secretive was because many of these sales were illegal.

The three also explained that they took certain jobs which entail killing people. Together they took down several local gangs and go after men who have wronged them or their allies. Similar what most people call a mafia, they believe they are more of a business and vigilante group than anything else.

"Yes, we have killed people." Cayden sighed, "But they deserved it! We would never kill an innocent."

I swallowed, "But you would kill Ramero. He's an innocent!" I pointed out.

Ryker shook his head, "No he ain't! He is one of our lead sales and hitmen. Ramero has made over three hundred illegal sales in the past five years and killed over fifty men."

Why wouldn't my friend tell me? They would kill him, I realized. I love my friend; I couldn't picture him being a killer. He's a teddy bear! Maybe it wasn't so far-fetched though. The hours that Ramero worked were always odd; especially for a manufacturing plant that he told me he worked for.

"Can I talk to Ramero now that I know? Would he be allowed to tell me anything?" I ask, wanting to confront my best friend.

"Sure. We are going to have a chat with him first. You aren't allowed to leave the house without us and lost access to all electronics for a week. This is one of your punishments for going outside last night, but we'll talk about that later." Ace replied, giving me a hint of my punishment.

All electronics? "Does that mean we can't have movie night this week?" I was concerned. That was our time, all of us cuddled on the couch. My favorite time of the week. We sometimes watched movies every night, but once a week we have popcorn and soda and just everything feels right.

Cayden shook his head, "You can watch TV with us, but not alone. Movie night is special, and we won't take that away. In fact, maybe we'll move it too tonight."

I nodded excitedly. "Thank you! I love you guys!" My excitement was interrupted by another thought. "Why couldn't Ramero tell me earlier? I'm not saying before, but once I started dating you all, why the secret?"

"We are so strict with our employees because our business may fall apart if the feds get wind of us. The city and state police are ours, but when you reach a federal level, we get screwed. We're working on securing our protecting, but nothing is set in stone yet. We told Ramero to stay quiet, you didn't need to know that side of us. We also didn't want

CHAPTER FORTY-FOUR: EMBER

you to know anything in case Lucas got a hold of you like he did." Cayden explained.

"Oh, why would Lucas care?" Then it dawned on me. "That night in the parking lot. You weren't beating him up for five dollars, were you?" I looked down sadly.

"No, he stole weapons from us and gave them to his friends. We didn't kill him because you loved him. A few weeks later we set up cameras in your motel room and saw what he was like. What did he tell you?" Cayden tilted his head curiously.

I sniffled; I thought Lucas was getting beaten up because he loved me. "He said that he stole five dollars for our rent. You wanted it back, but he couldn't pay. I never thought about the fact that rent was more than five dollars or that rent wasn't even due at that point. Lucas never liked me questioning him anyway. He told me he spent his rent money on me because I ate too much. I wasn't allowed to eat for a few days after." Wait, did they say cameras?

Before I could say anything, Ryker growled, "You need food to survive. Fuck him. You will never have to worry about not getting enough food. You eat three meals; you eat when you're hungry."

"Speaking of, we have to get you food." Cayden said as my stomach growled.

I nodded, "I guess I'm a little hungry. And I get why you didn't tell me, but you couldn't have made up something?"

"We don't like liars!" The three said at the same time.

"Okay. Did you say cameras? You spied on me? For how long? Why?" My voice got more frantic.

Ace laughed, "We put cameras in your room a few months after your 19th birthday. We wanted to make sure you were safe."

I bit my lip and got off of Ace's lap. "This is a lot."

Cayden walked over to me and put a finger in my mouth forcing me to stop biting my lip. "Suck." I lowered my eyes and did as I was told. "No more biting your lip. Every time you do, you will suck something. Next time it might not be my finger, so think carefully."

My cheeks heated and I mumbled "yes, sir" around his finger.

I was instructed to keep sucking while he spoke, "I know this is a lot, but we won't hurt you or kill in front of you." His eyes bored into mine, "Unless you want us to. It might be fun to fuck covered in someone else's blood."

I shuddered and closed my eyes. My pussy clenched at the thought. I bit down lightly on his finger, momentarily forgetting it wasn't my tongue. "Did you just bite me?" My eyes shot open. Cayden's hand went to my ass. I tensed, waiting for him to smack me. It was still sore, and I didn't know if I could handle another spanking. He rubbed it gently. "You like the idea of being bloody, don't you? Sweet firestorm, we won't do anything without your consent, no matter how horny you are."

I blushed and tried to look away. He took his finger out of my mouth and put it in his. He moaned, "Your spit tastes delicious."

"Cayden," I whined. Walking backwards towards the bed. I walked into Ace's waiting arms and jumped. "Wh-What are you gonna do?"

"Nothing you don't want, little flame. Say the word and I will stop everything." Ryker's hands roamed to waist and rubbed my hip gently.

I swallowed a moan, "Stop." His hands left me, and Ace let

CHAPTER FORTY-FOUR: EMBER

me go. "I-I'm hungry and I want to get my punishment over with."

Cayden nodded, him and Ryker left to go get lunch started. Ace was the only one who was left. "Ember, can I ask you a question?" I nodded and he took a step towards me. I forced myself not to flinch, this is Ace, my Ace. He got shot protecting me, he wouldn't do that for just anyone. I am safe with him.

"Baby blaze, you look scared. I won't hurt you. Why did you leave me? Would you have left Cayd or Ryk if they were the ones with you? I didn't scare you away, right?" His voice cracked and I couldn't resist hugging him.

"I would have gone outside regardless. I needed a minute, just my lighter and I. Last night was such a long night that I couldn't get my head together. I wasn't going to run away, I just needed to be alone. You were being so cold to me, and it didn't seem like you cared if I left or not. I'm sorry I scared you and made angry Daddy. That wasn't my intent." I was proud of myself for articulating what I felt in such a mature way.

The smile that Ace gave told me he was proud too. "Beautiful girl, I'm sorry I scared you or made you feel like I didn't care." He apologized? His apologies were rare, so this meant the world. "I was so scared that you hated us and would leave that I didn't want to leave you alone."

"You wouldn't kill me, right? You won't kill or hurt Ramero or Presley or Harper, right? You definitely won't kill Alyssa. Her ass will come back and haunt you." I smiled and put my lips to Ace's ear before whispering, "Alyssa scares the shit out of me."

Ace laughed, I never realized how much I missed it. "Alyssa would haunt me, wouldn't she? Ember, baby blaze, we don't hurt innocents and I know Ramero knows better than to get you involved. The only way I would kill him is if he were to talk to an outsider other than you. But we have a lot of trust in him, so I doubt that would ever happen."

I nodded before leaning my head on his chest. "How bad is my punishment gonna be?"

"You won't leave us?" I shook my head. "You won't tell anyone that we own ACR?" I shook my head again. "Then the no electronics is enough, we put you through a lot. Forgive me for being a dick?"

I giggled, "You are forgiven. Are we cool now? I might flinch or have my moments, but I promise I am not scared of you."

The rest of the afternoon and evening seemed to fly. We had a wonderful movie night watching stupid comedies and eating our weights in junk food. Before long it was bedtime and I was exhausted.

My men all went into the basement to say good night to me. I expressed earlier that I needed to be alone for a while. Ace conformed, "You still want to sleep alone?"

"I'm sorry, can I take some time to collect my thoughts?"

Ace looked a little hurt, but quickly schooled his expression. Giving me a sweet kiss, he smiled, "Good night, baby blaze."

"Good night, Daddy."

The familiar flash of red light blinked on the camera a few minutes later and I sighed. I dragged myself to the bathroom and decided to take a quick shower. The hot water calmed me a little, but I kept replaying the conversation in my head. They admitted to everything, I should be terrified of them. I'm not scared of them. I turned the handle until the water was hot enough to leave my skin red. The pain was a comfort.

CHAPTER FORTY-FOUR: EMBER

Before long the pain became almost unbearable causing me to get out. I wrapped a towel around myself and walked into the bedroom area. I found a shirt and a pair of sweatpants on the bed with a note. The note said: Comfy clothes for you. We love you so much! Love Ace, Ryk and Cayd.

I smiled at the note and looked at the cameras. The lights were still red and blinking. I said, "thank you," to the camera above the bed and put the clothes on. I hung up the towel and crawled into bed.

I tossed and turned for what felt like hours, before sitting up. I needed my men. I wanted to be held and protected by them. Chewing my lip, I got up and walked to the door. Turning the knob, I found it was unlocked. The stairs were dark and the door at the top was closed. Hesitantly, I walked up the stairs to the door.

The basement door opened with a quiet creak, before falling silent. I looked around the empty living room, before making my way to the stairs. These men had a hold on me, I wasn't going anywhere.

Tip toeing up the stairs, I winced when one of the stairs creaked. Who would be the best to go to? Ace would probably be too overbearing at the moment and Ryker might be with him after their scene today. I was glad my ass wasn't getting spanked like his. After a second at the top of the stairs, I decided I would go to Cayden's room.

I held my breath as my hand lightly knocked on the door. I heard a faint come in and squinted as the light from his room blinded me. "Cayden?" I dared say as he sat at his desk, back to me.

He jumped and turned to me, "Ember?" I fought back a cringe when he said my name. "What's up?"

"N-Nothing. Never mind." I turned to walk away, losing the confidence I had early.

He got up as I turned my back. I tensed when he crossed the room in only a few steps. "Sweet firestorm, what are you doing out of bed?"

I sighed, "Um, I-I couldn't sleep."

"Come on," he motioned me to go to the bed. I gave him a curious look. "You came up here because you didn't want to be alone. So, you can sleep with me."

"I'm sorry. I promised not to leave the room and I broke that promise." I waited for him to be mad, to punish me.

He smiled, "You came up here, you didn't run away. No harm done, now come here. You are allowed to come to us whenever you want. If we said not to leave your room but you need us, you come to us. Unless it is for your safety, like if someone breaks in or something. Understand?"

In almost a zombie-like walk, I walked over to his bed and perched myself on the edge. "Yes, sir."

He walked over to his desk, closed his laptop, and turned off the desk lamp. Cayden then moved to the bed, stripped off his shirt and pants, leaving him in his boxers. He slid under the covers and patted the bed, "Lay down. If you want me to hold you, I will. If not, then I will stay on this side of the bed."

I nodded and got under the blankets. I moved close to him, wanting to be held and cuddled. Cayden reached behind him and turned off the light before wrapping an arm around my waist. I sighed contentedly and settled in for the night.

Chapter Forty-Five: CAYDEN

Ember came into my bed late last night. I watched her sleep for a long time before drifting into a restless sleep myself. Waking up to find her watching me was another surprise.

It was even more surprising when she said, "You look like an angel when you sleep. Peaceful and unburdened."

My shock must have been evident when she giggled. I could listen to that sound every minute for the rest of my life. I never realized what she truly meant to me before she accepted our true selves. Even when Lucas kidnapped her, I knew we were going to find her. Here, she could have left. In this situation she could have hated us and then we would have been forced to keep or kill her.

Neither would have been an option. We would have gone to jail for her. We would have turned ourselves in just to protect her. Luckily that wasn't the case and she is right where she belongs.

Today Ace and I are going to visit Ramero. We need to see what his motives were and if we should keep him around. Ember loves him, which means we would probably have to lock him up and only release him to see her. He's young, but not dumb, so why would he say anything?

I swallow back a retort and smiled, "I love that sound. I hope to hear it more often." She shifted, her face red from my words. Ember rolled over to get up and I let her, "Bend over the bed."

"What?" She asked, wondering what I'm thinking.

A grin spreads across my lips, "Bend over and let me check your caning marks. If you're good I'll give you a fun spanking, if you are naughty," I trail off. A chuckle escapes my lips as she bends over the bed quickly. "Princess, this is your last chance to get into the correct position. What should you be wearing when I look at your ass?"

Her cheeks are a deep red as she locks eyes with me. "I'm sorry sir." She mumbles pulling down her pants and panties. Now naked from the waist down she bent back over the bed.

"Good girl." I rubbed her ass slowly admiring the fading lines. "These are fading nicely. However, I think you would do good with a red ass." She made a small noise. I smirked and gave her a sharp smack above one of the less faded lines. My handprint was left on her perfect ass.

Smack!

She jumped at this second spank. "Relax, sweet firestorm. Let yourself enjoy this! You take your spanking like a good girl; I'll fuck you until you can't remember your name."

My hand repeatedly spanked her over and over in slow, methodical movements. Her moans echoed in through the room, her body moving to meet my hand. I noticed Ace and Ryker standing by the door. They watched as her ass went from pink to a delicious shade of red.

I gestured to Ryker and passed him a condom. Ember was

CHAPTER FORTY-FIVE: CAYDEN

still bent over and had no idea that anybody else was here. I cupped her pussy and slipped a finger between her lips. She was soaked.

I moved my hand away as Ryker pushed into her. She gasped, "R-Ryker?"

His piercing was a giveaway. He started fucking her hard and fast, not giving her time to breath. Ace came into her line of sight and took out his dick. I did the same and before long Ace and I came on her face. What a beautiful sight to watch her come with our seed on her face.

"Beautiful, baby." Ace said, as he carried her to the bathroom.

I left them and went downstairs with Ryker to start breakfast. "Take care of her, we shouldn't be long. She might need extra love today."

Ryker nodded, "Why? I thought we were good. I don't mind giving cuddles, but aren't we all over it?"

I looked at him, "Ryk, she was just traumatized by what we do for a living. We might be okay, but she had a scene this morning after a rough few nights. You know how you get overwhelmed when you have a few bad days in a row?" He nodded. "That's what she's feeling right now. So, give her love, yeah?"

"Oh. Yeah, I can do that." He responded. Ryker sometimes needs things explained to him and typically Ace handles that. I wasn't always patient, but after a good session with Ember, I was relaxed.

I turned back to the eggs and toast I was making, "Make sure she eats all of this. She needs the calories." She loved cheese on her eggs, so I added a few handfuls of shredded cheddar to entice her to eat more. I slathered the toast in butter and strawberry jam before plating it.

Ace and Ember came down the stairs. He put a pillow on the hard chair and told her to sit. I served her breakfast and gave her a kiss. "Sweet firestorm, Ace and I have to go out for a little while. Be good for Ryker and eat all of your food."

She looked down, "You are going to see Ramero, aren't you? Please don't hurt him!"

It broke my heart to think she didn't trust us to keep our word. I was also proud of how observant she was and her ability to read the room. "Yes, and we promised we won't, so we won't. Be good." I kissed her cheek and walked to the car.

"You couldn't wait for me?" Ace asked, settling himself into the passenger's seat.

"I need answers, you were taking too long." I respond, to my surprise he let the disrespect go. I was going to pay for it later, but my behavior wasn't his top priority.

We pulled up to Ramero's apartment without bothering with a warning. Ace and I approached the door and forced our way inside. A startled yelp had Ramero scrambling to grab his gun. His hand wrapped around the gun just as I reached him.

"What the fuck Ramero?" I demanded, shoving him into the wall, my arm over his neck. He dropped the gun, knowing better than to try to threaten Ace or myself. His hands wrapped around my arms, trying to take pressure off of his throat. "You betrayed our trust. You have two seconds to start talking!"

He attempted to choke out words when Ace barked out a laugh, "He can't speak with your arm across his throat."

I eased up slightly. Ramero coughed, "I-I don't know what you're talking about!"

CHAPTER FORTY-FIVE: CAYDEN

His words seemed so sincere. I paused; he maintained eye contact as I debated the truth of his statement. The two of us always had the better relationship. If he was telling the truth, he would probably also feel betrayed. I relaxed my grip and shoved him onto his couch. Ace stepped next to me; he was also conflicted.

"Ramero, you sent a text to Ember telling her that we work for ACR. You told her who we are." Ace said, keeping his voice even.

He shook his head, "I haven't heard from Ember in a few days. I can show you my messages, you can stick Austin on me. I swear I would never break your trust like that. Besides I've been watching Trevor's bar for the past two days. My personal phone wasn't on me."

"Give me your phone." He handed his phone to Ace who looked at it. "Password?"

"052306, my sister's birthday." Ramero was clearly uncomfortable. It was odd seeing him so unsure and nervous, he was typically the definition of calm and collected.

Ace tilted the phone to show me that the last message from Ember was two days before we went to the mall. He could have deleted it, but somehow, I doubted it.

I took my phone from my pocket and called Austin, "Go to my house and get Ember's phone. Look at the messages from Ramero, trace the last one sent." I hung up without any other detail. Ace messaged Ryker and let him know. Ember was banned from electronics anyway, so that didn't matter. I'm sure he would tell her anyway.

Ember wasn't stupid. The minute she saw Austin, she would question everything. She would probably interrogate us about Alyssa too. Now, she will want to know who else is involved with ACR Empires.

"Ember loves you, man. She begged us not to hurt you. Sacrificed her life for yours. That is the only reason you don't have a black eye and broken face." I mumble falling next to him on the couch.

His apartment was small, with the couch against the wall that lined the kitchen. The kitchen was small, the fridge door would hit the shelf across from it when it opened. There was a small bedroom that sat next to the bathroom. There was barely enough room for the shower, toilet, and sink. We pay him well, why was he in such a small place? He looked almost comically giant compared to his surroundings.

Along the wall was pictures of him and his sister, him and Ember, and him and the RHW roster. There was nothing else to show any sort of personalization. He had a TV facing the couch and a bookshelf filled with books. He must have been reading when we came in, there was a book on the floor next to the couch.

"We are going to hang out until we hear back from Austin." Ace started walking around the apartment, entering his room, and looking though closets. This was more of a scare tactic than anything else. He did not protest, although I'm sure he wanted to. Ace didn't care what was in his apartment.

"Why are you living here?" I asked, turning my body to face him. "We pay you well, why are you in a shitty apartment?"

He shrugged, "Why does it matter? I do good work for you, right?"

I nodded, any other person I would drop the topic. Ramero is Ember's friend, it would be wrong to not look out for the kid. He was only 22 and dragged into this shit life. "You aren't doing drugs, are you kid?"

CHAPTER FORTY-FIVE: CAYDEN

"Hell no!" Ramero sounded offended that I would even ask that.

We were interrupted by Ace's phone ringing. Followed by Ace's roar, "WHAT THE FUCK DO YOU MEAN?"

Chapter Forty-Six: EMBER

I shivered as the cold hit me, where am I? I looked around the room and saw the concrete walls. I sat up and jumped when the chain rattled. The cold chain was cuffed to my ankle and connected to a hoop in the wall.

"Ember?" A familiar voice asked. I turned to see a familiar mess of brownish hair.

"Alyssa?" I tried to move to her, but the cuff around my ankle didn't let me. "Are you okay? Are you hurt?"

She shook her head, "N-no, I think I'm okay." She also had a cuff around her left ankle. Alyssa, ever the motherly figure gave me a small smile. Her words, true or not calmed me, "Everything's going to be okay, honey."

We had to be in a basement. There were no windows and only one door at the top of an old wooden staircase. Alyssa and I were spaced far enough apart that we couldn't touch.

"Do you recognize where we are?" She asked, in a somehow calm voice.

I shrugged, before it hit me. I knew where we were. We are in a basement. Lucas's basement or whoever's basement that

CHAPTER FORTY-SIX: EMBER

was previously held in. Memories of this afternoon hit me.
Ryker and I were sitting on the couch watching a movie. The doorbell rang and it was Austin and Alyssa. Ryker told me that Austin was going to look at my phone. He said that Austin was a tech geek and wanted to make sure my phone wasn't bugged.
I knew him. Austin was some wrestler from bumfuck nowhere. A bunch of us called him country boy, as he was from the south. He was attractive, with his shaggy brown hair and big muscles, however my men are hotter.
Alyssa and I sat in the living room. The other two were in the kitchen doing whatever work they needed to. She told me about how Austin and she were dating. Alyssa asked me about my submission to my men and if I enjoyed it. After that question there was a loud crash at the door and five men rushed into the room.
Ryker and Austin came flying out of the kitchen, guns drawn. The two of them were no match for the five men who already had the upper hand. I grabbed Alyssa's hand and made a run for the basement. My room had a lock and maybe I could find my tablet still on the table if they haven't taken it yet.
Alyssa screamed as she was grabbed from behind. I could do nothing as another person gripped my arm and dragged me into him. The last thing I heard was Lucas tell me to be a good girl as a needle pierced my neck.

It was Lucas who did who knows what to Ryker and Austin. It was Lucas who kidnapped us. I choked back tears as I stared at Alyssa chained to the wall.

"I'm so sorry!" I cried out. "If it wasn't for me and my idiotic thinking you wouldn't be in this situation!"

She looked horrified before her face changed to anger, "You will not speak like that. This is not your fault; it is your brother's fault. Your men really need to spank you more if this is how you think."

I flinched; Alyssa was being harsh. She terrified me before, but this was her first time being so harsh. I would give anything to be over any one of my men's knees right now. Anything was better than being here.

"Maybe they do," I respond.

The next few hours consisted of us playing games to pass the time. Sometime after we woke up a bottle of water and two apples were thrown down the steps. The apples landed by Alyssa and the water rolled just within reach of me. I took a sip and then rolled it to Alyssa. She rolled me an apple as a trade.

The apple was red and covered in dirt and dust, but I was hungry. Wiping it off on my equally as dirty shirt, I took a bite. It was juicy and if I ignore the dirt seasoning, it wasn't half bad.

Soon enough we both had to pee. There was nothing in the room except for an empty bucket that was just within reach. I looked at Alyssa and then to the bucket.

"I'll keep watch at the door. I won't look, I promise." She reassured, knowing that I was going to burst at any second. Finishing my business, I awkwardly passed the bucket to her. Nobody came down the stairs.

We decided that we would take shifts keeping watch. With no way to tell time, we agreed to estimate a few hours. If the other was really tired and couldn't stay awake, then we would wake the other up. She took first watch, and I was grateful.

Struggling to find a comfortable place on the hard concrete floor, I let my mind drift. Ryker isn't dead. That's what Lucas wanted me to think, so I know it can't be true now. My men will find us soon, they have to.

47

Chapter Forty-Seven: RYKER

Ember was gone... again. I would have been dead if it wasn't for the three-armed people that we keep down the street. Lucas had gotten to Ember and Trevor got Alyssa before I could get to them. Ace and Cayden were furious. Austin was scared and angry. Him and Alyssa had just officially given their relationship a name.

Ramero was out searching the usual hideouts of Lucas and Trevor. It has been almost twenty hours since they were kidnapped. He thinks he pinpointed where they were. Ramero saw Trevor's truck outside the Greasy Chick.

Lucas kept Ember there last time, was he really dumb enough to do that again? Ace stopped Cayden from jumping into his truck. In typical Cayden fashion, he blew up.

"Why the hell aren't we going to that fucking bar?" His demands only made Ace more upset.

Ace took a deep breath, exhaling sharply through his nose. "Cayden, relax. Lucas would be stupid to keep the girls at the bar. Or he could be smart to do so. If this is a trap to lure us in and kill us or kill the girls in front of us, we would be walking right into it."

Ace was right, of course Ace was right. "So, what do we do?" I asked, my mind still trying to wrap around her kidnapping. It was my fault.

"We put together a team, get Gianna, Ramero, and Micky to lead teams into the bar. The three of us will follow and go to the basement. According to Austin that is the only place in the bar that they could be keeping them."

"I want to go to." Austin joined us in the living room.

We all immediately shook our heads. Austin was the clumsiest member of our company. He fell over the coffee table during the fight earlier, nobody was even near him.

"Austin, you don't go into the field for a reason. We need you here more than out there." Ace tried to reason.

"No, my girl got kidnapped too. How would you feel if I told you to sit back? I failed Alyssa, I need to rescue her." Austin took a chance and confronted us.

Cayden glared at him, "Yeah, but we don't trip over ourselves as we walk."

I snorted as Austin rolled his eyes, "It was one time. Let me save my woman. Please."

He sounded desperate and weak in that moment. Ace sees Austin as his little brother. He was two years behind us in school, a tech genus even then. He's family.

Finally Ace nodded, "Let's go, stop wasting time. Cayd, get Ramero and the others ready. Go with Austin in his truck. Ryk, you're with me." He then turned on his heel and walked out the door.

I looked at both men and followed Ace outside. He was already in his truck and impatient. His eyes watched as I moved to the passenger side and opened the door.

CHAPTER FORTY-SEVEN: RYKER

"It's not your fault." He said as I buckled my seatbelt. He threw the truck into reverse and sped out of the driveway. "You did the best you could to protect Ember."

I licked my lips and stayed silent. Whatever I say doesn't matter. Whatever he says doesn't matter. Ember being gone is my fault. If she dies, then so do I. My thoughts started to spiral as I forced back the tears that threatened to spill.

"Baby boy, we are going to save Ember. If you still feel like it is your fault, we can deal with it later. Okay? I need your head clear. We don't have time for a release right now. I'm sorry." I nodded along with his words.

"Can you not be right for once?" I asked with a laugh.

Ace smiled, keeping his eyes on the road. We drove for another hour before we came across Trevor's bar. The parking lot across the street was abandoned. This would be our rendezvous point before and after the attack. Ramero, Gianna, and Micky were already waiting with teams of four. Cayden and Austin pulled up behind us.

We sent Ramero through the back door, Gianna through the front and Micky through the side door. Ace, Cayden, Austin, and I followed Ramero's team, but hung behind as they went in. The alleyway was dirty and covered in alcohol bottles, cigarette butts, and used condoms.

"You gonna join us or hide?" Ramero's voice crackled in our earpieces.

One look to Ace and Cayden and off we went. The back door was kicked open and the sounds of fighting, bones breaking, and skin being torn filled the air. The echo of gunshots was deafening as we made our way to the basement door.

A man jumped in front of Austin, but Cayden was able to

knock him down with one punch. I turned in time to find two of Trevor's guys approaching. I bare my teeth, loosen my knife, and rush forward.

   This is going to be fun.

48

Chapter Forty-Eight: EMBER

It was my watch. Nobody bothered us for hours. I heard movement and voices near the door and threw an apple core at Alyssa. She awoke with a jump and turned to me.

"What?" She questioned to which I put a finger to my lips. I motioned for her to listen for the voices by pointing to the door.

Alyssa nodded as a loud slam echoed in the quiet room. We turned to the stairs, fearing who was coming down. It could be anyone, but we knew it had to be Lucas. Who else would it be?

"Hi girls!" Lucas practically sang as he entered the room. I pulled at the chain that was connected to a metal fixing on the wall. "Stop that Ber! You're already in trouble." He turned away from me. I watched as the unkempt blond moved closer to Alyssa. "Hi Lissy!"

"Don't call me that!" She spat, standing her ground. I watched in horror as he shoved her to the floor. Alyssa fell with a grunt. She clutched her elbow, fighting the pain that had to be there.

"Lucas!" I shouted, desperately trying to run over to my friend. "What the fuck is wrong with you?"

He turned and grabbed me by the neck. "Who the fuck do you think you are?" He demanded, shoving me back against the wall. "I saved your life! I kept you safe, fed, and clothed. This is how you repay me? This is how you fucking repay me?"

I closed my eyes and tried to ignore him. I thought of my men, of being with them in their bed. Cayden and Ryker this morning, spanking and fucking me. "Look at me!" My twin demanded, crushing my windpipe. I whimpered and opened my eyes.

"Leave her alone, Lucas!" Alyssa said, getting back up to her feet. She was cradling her arm; she broke her elbow too many times before.

He laughed loudly, "I'm glad you have such a strong friend. She's gonna be fun to break!"

I couldn't speak, only stare wide eyed at him. He dropped me and I fell to the floor coughing. He turned away from me and stalked over to Alyssa. She seemed unafraid, however her eyes said otherwise. He gave her a wide smile and punched her in the ribs.

"It really is a shame, such a beautiful face on such an ugly body." Lucas said, squeezing her cheeks. Alyssa spat at him. He flinched and smacked her hard across the face. "You stupid bitch. I'll have you begging for mercy."

I choked out a scream and he walked over to me. His boot landed hard in my ribs before turning away from us. Lucas stormed out of the basement, cursing us.

We waited until he left before speaking. I looked at her, her hand on her throbbing cheek. "I'm sorry! I never thought

CHAPTER FORTY-EIGHT: EMBER

you'd get roped into this!" I apologized, wiping the tears that were falling from my eyes.

Alyssa shook her head, "Em, this isn't your fault. Look at me, hun!" She moved as close as the chain would allow. I couldn't look at her, I felt so much shame and guilt. "Ember, I don't blame you. We need to get out of here though."

I nodded, sniffling a little. She was right, we needed to get out of here. I bit my lip and looked at her, not meeting her eyes. "How?"

Alyssa looked around the basement. There were no windows, and the only door was at the top of the stairs. She looked at the chain before kneeling down and looking at the lock. "We can get ourselves unchained, but I'm not sure about getting out. Presley taught us to pick a lock, remember?"

I nod, "I can also distract Lucas when we get upstairs, as long as he's the only person, we should be fine."

We formulated a shitty plan, but it was the best one we could come up with. I watched Alyssa focus on undoing the chain on her ankle. She took a bobby pin from her hair and bent it. She worked on picking the lock as I watched the stairs.

"Alyssa!" I whisper shouted when the door opened. I heard the stairs creak, and my friend stopped her efforts immediately. She hid the pin and stood up.

"Are you girls gonna behave now?" Lucas asked, as he walked down the stairs. I backed into the wall, looking at the ground. Another man walked down the stairs behind him. I didn't recognize the man. He was the same size as Lucas, with dark brown hair that was slicked back.

"Ber! You can't get away that easily. Come to big brother!" I shook my head. He rolled his eyes. "So skittish, come give your twin a hug!"

"She doesn't listen very well. Might want to teach her to obey." The man's voice rumbled.

He stormed over to me when I made no effort to move. His hand collided with my face causing me to shriek. "When I tell you to do something, you do it! Now give your brother a hug!"

I hesitantly wrapped my arms around him. He chuckled and shoved me away, "You don't deserve love!"

Alyssa's chain rattled, "She does, and she found it!"

"Shut up her up, Trevor!" Lucas demanded.

Trevor walked over to her. I watched in horror as he grabbed her hair. "Maybe this will help teach you to be a proper girl!" The larger man forced the woman to her knees. He grabbed a length of rope from a bench by Alyssa's chain and tied her hands back.

My friend struggled and pulled against the ropes. The guy, Trevor, smacked her hard and grabbed her chin. "Open!" He demanded as I heard his zipper being pulled down. She shook her head. He kicked her stomach and she gasped for breath. At this moment, Trevor shoved his dick in her mouth.

Alyssa reacted quickly and bit down. Trevor's screams echoed through the basement. He jerked away, however that made things worse. I watched as the man grabbed his crotch and Alyssa spit out part of his now detached dick.

Trevor fell to the ground, cursing her and her teeth. Alyssa stood up and walked over to the bench. She could barely reach the corner but managed to use the sharp edge to cut herself free. While Lucas stood shocked.

Finally, Lucas rushed over as Alyssa finished uncuffing herself. She ran around him and grabbed a large piece of wood. Bashing it over his head, she passed me the bobby pin.

CHAPTER FORTY-EIGHT: EMBER

I went to work uncuffing myself.

"Are you okay, honey?" She asked as if she didn't just bite someone's dick off and knock the shit out of my twin.

I nodded, suddenly fearing her. I picked my lock quickly as we heard the door being thrown open. We stood and prepared ourselves for the other goons that helped kidnap us to appear. Instead, we were met by Ace and Alyssa's boytoy Austin.

Our men looked between us and the two men on the ground. I ran into Ace's arm, sighing as his strong arms locked around me. I heard Austin walk over to Alyssa who was calmly walking to meet him in the middle. I wondered how she wasn't crying or upset. I wish I could be as strong as her.

"Who bit Trevor's dick off?" Cayden asked, walking down the stairs.

I laughed and pointed at Alyssa as I wrapped my arms around him. I watched from Cayden's arms as Austin's eyes widened. "Don't fuck with Alyssa. She'll bite your dick off country boy." Ryker said, walking over to me. He took me from Cayden as we all laughed.

Ace and Cayden grabbed Lucas and Trevor and tied him up. Trevor was still crying over his missing body part. Lucas was still out of it. I somehow knew that this would be the last time Lucas messed with me. Country boy held Alyssa close as we walked out of the basement and to the car. I rolled my eyes at his pickup truck. How was this asshole so stereotypical? They were cute together though.

Alyssa gave me a huge hug and whispered, "You were so brave. I love you. Stay safe." She still held her arm, hopefully Austin could convince her to get it looked at.

I nodded, fearing that speaking would make me cry. She understood and patted my back. I watched as her guy helped her into the truck. Ace called out, "Have Jacob look at her arm! She can't afford to have another broken elbow!"

Ace led me into the truck. I snuggled into his side as we drove home. Cayden drove, Ryker sat on my other side holding my leg. It wasn't until we entered the house that I broke. My men could do nothing but hold me and console me until darkness finally consumed my tired body.

49

Chapter Forty-Nine: ACE

She wants to what? Ember looked at the three of us through teary eyes. I look to Cayden and Ryker, both stared at her with shock. We sat on the couch, holding her as she cried after Lucas kidnapped her. The silence in the room had her looking between all of us. Ember's face was red and splotchy from the tears and emotions she was going through.

"Say something, please!" She encouraged, her voice shook with anticipation.

"You want to," I paused and wrinkle my nose, "kill him?"

She nodded. "You said that he's alive. I want to kill Lucas. I want him to suffer at my hands."

Cayden was shaking his head, "You are innocent, sweet firestorm."

She shook her head, "This is MY way of handling MY trauma. Please! You will be there the whole time!"

"No!" Ryker bellowed. Ember flinched and Ryker winced. "Little flame, once you kill someone, you can't get rid of that mark. You can't undo a murder."

She looked down for a moment, then stood. She looked at all

of us, almost like she is giving a presentation or a speech. She took a deep breath and said, "Killing Lucas will mark my soul. I can almost guarantee that you have several black marks on yours. Right? So what? When I die I go to whatever paradise there is? You go to Hell or whatever? We are separated for eternity because you wanted to protect my innocence. I would rather go to Hell and stay with you, than be in paradise without you guys. Lucas hurt me. He cut, kicked, burned, punched, and tortured me. Let me do this."

I licked my lips, "Come here." She obeyed without question. "I love you. If we let you do this, how would you kill your twin brother?"

She gave us a sinister smile, one that I have only ever seen Cayden or Serpent give. Maybe she really was a sick fuck like the rest of us. I knew there was a reason we were drawn to her, but what is her plan?

50

Chapter Fifty: EMBER

I can't believe I convinced them. The four of us stood outside the room where Lucas was being held. There was a really large guy with us, his eyes were tattooed black. He was very intimidating. He told me his name was Serpent. The man gave me a smile, he had fangs accompanying his teeth. I shivered. I don't judge based on appearance, but I was questioning that decision now.

"You must be the girl that these three are batshit crazy for? Beautiful curves, round ass, blonde hair, why wouldn't they?" He commented, earning a growl from all three men. "Calm down. Ember, control your wild dogs. I'm not interested in you or anybody for that matter. I'm just here to collect his remains."

"I don't know what will be left for you," Cayden retorted.

"You eat human too? We can share recipes! Have you ever had barbequed human thighs?" Serpent said with plenty of enthusiasm.

I felt my eyes widen and quickly looked at my men. They were equally amused and horrified, as I tried to make sense of what he said. "I-I don't eat... what?"

He laughed, "Guess I was wrong. It would be weird to eat your own twin, I guess. Unless you're in the womb, then it's apparently acceptable."

"That's not ho-" I paused, "never mind. You eat people?"

"Don't worry, I won't eat you, little girl. You men should do that enough." Serpent said, causing a deep blush to form.

"Serpent! Stop messing with her!" Cayden demanded, clearly hiding his laughter. The chill atmosphere had me feeling relaxed and safe amongst this group.

Ramero opened the door leading to the room that Lucas was in. I looked at him in shock, he was covered in blood. "Ramero?" I asked shocked, even though I knew that he worked for my men. I guess I never thought he would be torturing people. He wasn't allowed to see me when I was rescued, which meant I couldn't confront him. This wasn't the time or place.

"Hi Ember," Ramero sheepishly responded. "I think he's ready for you. It's not pretty, pumpkin. Please be prepared."

I nodded and looked to Ace. Ryker opened the door and we all filed in. Ramero and Serpent entered the room with my men and me. I wasn't as scared having all of this back up. My lighter felt heavy in my pocket. So, I took it out and flicked it open. Ramero retrieved my old lighter yesterday and gave it to Cayden.

"Ember!" Lucas cried as I continued playing with my lighter. When I refused to look up Lucas continued, "Help me! Please, Ber! My beautiful, wonderful sister!"

I laughed, a maniacal, violent, lunatic laugh. It lacked humor and made me look insane. I snapped my head up to look at my brother. Swallowing my shock, I observed Lucas. He was

CHAPTER FIFTY: EMBER

beaten within an inch of his life. His face was broken almost past recognition. Lucas had his arm bound behind him and his legs tied to the legs of the chair with scratchy rope. He gave me a pleading look with his left eye, the only one that would open.

"Ember?" He asked, slowly realizing I am not his savior. "You bitch! You would let your twin die? I did everything for you, and you repay me by being a fucking whore?"

My three men started to raise their voices and tell Lucas off, but I raised my hand. With them silenced, I took a step forward and opened my lighter. Focusing on the flame, I brought it to his unkempt hair.

"No!" He begged as I lit the tip of his hair on fire. I quickly put it out, I was just scaring him like he scared me. "Please, Ber! You're my sister, my twin! I love you!"

I said nothing. I lit another chunk of hair on fire. He shook his head trying to extinguish the fire. I put out the fire with a towel that Cayden handed me. Lucas was begging and whimpering as the fire was lit and put out several times. I then did the same thing he did a few years back and put the lighter to his feet. He screamed as the bottom of his feet turned red and I refused to move the lighter. Serpent was tipping the chair backward so I could keep the lighter in place comfortably.

When his feet really started to look ugly, I stepped back. I motioned for Serpent to stay where he was as I grabbed a bottle of rubbing alcohol from the cart on the other side of the room. I gave a list of what I needed for this afternoon and my men delivered.

My list had included several bottles of rubbing alcohol and lighter fluid, sharp pocket knives, six towels, and a dozen red roses.

Without looking at my men or Ramero, I poured the rubbing alcohol on his burnt feet. His screams forced a wide smile onto my lips. Despite my attempts of staying neutral, my happiness was brought to the surface. Serpent put Lucas down so his bare feet were forced to the dirty ground.

For the next forty-five minutes I burned, cut and covered Lucas in rubbing alcohol. He cried and screamed and begged which only made me laugh and hurt him even more. This man harmed me for so many years, I couldn't even remember if I loved him, or he loved me.

This is it, I thought. It's time to end this asshole once and for all. This chapter of my life was about to close. I dumped two full bottles of lighter fluid over him. He screamed as the fluid got into his eyes, his cuts, and the already burnt flesh.

"Lucas, my dear twin." I smiled and twirled his burnt hair. "You can burn in Hell."

I took my lighter, the same one he used to torture me and lit a rose on fire. The flames danced on the plant; I held it up to my twin's face. His eyes widened with fear and his struggle doubled. I threw the burning flower it onto his body.

I repeated this until all the roses burned along with my twin. His tortured screams were beautiful. The smell of lighter fluid, fire, and burning human flesh filled the air. I stood back and watched him squirm, trying to escape his bonds and put out the fire.

My loved for him burned faster than the flames that wrapped around Lucas's body. The flames danced in a wonderful blue, yellow, and orange tango. My eyes were glued to the burning man. My lips curled into a sadistic smile. The fire slowly stopped burning leaving a darken, burnt corpse in

CHAPTER FIFTY: EMBER

the chair.

I walked over the charred body and kicked it. That wasn't enough for me, I grabbed another bottle of lighter fluid and set him on fire a second time. I wanted him to be nothing but ash.

Cayden wrapped an arm around my shoulder and pulled me away from the second fire. A wicked smirk on his face told me that he was proud. "Sweet firestorm, how do you feel?"

"Powerful, strong, on top of the fucking world!" I stated, watching the second fire burn out.

"Ramero, Serpent, please leave. I appreciate your help." I commanded.

As soon as the door closed, I turned to my three men. "Fuck me." I licked my lips, "Fuck me on top of my twin's ashes. Disrespect him like he did to me."

"Yes, ma'am!" My men say in unison.

51

Chapter Fifty-One: CAYDEN

"Cayden!" Ember screamed as she came. We collapsed onto the warm ashes that were once Lucas. The four of us were naked and Ember took turns riding Ace, Ryker, and I. I went last, watching the others made me harder than I've ever been.

After our fun filled afternoon, I picked up Ember and brought her upstairs to Ace's office. There was a private bathroom with a shower close by which we took advantage of. Ryker held Ember up as Ace and I washed her ash covered body. We then took turns washing ourselves and holding Ember close. Her eyes were closed, and her head rested on Ace's tattooed shoulder.

Ryker dried off as Ace dried Ember. Ryker carried her into the office to the couch and placed her naked body on his towel wrapped lap. Ace and I joined them on the couch, wearing only towels.

Ember smiled, "Thank you."

"For what?" I asked softly, playing with her wet hair. She shrugged and nuzzled into Ryker's chest. "She's tired we should get her home for a nap. No reason to stay here."

CHAPTER FIFTY-ONE: CAYDEN

Ace nodded and stood up; he walked over the set of drawers that were built into the wall. Pulling out four shirts, three pairs of sweatpants, one pair of jeans and three pairs of socks. I took a shirt, a pair of pants and socks from him before quickly changing.

I helped Ember into a shirt and a pair of sweatpants. Carrying her to the parking lot was a little more than a struggle. Poor Ember was half asleep and upset at being moved. She whined and tried to hold onto Ryker while I attempted to lift her. When Ryker went to get up, she cried out and demanded that we leave her be.

Ace had just finished putting on his jeans when she started her demands. Which meant that he was ready to leave. He was in no mood to play; Ace pulled her up and landed four heavy handed smacks to her ass.

"Little girl, we are going home. I promise you can rest there and in the car." Ace's tone must have sparked something as she nodded. Her arms wrapped around my neck, and she clung onto me as we walked to the parking lot.

The trip home was silent, Ember was snoring lightly before we were even out of the parking lot. I stroked her hair and watched as she slept peacefully. I just needed to get her inside without waking her. She doesn't like to be woken up, especially after sex.

Today was a stressful day for all of us. Taking a life, especially your own brother's life, must have been difficult. She needed her sleep.

She whimpered slightly as I lifted her up, still asleep. Ace pointed downstairs to which we all went to her room. I settled her down on the bed, stripped both her and me naked to cuddle her. Ryker did the same and Ace took a phone call outside the room.

Ember needed someone to talk to when she wakes up. Her mental health can finally take priotiy now that the threat of her brother and Trevor was neutralized. Ace, Ryker, and I discussed therapy for her. She has a lot of trauma and killing her brother will only help with so much. In the dark room, I watched her chest rise and fall. She was so peaceful when she slept, I wish she was like that all the time. A therapist might help.

We first met Ember when she was really young, but her nineteenth birthday changed everything. Her nineteenth birthday is the first time Lucas hit her in public. He played it off as accidental, but we knew better. We knew him.

"Ember!" Lucas yelled across the parking lot.

Everybody already went home, expect for the three of us and them. Lucas either didn't know or didn't care that we were still outside the building. He grabbed Ember by the arm from where she was puking her guts up.

Ember was pale and shaky the entire day. We took turns following her outside to make sure she was okay. Unfortunately, we agreed not to help her or make her feel uncomfortable. After the show she ran outside and hid behind the dumpster to hide her sickness. The poor girl had a stomach bug, and her brother wasn't doing anything to help her.

"Ow! Lucas, please let go!" She begged her twin to let her go.

That's when he smacked, twice across her face. She yelped and we watched her eyes fill up with tears. My entire body called out to murder Lucas right then and there. Ace put a hand on my shoulder and shook his head. The next day we installed cameras in their motel to watch them.

From then on, we made a vow to protect her. We called

CHAPTER FIFTY-ONE: CAYDEN

Lucas when he got angry and started to hurt Ember. That was also one of the reasons we kicked his ass a few years back. Ember was there unfortunately, but we took our shot.

I was elbowed in the side, and I looked down at the sleeping form next to me. She was having a nightmare. Ryker sat up and tried shaking her, but she wouldn't wake up. She was now struggling and crying before she suddenly sat up and screamed.

52

Chapter Fifty-Two: EMBER

"I'm going to make you an obedient girl, Ber!" Lucas growled. *I was gagged again and hung by arms to the celling of his basement. I heard the belt buckle behind me, it was almost as loud as my screams.* "You are going to be such an obedient sister by the time I'm done with you."

"No! No, Lucas! Please don't hurt me!" *I pleaded with my brother.*

I heard the belt whistle in the air before my back exploded with pain. I screamed!

"Ember?" Cayden's concerned voice cut threw my panic. "You had a nightmare, you're safe!" He pulled me into his bare chest. My eyes wouldn't focus through the waves of tears that continued to fall. My breathing came out in choked pants. Cayden whispered to me, but I couldn't hear him around my breathing and sobbing.

"Baby blaze," Ace knelt down in front of me. I couldn't tell where he or any of my other men came from. My eyes were so teary that I didn't know where I was. If we are still in the room with Lucas, I will burn him again for this nightmare.

CHAPTER FIFTY-TWO: EMBER

My men worked on focusing my breathing to a normal rhythm. Ryker cleared his throat, "What were you dreaming about?"

I sniffled and leaned my head into Cayden's chest. The soft beating of his heart was my focus as I whispered, "Lucas whipping me." It came out more of a gasping breath.

"Baby, I'm sorry. Can I hold you?" Ace asked, I knew that he needed me as much as I needed him. I nodded, feeling slightly guilty that Cayden had to pass me to him. Cayden didn't make any comments, he knew how important this was to both Ace and I.

It felt weird to be naked on his clothed lap. My body still tingled from the earlier sex and being without clothes made me wet. Ace's jeans were rough against my sensitive body, causing me to squirm slightly.

"Stop squirming." He demanded.

"Your jeans bother me though!" I whine, moving off his lap.

Ace stood, took off his jeans and shirt, then pulled me back into him. I settled, my ass between his thighs and head cradled against his chest. "Better?" His chest rumbled as he spoke.

"Yes Daddy." I mumble, suddenly exhausted.

He rocked us gently, luring me back to sleep. I woke up again in his arms. This time we were all laying down on the bed in the basement.

"Little flame, are you okay?" Ryker asked, as I stretched. My shoulder let out a satisfying pop and I smiled.

"Yeah, I think so. I'm, never mind." I chewed on my lip. Was it wrong to want them to fuck me?

I looked at the ground. Cayden shook his head. A finger forced my lips apart, "Stop biting your fucking lip, Ember."

I mumbled an apology. Cayden pressed down on my tongue

forcing a whimper from my throat. I was soaked, I could feel my juices dripping down my leg. He released me and nodded for me to speak. Ryker and Ace also stared at me, waiting for my answer. "I shouldn't feel like I want to be fucked. I just killed my brother." I say quietly. "I just don't think my heart can take any more pain in this lifetime. I'm scared, I don't want to be hurt again. I feel stupid to ask you to fuck me. I feel stupid to enjoy being spanked and punished by you three after Lucas. Am I stupid?"

"No! You enjoy what you enjoy. The difference between Lucas and us, is that we love you. You trust us." Cayden forced eye contact. I nodded in agreement.

Ryker smiled, "You said two years ago that men only think with their dicks. Do you still think that?" Ryker gave me an innocent look. He looked like a puppy, innocent and harmless. "Little flame, we want you to let us make you feel good, let us hold you and love you. I'm not thinking with my dick, I'm thinking with my heart. I want you to be happy."

How he remembered that was insane. I said that to Alyssa when I first developed my crush on these men. Now, I disagree with that statement. They rarely if ever thinks with their dicks. My men enjoy my pleasure and happiness. Even when they shove their cocks down my throat, I still enjoy it. They know that and they know how to make me feel like I'm floating.

"Let us prove that not all men think with their dicks. Will you let us baby?" Ace asked.

They knew that I disagreed with that statement, I also knew that Ace could feel how wet I was. I smiled, "What do you want me to do?"

All of their faces lit up. Cayden cleared his throat, "Be our good girl and listen to us. You can safeword anytime. What's

CHAPTER FIFTY-TWO: EMBER

your safeword?"

"Thunder, sir."

Cayden gave a big smile, "Lay on your back and spread your legs open for us."

Their hungry stares followed my actions as I moved myself so that my back was down on the bed. My knees fell to the side, exposing myself to the men who promised to take care of me. They all looked at me like I was a meal, and they haven't eaten for months. The three settled around the bed. Ace sat by my head, Cayden at my boobs and Ryker between my legs. They all looked to me for permission, another sign that they didn't want to hurt me. I needed them to touch me. I wanted their hands, mouths, and cocks to make me feel good.

"Please," I moan, hoping they catch the drift.

That one word sent them to work. Ryker was kissing my thighs; Cayden was kissing my breasts and Ace was kissing... me. He kissed me like this would be his last time. Like he was trying to memorize my taste and the formation of my lips.

I bucked my hips towards Ryker who took him time working towards my core. Cayden nipped and pulled at my nipples, making them hard and aching for pleasure. I let out a moan which Ace swallowed. Ryker blew on my swollen clit and Ace pulled away from my lips.

"Tell us what you want, baby girl." He muttered, taking my lip lightly between his teeth.

I arched my back, "I want to feel good!" My voice was breathy and barely more than a whisper.

My three men chuckled, and Ryker blew another breath. "Do you want Ryker to eat your pretty pussy? You want his mouth on your sweet clit?" I shuddered at Cayden's bold words.

"Please!" I whimper, moving my hips towards Ryker's mouth.

"Our dirty girl! What do you think Ryk, you gonna give her what she wants?" Cayden sucked a nipple into his mouth. I yelped when he bit down hard on the bud. I groaned and almost screamed when Ryker sucked on my clit. His mouth teased my sensitive pussy. Ace put a finger in my mouth and moved to my other breast. Ace was using his finger to fuck my mouth as Ryker entered two fingers into me.

The pleasure was building, and I started to thrash and move away from them. I was held down as Ryk entered a third finger. Ace added another two fingers to my mouth and a hand moved to my hair. They all picked up the pace and I screamed around Ace's hand as waves of pleasure washed over me. My orgasm was quick and came from out of nowhere.

I was still shaking slightly when someone cleaned my up with a warm washcloth. They each kissed me before Ryker lifted my body off the bed. I whined, but Cayden's sharp spank caused me to stop. He really hated whining.

"Let's get you fed and then we can snuggle on the couch for a while. I think you deserve a movie night." Ace murmured to me before leading the way out of the room.

I grinned; my men know me so well.

53

Chapter Fifty-Three: RYKER

Ember took care of Lucas, which left Trevor. Dickless Trevor. Ember was asleep on Ace's shoulder. The four of us sat on the couch for hours, watching movies and eating popcorn. Ace tried a new seasoning that was buttery garlic and we all loved it.

Ember ate an entire bowl and then passed out. It was wonderful to see. She has never been this comfortable around us. We showed her that her size no longer matters and that we will love her no matter what.

"Maybe we should have little flame burn Trevor. She's damn good with a lighter and has the same kill streak that Cayden has." I whisper to the other two.

Cayden shook his head, "No, she's too innocent."

"Yeah right. She killed her twin and burned him to death and then once more for good measure. Maybe we should let her work with us. She could be the fire queen of ACR?" Ace suggested.

I tilted my head. "Fire queen?"

"This is ridiculous! Do you really want to subject her to

more death?" Cayden whisper yelled.

"Let me be your fire queen." A sweet voice said. We all turned and looked at Ember. She smiled, "The nickname will fit my hair when I redye it. Plus, how could I be scared of you if I am like you? Let me prove myself!"

"Ember," Cayden started, and Ember cut him off.

"With all due respect, this should be my decision. You can help me feel empowered and like I really am the queen you see me as." She straddled Cayden.

He looked to Ace who shrugged, "Baby boy, this is her decision. Let her make it. Just know Ember, that you can back out at any time. We also need to deal with Trevor soon."

Ember smiled and I smirked, "First thing tomorrow morning?"

"Second. I think I'll need a good luck gift before we leave tomorrow."

* * *

Ember is a force to be reckoned with. After two rounds with each of us, she got up this morning to eat breakfast. Ace made eggs, bacon, and toast for her before we left for ACR headquarters. Currently we were watching her torture the already broken man in front of us. Trevor hurt his family, his father, which meant that he was going to die. He also hurt Ember and Alyssa which was punishable by an even more painful death.

She was dangling Trevor's foot above her favorite green lighter. He was screaming in pain, which was making her giggle. Our little sadist enjoyed the torture. Serpent was holding the chair up for her. He looked at us with a lopsided

CHAPTER FIFTY-THREE: RYKER

grin. The large man was clearly enjoying Ember's violence.

"Remind me to never piss her off," I whispered to Ace and Cayden. Both men chuckled and agreed as Ember slowly and methodically placed the flame around Trevor's body.

"Serpent?" She looked up at him. He nodded for her to continue. The two of them were best buddies. Both were joking lightly with each other as we watched Cayden get the remaining information from Trevor. Ember grinned, "Hold out his tongue." She walked over to the table that held lighter fluid and other tools. She grabbed a pair of dirty pliers and walked back to Trevor. Serpent was holding Trevor's tongue out for Ember. She was already making commands like a true queen.

I looked at Ace in shock. He shook his head as I heard the familiar flick of the lighter. I turned and watched Ember hold the lighter under his tongue. He tried to yank his tongue back but failed. Ember reached into his open mouth with the pliers and ripped a tooth from his mouth. An unconscious response to that pain was to scream and snap his jaw shut.

His tongue was now held in Serpent's hand. Serpent stared at it for a moment before slapping it across Trevor's face. Ember let out a shrieking laugh of pure joy. Our beautiful flame continued smiling as she noticed Trevor's bleeding mouth. It was unfortunate that the asshole was going to bleed out.

"Time to end him," she said almost upset that her fun had to end. She skipped over to the table and grabbed two bottles of lighter fluid. She dumped the contents all over Trevor's shaking and bloody body.

One last flick of the lighter was all it took before Trevor went up in flames. She stepped back and leaned her back against Cayden's front. She kept the sadistic smirk until the flames died out. She turned around and looked at us, "This is a lot of fun, can I do this again?"

  I love my little flame, our fire queen.

54

Chapter Fifty-Four: EMBER

Five days have passed since I killed Trevor. My men are more protective than ever. I was only allowed to leave with them or Ramero. Now that Ramero didn't have to hide his job, we were closer than ever. We went on "friend dates" once a week that consisted of getting food and then going to the movies or bowling or some fun activity.

As for my men, we were also closer. We were fucking like the world was ending. I would wake up to a tongue between my legs and a hard dick being shoved roughly into me. Every night I get a spanking to keep me in line before being passed around to satisfy all four of us.

This night was no different, after my spanking I was settled on Ryker's lap. The three of them had mischievous grins all night and I had a feeling I was going to find out why.

"Do you wanna have some fun, sweet firestorm?" Cayden asked, kneeling in front of Ryker and me.

I looked at him nervously, "Um, sure?"

He grinned and lifted me off of Ryker's lap. I didn't fight as I was carried to the room next to my former prison. He sat me on the bed in the playroom and started kissing my neck. I tilted my head to give him access.

"Safe word?"

"Thunder!" I said, enthusiastically.

Ace petted my hair, "New game, ready for the rules?"

I moaned, "Yes, Daddy!"

"You are going to have a vibrator in your cute little pussy, that tight asshole and on your clit. We are each gonna take a remote and have some fun. All you need to do is pick a number 1 through 10, the closest number gets to increase the intensity. Understand?"

"Yes, Daddy!" I said again and allowed them to remove my clothes the rest of my clothes. I was already undressed from the waist down because of my spanking.

When I was naked, a pair of leather cuffs were placed around my wrists and ankles to secure me to the bed. A blindfold was placed over my eyes as something cold teased my entrance. A large dildo was pushed inside, leaving me full and needy. More cold liquid was rubbed against my ass, and I whimpered as a finger went inside me.

"Shh, little flame. Relax for us." Ryker petted my hair as my ass was stretched. They have been working to get me to take their dicks up my ass. The man playing with my tight hole stuck two fingers in and started scissoring them. I whimpered and tried to squirm away. Ryker kept talking me through the pain. Soon they put a thin vibrator in and gave my red ass a gentle smack. I was panting from the feeling of being so full.

Finally, one was placed on my clit. Ace smiled, "Choose a number one through ten, baby girl." They all had whiteboards and wrote down a number. I had no idea what vibrator they each had, and the unknown made me nervous.

CHAPTER FIFTY-FOUR: EMBER

I gulped, "Three."

I felt the vibrator in my ass turn on. "I wrote three!" Ace exclaimed. They all erased their numbers and wrote down something else. "Choose another one!"

I bit my lip, "Six."

The other two vibrators turned on. I moaned; the sound of buzzing filled the room. We played this game for another painful ten rounds. I was a shaky moaning mess. I had cum three times during this game. At the tenth round, I chose the number eight.

Ace smiled and pressed a button. The vibrator in my ass was now at its highest setting. I screamed as I came again for the fourth time. All the vibrators jumped to full power and my men turned away.

I whined, "No more, please no more!" They ignored me. I knew that the only way to stop was with my safe word or when they were done. I was overstimulated and tired, but they were not done yet.

"Well baby blaze, you seem tired. I'm gonna take the vibrators away. You aren't done though; you can handle more. Right, baby? You want to take more for Daddy?"

"Yes Daddy!" I breathed as all the vibrations stopped. I was left feeling empty as they were pulled out of me. Ace started directing traffic.

At Ace's words, Ryker was kneeling in front of me. I felt his breath on my pussy as he fell to all fours. His breathing changed and he let out a light whimper. I looked up at Cayden who was standing behind Ryker.

"Relax Ryk, focus on our queen." Cayden rubbed his friend's back. Ryker's pants were down, and Cayden was sticking a finger inside the other man. I felt his tongue dart out and circle my clit.

Both of us moaned together and Ace laughed, "You both sound beautiful. My sinful symphony." He patted Ryker's head, "You like Cayd stretching that tight ass, baby boy? Imagine how nice his dick will feel." Ryker moaned and Ace reached down to his hardening cock. "I think he's ready."

Ryker made a noise of protest when Cayden removed his fingers. It was soon replaced by a whine when Cayden pushed the tip of his dick against Ryker's ass.

Watching this felt like a dream. The combination of watching my men's pleasure and Ryker's tongue made me feel like I was floating. Ace was whispered to Cayden before moving to me.

"Do you think you can take my dick into your tight ass? Let me in, baby blaze. Show your men how good you can be." My moaned at his words alone. My body was untied and maneuvered so Ryker can fuck my pussy while I sat on Ace's dick.

Ryker's panting and moans made me even weaker. I slowly slid onto Ace's lubed dick, my ass felt like it was being split into two and the burn had me crying out. I winced at the feeling of being so full.

"Such a good girl for Daddy. You are going to be so sore, but you like that feeling, don't you?" Ace murmured in my ear as his hand went to circle my clit.

Ace was fucking my ass as Cayden's thrusts got faster. Each of Cayden's thrusts caused Ryker to be pushed deeper into me. Ace's hand teased my clit as I was bounced up and down on his cock. I was already so sensitive and was barely hanging out.

Cayden pounded into Ryker. Ace was close, his breathing

CHAPTER FIFTY-FOUR: EMBER

was coming in pants, and he gave me a wicked smile. "I'm going to be dripping out of your ass, little girl." He grunted as he came down my throat. I struggled to swallow without choking, however my focus was on my Ryker's mouth before long. Ace pulled out and commanded that the remaining three of us to come.

I yelped and came hard for the fifth time. My eyes rolled back, and I was only faintly aware of Ryker and Cayden's actions.

Ace was talking to me about something. I looked at him, watching his lips move. "Daddy?" I mumbled.

He smiled and said "You're in subspace, baby girl. It's okay."

I nodded. I was aware of being lifted and carried upstairs. I slumped against Ace's chest as I was brought into the bathroom. He had me stand against him as he started a shower and pulled us under the steaming water.

He massaged shampoo into my hair and washed our bodies. He dried me off and brought me downstairs. We sat down at the dinner table where Cayden had placed two plates of food in front of us. I yawned and nuzzled into him. "Not yet, baby girl, you need to eat." I shook my head. "Don't fight me Em, you are too tired to take a punishment."

I whined but allowed him to force some food into my mouth. I took the fork from his hand, feeding myself quietly. Cayden and Ryker joined us. They all praised me, told me how good I was. I blushed and tried to hide my face. Ace pulled my face away from his chest, "No hiding, love."

I nodded, not wanting to upset them. I was still floating high as we ate in a comfortable silence. After dinner we watched a movie on the couch. I watched Ryker shift uncomfortably and smiled remembering the night fondly. We all cuddled on the couch, and I allowed the world to disappear. Cayden's warm chest had me to drifting into a peaceful, warm sleep.

55

Epilogue: EMBER

One Year Later

"You ready fire queen?" Serpent asked joining me outside the ACR cell. I nodded happily, the weight of my lighter a comfort in my hand. "After you," Serpent held the door open, and I walked into the room.

The smell of metallic blood and piss assaulted my nostrils. This was the only annoying part of my job; the smells were often nauseating. Often the men in these cells shit themselves or piss themselves before or during my play.

Over the past year I perfected my torture. I now wore red contact lenses and dyed my hair with oranges, reds, and yellows to replicate the beauty of my flames. Although my green lighter was my favorite, my men didn't like that I burned my fingers. Despite saying I didn't mind, they got me an assortment of grill lighters and blow torches. Serpent worked on my control and the best ways to inflict the most pain for the time that was allotted.

I was known around the ACR office as the fire queen. I was feared by most and they all knew that Ace, Cayden, and Ryker would stick them in a cell with me if I was crossed. I've never felt this powerful or confident in myself. My men never let the power go to my head, the nightly spankings, both fun and punishment kept me in line. I knew that if I was ever out of hand, it would be taken care of in a loving and healthy way.

Serpent cleared his throat which indicated that it was time to end the man in front of me. This was going to be quick. Unfortunately, this was just a way to get rid of the body. Serpent couldn't fit anymore in his freezer, so we needed another way of disposal. Tonight was event night and I needed to get ready in about an hour and a half.

I would have had more time, but Ryker wouldn't let me out of bed. My ass was still sore from the spanking he gave when I demanded from him to let me up. I should have known better than to demand my way.

I grabbed the lighter fluid and my trusty green lighter that I wasn't supposed to use. Dumping the liquid on the man, I grinned as he screamed.

"Bye scumbag," I taunted and used my lighter to set him ablaze. His screams filled the air as Serpent, and I walked out the room.

Ace met us outside the room. "You ready baby blaze?"

* * *

I stood in the ring. I was the RHW TV champion. It was a long way from when Lucas refused to let me wrestle. It turns out I am way better than he ever was and would have better. Ace was screaming into the microphone about his upcoming

EPILOGUE: EMBER

heavyweight title match and Cayden and Ryker's tag team title match. We were all champions, and we worked our asses off to be the best in Jeremy's company.

At the end of his promo, we posed in the ring as our music hit. We were still hated by fans, but it did nothing to deplete my confidence. Walking back to the curtain I realized I was finally happy.

My men pulled me aside and Ace wore his signature grinned, "Green lighter equals a spanking, baby blaze." My ass clenched in anticipation. "Let's go home, my fire queen."

There is no place that this fire queen would rather be.

Acknowledgements

Thank you to the amazing people that read this and felt even the slightest emotion while reading this. Thank you to my amazing friends and family who listened to me ramble on about my characters not behaving. Special thank you to Jazz who put up with several drafts of this book. Special thank you to Alyssa and Suki being there from the start and not throwing me out a window every time I mentioned hurting Ace or killing off everybody when I got frustrated. Special thank you to Waterbottle for helping me design a cover. Special thank you to Sam who providing the best moral support and cheerleading no matter how outrageous the idea was. Special thank you to Emmelia who helped me collect my ideas and create nicknames for my future characters. Finally, I would like to thank my grandmothers who always encouraged my writing... despite the topic... but never failed to push me to be better. Until we one day meet again.

About the Author

Cassy Oak is a writer of dark romance that often talks to her characters before they even hit the page. She can be found speak nonsensical gibberish to herself while working on her latest work. Cassy is often seen with a book in one hand and a hot chocolate in the other. When not writing, she is out playing with her dogs or trying to catch up on some much needed sleep.

Made in the USA
Columbia, SC
07 May 2024